shock
wave

also by james o. born

Walking Money

g. p. putnam's sons   new york

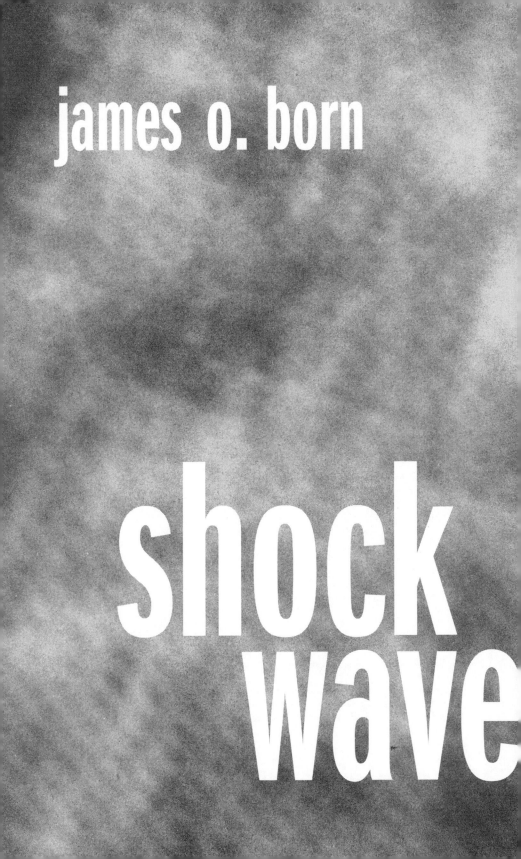

james o. born

shock wave

G. P. Putnam's Sons
Publishers Since 1838
Published by the Penguin Group
Penguin Group (USA) Inc., 375 Hudson Street, New York, New York 10014, USA • Penguin Group (Canada), 10 Alcorn Avenue, Toronto, Ontario M4V 3B2, Canada (a division of Pearson Penguin Canada Inc.) • Penguin Books Ltd, 80 Strand, London WC2R 0RL, England • Penguin Ireland, 25 St Stephen's Green, Dublin 2, Ireland (a division of Penguin Books Ltd) • Penguin Group (Australia), 250 Camberwell Road, Camberwell, Victoria 3124, Australia (a division of Pearson Australia Group Pty Ltd) • Penguin Books India Pvt Ltd, 11 Community Centre, Panchsheel Park, New Delhi–110 017, India • Penguin Books (NZ), Cnr Airborne and Rosedale Roads, Albany, Auckland 1310, New Zealand (a division of Pearson New Zealand Ltd) • Penguin Books (South Africa) (Pty) Ltd, 24 Sturdee Avenue, Rosebank, Johannesburg 2196, South Africa
Penguin Books Ltd, Registered Offices:
80 Strand, London WC2R 0RL, England

Published simultaneously in Canada

Library of Congress Cataloging-in-Publication Data

Born, James O.
Shock wave / James O. Born.
p. cm.
ISBN 0-399-15263-6
1. Police—Florida—Fiction. 2. Undercover operations—Fiction. 3. Florida—Fiction. I. Title.
PS3602.O76C47 2005 2004048865
813'6—dc22

Printed in the United States of America
10 9 8 7 6 5 4 3 2 1

This book is printed on acid-free paper. ♾

Book design by Victoria Kuskowski

to john, jane, george and murray.

great people to grow up with

acknowledgments

I want to thank my friends at Putnam, especially Neil Nyren and Michael Barson, for guiding me through my first year.

I should acknowledge my agent, Peter Rubie, whose odd mind provided the impetus for the story.

My good friend Reed F. Coleman came up with the title *Shock Wave*. I am in his debt.

I would also like to thank all the cops out there who supported me on the launch of my first book. You guys are the best.

shock
wave

one

he took a deep breath, not only to calm down, but in response to the Latina in a red bikini crossing Ocean Avenue. Her abdominals formed an olive-colored sign pointing to her pierced navel. She held that South Beach–distant attitude on her precise Cuban features as her long, jet-black hair fanned out behind her. She was one of many, but he definitely noticed her.

Looking down at the gym bag, he felt for the SIG-Sauer P-230 pistol he had tucked in between the seats in case of emergency. Really, it was in case of disaster. In an emergency, the six other cops watching him would swoop in and rescue him. If that failed, he might need the little .380 with its eight shots. The last thing he wanted today was a disaster. His first undercover gig since his *last* disaster. Even though that one had had nothing to do with undercover, or even a fuck-up on his part. He patted the gym bag to reassure himself. It was small scale as far as undercover deals went: five pounds of pot for some supposedly untraceable handguns. But there would be a good payoff. Many times, guns like these were used in homicides. Once they had the firing marks and ballistics, he figured they'd be able to connect one of them to something good. If not, they had a creep willing to trade guns for dope off the street.

Bill Tasker scanned the street in front of the Clevelander Hotel to make sure all his covering surveillance was in place. Working with his own guys from the Florida Department of Law Enforcement made him feel a lot more comfortable. God knows he didn't want to deal with the Bureau right now. He'd seen firsthand how they could lose targets on surveillance. The FDLE agents had two Miami Beach cops with them, but it was for courtesy as much as to be able to call in every cop in the city if there was a problem. Everyone had been briefed and knew what to expect. He wasn't too worried.

He caught the last possible glimpse of the girl in the bikini as she headed down the slightly elevated dune toward the water. At this part of the beach it was a fifty-fifty chance she'd go topless, maybe even nude. Tasker didn't have to check to see if the other FDLE agents saw her; they didn't miss much. She wasn't even his type. He went for the natural-girl-next-door, not the if-you-don't-have-a-Porsche-I-won't-talk-to-you type. But he couldn't deny her obvious attributes, real or store-bought.

Tasker snapped up his head as he caught sight of the Ford F-150 coming down the street.

He tracked the truck with his eyes and grabbed his cell phone. He never used a radio on an undercover, just in case he forgot and left it on or the bad guy found it. Whatever could go wrong during an undercover did go wrong.

"You guys see him?" he asked over his Nextel.

"No problem, Billy. We're set," a voice answered. Then, "He's not alone. Be ready."

Tasker tensed. Could be a rip-off. The team had discussed this but everyone figured no one would rip a lousy five pounds of pot. The big deal here was the fact that the guy wanted to pay with guns. Tasker watched as an older white Ford truck crept toward him. That was one of the reasons he'd chosen South Beach as a meeting site: over here, a pickup stuck out like a porn star in Utah.

Tasker pressed the button on his Nextel. "It's cool. I'll see what they have to say. Tell everyone to stay back."

"Ten-four," the voice said.

The truck was now half a block in front of him. The bearded driver recognized Tasker sitting in the driver's seat of the rented Suburban. FDLE liked using big rental cars so they had room to put in a camera, and if the car got trashed during an arrest or shot up somehow, all they had to do was turn it back in. They were down to one of the last rental companies in Dade County.

The pickup made a quick turn across the oncoming traffic, pulled down the side street and parked in the space for people checking into the hotel. The big bearded guy named "Bud" stepped out of the driver's side and gave the area a good look. A smaller guy, about thirty, dressed sharper in slick pants and a silk shirt, spent a few seconds checking his look in the truck's side mirror.

Tasker could see right off that this was the man with the guns. The redneck he'd dealt with the last time was just a middleman. That was always what happened. You meet someone, identify him and then have to arrest someone else. In this case, Tasker had had an analyst do a workup on Lloyd "Bud" Wilson, a landscaper from south Dade, and now he saw that Bud wasn't any smarter than he'd seemed when they met last time. He just knew someone with guns.

Tasker made a quick safety check of the Suburban. He glanced up at the passenger-side visor, just able to see the tiny microphone for the transmitter. If it worked, the surveillance agents would hear what was going on. His Nextel was on private and the gun was still hidden in the seats.

The big redneck, Bud, waved as the pair approached the truck. Tasker rolled down the passenger window so they could talk to him without walking into the street.

Tasker leaned over and said, "Hey, Bud, who's your friend?"

Bud ran his thick fingers over his sunburned face, "Well, Willie, this here is the fella that can put his hands on the guns."

"Thought you were bringing them today."

"We brung a sample."

The smaller man held up a small satchel.

"Sorry, Bud, we had a deal. Don't have time to waste on a guy that dicks me around." Tasker started to roll up the window.

The smaller guy stepped in front of Bud. "Willie, I thought we could talk."

Tasker ignored him. Bud had obviously told him Tasker's undercover name and didn't seem to mind having this slick little bastard cut in.

Tasker paused and looked at Bud. "I don't hear anyone talkin', Bud, 'cause you're the only one I know. Now, I came in good faith and expected at least six handguns. I don't see them, so I'm leaving." He put the big Suburban in gear, but gave the two crooks a second to convince him to stay.

Bud put his hand on the half-closed window and said, "Now, hold on there, Willie. Gene here is gonna get the rest from the truck." Without waiting for Tasker to reply, the short guy, Gene, grabbed the keys from Bud and scurried back to the truck, cutting across the open courtyard of the Clevelander. Bud leaned into the window. "I'm sorry about this, Willie."

"Who is that guy?"

"Gene—he's a mover and shaker down in Homestead. I had a little trouble coming up with the cash for the guns, so he's fronting them. He's just watching his investment."

The idea that anyone in the rural community of Homestead would be considered a mover and shaker made Tasker smile. He kept his eyes on the short man as he headed back with a heavy backpack he held across his shoulder. Bud opened the rear door and slid in before Tasker could say anything. Gene jumped up front with the bag. Tasker hoped that move wouldn't prompt the surveillance guys to come in. No one liked a bad guy behind the undercover agent.

Gene said, "Sorry, Willie, I just wanted to make sure you weren't a cop."

Tasker finally acknowledged him. "What made you decide I wasn't?"

"You were ready to drive off. Just a businessman." He had a harsh, Brooklyn accent. His hair was combed back, but it was a cheap cut. His watch looked like a Cartier but had an odd band. "Besides," Gene added, "if you're a cop and I ask you, you're required by law to admit it."

Tasker stared at him, then at Bud, trying to decide if one or both of them might be mentally challenged.

Gene asked, "Are you?"

"Am I what?"

"A cop?"

"No, I am not now and have never been a cop. How's that?"

"That's good. Now, what've you got?"

Tasker kept a close eye on Bud, then said to Gene. "What have *you* got?"

Gene started to say, "We can play games all—" when Tasker just reached over and grabbed the backpack off his shoulder.

Gene cleared his throat and said, "Or you could take a quick peek." As Tasker rummaged through the bag, Gene continued. "I brought a good assortment. Three Tec-9s, two Taurus nine-mills and a couple of Smith .38s."

Tasker nodded, still looking in the bag. "Not bad. Where'd you get 'em?"

"That's on a need-to-know basis."

"Can I sell 'em or will they be hot?"

Gene smiled. "I wouldn't sell them to a gun shop or nothin'. Now, what do you got?"

Tasker set down the pack and leaned down to retrieve his gym bag. He slid the brick of pot he'd checked out of evidence for this reverse sting and held it in his lap. "Five pounds of Colombian gold. Fresh and wrapped tight from the field." He held up the brick so Bud in the backseat could see it. As he did he noticed the backside of the brick for the first time. On the inside of the wrapper, where he hadn't felt it, was an evidence tag that read in bold letters: FDLE EVIDENCE MIAMI OFFICE #1043.

Tasker thought, Holy shit, how did I miss that? He held the brick firmly with the back to him. Gene tried to take it, but Tasker wouldn't budge. A thin film of sweat formed over his forehead.

"Let go. Let me take a look," said Gene, tugging on the pot.

Tasker said in a louder voice, "Looks like we're good to go." That was the verbal signal over the transmitter for the arrest team to move in. He kept his hand on the pot.

"Willie, what gives?" asked Bud from the backseat.

Tasker looked up and didn't see anyone moving toward him. He knew that time seemed to stand still whenever an undercover agent gave the arrest signal, but this was ridiculous. Maybe they hadn't heard him. He needed to give the visual sign, too. All he had to do was flash the lights, but the only way to manage that was to let go of the pot.

Gene finally pulled the pot brick loose, freeing Tasker to flash the lights.

"What are you doing?" asked Gene.

Tasker saw a blocking car coming from the south and then a couple of the agents sitting around the hotel bar and pool ease toward them. Then everything happened at once.

Gene flipped over the pot, Bud saw the activity outside the Suburban and pulled a Taurus nine-millimeter and Tasker knew he had to bail to stay out of the line of fire. He reached for the door handle.

Gene realized what the sticker was, and said, "He's a fucking cop," as he swung the brick hard into Tasker's face, slamming his head against the window.

Bud panicked and slid to the rear driver's-side door, away from the approaching agents and, without looking, kicked open the door and jumped out.

That was a mistake. A kid impressing a model in his dad's Jaguar XJ-8 was taking advantage of a break in traffic and caught the slow-witted Bud clean at about forty miles an hour. The door to the Suburban and Bud seemed to mix into a crumpled mix of man and metal.

Tasker, coming out of his daze, saw Bud's blood-streaked face, an eye already out of the socket smeared across his side window. The body, stuck on the grill of the Jag, slid past the end of the Suburban's hood, then onto the pavement, until poor Bud slipped under the blue Jag's wheels just as the kid brought it to a stop. Even Gene and the arrest team were momentarily stunned by the sight.

Then Gene made a ballsy move. He jumped into the backseat and out the missing door. He sprinted like a scared deer, his short legs pumping in fast motion. He shot past the stopped arrest team car and headed south down Ocean. Easily the fastest guy Tasker had ever seen in person.

Tasker got out, hearing another agent asking if he was okay. It still sounded like he was in an echo chamber. He nodded, waving the agent off to go chase Gene. Three other FDLE agents with their badges on chains around their necks and their heavy ballistic vests showing from under large untucked shirts gave chase to Gene, the would-be gun dealer.

Someone handed Tasker a handheld radio so he could hear the gasped description of where the chase was headed. Two agents were trying to free Bud's lifeless corpse while the others fanned out to see if they could help corral Gene.

Tasker monitored the radio as he retrieved his gun from the battered Suburban and started walking west on a side street, still listening as the arrest team would lose, then find Gene. He pictured the foot chase and started to see a pattern. Gene wasn't the dumb-ass he seemed. He had led the arrest team away from the hotel and now seemed to be heading back. Back to the truck, for which he still had the keys.

Tasker waited, and then, as the chase came back his way, ducked into the covered entrance for some construction going on a block west of the old run-down Clevelander. He quickly looked around and picked up a piece of scrap three-quarter-inch plywood about the size of his leg. He heard someone call out that Gene had turned down the street and Tasker caught a glimpse as he approached. He owed this mope a swat in the face, so without any warning he calmly stepped to the edge of the temporary construction wall and swung just as Gene appeared.

The old plywood split easily across Gene's face, but the effect was spectacular. The short man flew back off his feet and landed with a splat on the cracked sidewalk.

Tasker leaned over the gasping, bleeding man and said, "You're under arrest."

The man scanned the clearing in both directions for a good two minutes. As quiet as he expected it on a Thursday afternoon. He'd used this open lime pit west of Krome Avenue once before, but the amateur shooters on the weekends made him nervous. He didn't want someone he knew to wander by and recognize him. Even though people in the area mostly minded their own business, he liked to keep a very low profile. Except where women were concerned. That was definitely a weakness.

He stepped back from his experiment. The thick metal cap had just fit into his oversized step van with his business sign faded to almost nothing on the side. Although it had been fairly easy to drag out of the van, loading it at the scrap yard had been very difficult. The heat didn't make it any easier. The tropical humidity and brutal sun sapped most of the energy out of him. Still, he did what he had to do.

Stepping back, he made sure the metal sheet was braced against a small tree. He had used only about a quarter of the explosives he had had for over two years. He had about ten ounces left and he had calculated that to be plenty for his plan. He realized that the four ounces in the suitcase had been too much and he'd obviously set the timer improperly. He'd been rash, only doing the one test out west of Hollywood. Now there were houses all around and he'd had to move down here. He still had the crease on his Corolla where the rebar had blown straight in the air and hit the car. It was his badge of honor.

He took no chances this time. He'd moved his van two hundred yards away. He had a transmitter that would allow him to detonate the homemade explosive remotely from at least that far.

As he trotted back to the cover of the van, he let his eyes roam just in case he'd missed someone or something that could be a problem later. He wanted to hurry so he could be back for the kids when they got home from school. His wife was notably unreliable about being home in the afternoon.

Crouching next to the van, he looked at the transmitter in his hand. His blood rushed as he thought about the imminent explosion. He had just calmed down from watching the spectacular Miami riots and knew he needed another dose of destruction. The devastation he created himself was always better than watching the work of others. Sometimes he'd help others by making something or giving advice on where to plant a bomb, but he liked his own projects more. Helping others was better than nothing. Whether it was Arabs, the Puerto Rican guy or some of the local Nazis, he loved to see confusion and know that he had something to do with it. It had started small when he was a kid. A smoke bomb in the cafeteria made everyone run around like a cat with its tail on fire. The emotional jolt he'd felt had lasted for weeks. The only problem was that he needed a bigger stunt every time to feel the same charge.

He squeezed the transmitter's small trigger. Instantly the pack of explosive detonated in a sharp crack and a near-blinding flash. He could see the five-foot metal pan fly into the air and crash back onto the hard lime ground.

He drove the van back to the experiment. He planned to clear the area in case anyone had heard the explosion. Stopping twenty feet away, he approached it slowly. There in the center of the metal sheet was a six-inch hole. Perfect. That would do the trick nicely. He gazed at the scorched metal and wondered if this was how Oppenheimer had felt.

Traffic had been rerouted, and Miami Beach patrol cars with their lights flashing were at each corner and along the road. This was a lot of excitement for a Thursday afternoon on South Beach.

Tasker sat, holding an ice pack to his head where Gene had whacked him with the brick of pot. He watched the paramedics load what was left of Bud Wilson into the ambulance and then looked over to Gene sitting in the backseat of one of the FDLE Crown Vics.

"You okay?" asked his supervisor, sitting his squat frame on the step next to him.

Tasker nodded.

"Hey, shit happens. You can't keep a guy from jumping into traffic. This is a good arrest." He slapped Tasker on the shoulder, jarring his already aching head. "Good to have you back," the older man said, standing up to start pulling order from the chaos around them.

Tasker said, "Thanks, boss. Guess I better have Gene booked."

He padded over to the car holding the surviving prisoner, each step pounding in his head, and opened the door.

Gene's face had a good-sized red splotch where Tasker had hit him with the plywood. "Where are we going?" asked Gene.

Tasker said, "You're headed to TGK." The main holding facility in Miami–Dade County was the Turner Guilford Knight Center. No one seemed to know who Turner Guilford Knight was.

Tasker's supervisor came up next to him. "Make sure you throw in a felony murder charge for his friend gettin' squished."

After what Tasker had seen, the phrase turned his stomach.

Gene started talking fast, "I'll cooperate, I'll talk, just give me a break."

Tasker said calmly, "Gene, there's nothing to cooperate on. You're arrested and Bud is dead." His supervisor came over to the car to hear what was going on.

"I can give you someone else."

"I'm very satisfied with *you*. Now, I got a headache, Gene. Can you shut up?"

"Please, I'm tellin' you, I got something for you guys."

"There's nothing you could say that would make me want to listen to you right now, Gene."

"I know a guy who's looking to sell a Stinger missile."

Tasker and his supervisor froze and looked at Gene. Tasker said, "Okay, we'll listen."

two

bill tasker watched his supervisor lean back in his cheap, prison-made chair. The heavyset man defied physics every time he stretched his girth across it. Tasker always held his breath during this movement, but so far he'd never had to take any emergency medical action.

"Billy," started the fifty-five-year-old supervisor, "I just wanted to say you done good yesterday. Made a good arrest. Had one dumb-ass killed, but that was his own fault. Just wanted to say you done good."

"Thanks, boss." Tasker knew where this was headed, because he had been waiting for a talk like this the last few weeks.

"I know you got roughed up by the FBI pretty good over this Alpha National Bank shit. But no one here ever believed anything the Bureau was saying."

Tasker nodded. At night, when things were quiet, all he thought about was his recent brush with the FBI. He knew he'd been the victim of a frame-up, pure and simple. Even though frame-ups are largely a Hollywood invention, Tasker had had an FBI agent named Tom Dooley plant evidence that pointed to him stealing a satchel of cash from an Overtown bank during the recent riots. The real story was still confused, but it looked like Dooley himself had taken the money, though nobody seemed to know where it was, and now Dooley was in jail waiting for trial and the FBI was embarrassed by the whole situation.

The supervisor said, "I know people wonder where the cash ended up, but no one I ever talked to thinks you had anything to do with it."

"Thanks, boss."

The supervisor went on. "That's why I'm glad you got a good long-term case going now. I'm just sorry you're tied in with the Feds on it."

"No, you were right, we need the ATF in on this. They know Stingers. And they're a good outfit. Hard workers, regular guys. I like working with them."

"I know you'll do us proud."

"Thanks, boss."

Later that afternoon, Bill Tasker sat on an intracoastal seawall near the Bay Front area, talking with a lean City of Miami cop named Derrick Sutter. Sutter had been on the original robbery task force with Dooley and Tasker that had started it all. The two of them caught up on news as they spilt a bag of plantain chips. Sutter had saved his ass during the ordeal over the stolen money, even caught a bullet from Dooley. Tasker wouldn't forget that.

Sutter stretched his long thin arms as he took a deep breath of salty air. He cocked his head, giving Tasker a look. "You want me to work on another task-force investigation?"

Tasker nodded. "Technically, this is a joint investigation, not a task force."

"What's the difference?"

"Task force is a long-term, multiple-case commitment. A joint investigation means we don't have to get friendly with the Feds because it's a one-shot deal."

Sutter was still on edge. "You remember the last one we was on?"

"I recall a little of it."

"I remember 'cause I got shot."

"Yeah, I know. But this could be a good case. I figured it wouldn't hurt to have someone I trust in with me."

"I don't understand why the Feds are involved at all. FDLE has all the jurisdiction we need, unless you set the deal up in Texas or something."

"We called ATF because they have the expertise on Stingers. Hell, they made a great case on the IRA with a Stinger in West Palm. Then ATF had to call the FBI because there must have been a terror-related angle."

"How'd the Bureau link terrorists to a redneck selling a Stinger?"

"What else is a Stinger for? Doesn't matter, anyway. They're in the case, and I want you, too."

Sutter ran his dark hand over his darker face. "You know I'm still pissed off the damn FBI rejected my application. I think it was a racial thing."

"I thought it was because you were nine hours short of a bachelor's degree."

"That's what I mean. It was a racial thing."

"I thought you got booted out of Florida International for missing class your last semester."

"It was a racial thing."

Tasker just looked at him.

"Yeah, little white French-Canadian girl from Hallandale. She never let me go."

"That's how you were oppressed?"

"Let me have a little racial anger, my brother. I'll help you on the damn case as long as the Feds leave us alone and no FBI guys shoot me again."

Tasker had to crack a smile at that one. "I can almost guarantee no one in the FBI will shoot you during this case."

At the Miami field division's main office of the Federal Bureau of Alcohol, Tobacco and Firearms, known simply as ATF, Bill Tasker sat at a desk, shaking a Magic 8-Ball.

"Will I see a naked woman in the next twelve months?" he asked the ball quietly.

NOT LIKELY, showed on the octagonal globe inside the ball.

"Figures," muttered Tasker, placing the ball back on the desk.

"What figures?" asked Camy Parks, the ATF agent working on the Stinger case with him.

"Just testing my luck." He said it staring at the ball so his eyes didn't try to involuntarily dart toward the gigantic opening on Camy's low-cut white blouse.

"Guys worry about luck. Women worry about skill."

Tasker quickly moved his gaze up to Camy's delicate face.

She smiled and said, "Guys worry about those more than women, too."

Tasker blushed at being busted.

"Things still not on track with your ex-wife?" she asked.

"Not yet. What am I saying? Not at all."

"What's her beef?"

"She isn't ready. That's her best answer. Her worst is that she still has feelings for some lawyer she was dating."

"A lawyer—yuck. Why?"

"Don't know. I don't think she even knows."

Camy sighed. "Women, what a pain in the ass." Her delicate Tennessee accent made every word sound like a compliment.

Tasker nodded, keeping his eye on her for any hint of a joke. Maybe the rumors he'd heard about her were true. He watched her compact, incredible frame move as she cleared some of the folders off her desk.

"It'll be a relief to take a break from this stuff."

"That all the cruise-ship case file?" asked Tasker.

"These are just the reports. I have a file cabinet full of photos and a whole aisle in the evidence room."

Tasker looked at the photographs taped on separate sheets of paper. The first was of the Krans-Festival flagship, the *Sea Maiden*. One porthole was burned black around the edges. The second photograph was of a red suitcase.

"This couldn't have held the bomb?"

"No, that's the same model and color. All we had left was a handle and some of the top of the bag."

Tasker read the label: Samsonite.

"You worked this all by yourself the past two years? What about the Bureau?"

"They had a guy on it for the first month, then something happened and they pulled him off. I got a Department of Transportation agent on it with me, and we're in good shape with the leads."

"You close to an arrest?"

"Not at all. Just caught up on leads and lab work. Nothing new in eighteen months."

"Any other hard evidence?" asked Tasker, trying to remember the details of the two-year-old case.

"Just the handle to the suitcase that contained the explosive, a photo of a car we believe was involved and the explosive fingerprint. And about three hundred bogus leads." She pulled out a black-and-white security-camera photograph of a light-colored Toyota Corolla with a big dent in the roof where the windshield met it.

"What kind of explosive did they use?"

"It's called TATP. God help me, I can never say the full name. It's homemade and really unstable and nasty."

"You think the bomber killed himself since this attack?"

"I doubt it. We checked all the unattended death records for the tri-counties. There are just too many missing persons. For all I know, he's rotting out in the Everglades after standing too close to one of his own bombs."

"One can only hope."

She smiled at him. "People were real interested in the case, but then interest just dried up."

"I remember the news coverage—for a week. The people at Krans-Festival fell all over themselves saying it was an isolated incident."

"Yeah, they thought it would hurt the cruise industry, but it really didn't. The one baggage handler was killed. The city is holding it as an open murder case, and the survivors didn't see anything unusual."

"Why wouldn't the FBI be all over that?"

"Maybe because the casualty was an Italian laborer on the ship. Maybe 'cause there wasn't much damage and it didn't look too sophisticated?"

"That wasn't big enough, but they want a piece of my Stinger deal?"

"It's crazy, I know. At least I know the agent they assigned to us."

"Lail?"

"Jimmy Lail."

"What's he like?"

"Different."

The test was perfect. He felt more and more comfortable with the TATP. The liquid explosive was a little unstable, but that only added to the fun. For a homemade explosive that couldn't be traced, he'd take the risk. Even though it had been made in a wash basin in an old dilapidated garage, he had to admit that in the couple of years he'd had the explosive it had held up well. He didn't take any chances with it, either. That was the saving grace of the tiny detached garage. He kept his Corolla, his tools, three hidden guns and the explosives in it, away from everything and everybody else.

He walked in through the rear kitchen door, wiping his feet carefully to avoid his wife's wrath. She was peeling carrots for a salad at the cheap, uneven kitchen table, and as he came inside, he leaned down to kiss her.

"How was work?" asked his wife.

"Good, no problems."

"Carlos called for you about an hour ago."

He nodded silently as he tramped through the cluttered house out to the garage. He always parked the Corolla behind it so no one could see it from the street. Sometimes he even pulled an old parachute over it because the crease in the car's roof caused it to leak a little and the old silk parachute deflected light rain. It also hid the car completely. Just in case.

three

bill tasker sweated as he cranked the pedals of his Trek mountain bike. He rode on the grass swale while his eight-year-old, Emily, steered her smaller Mongoose on the road next to him. Her long blond hair, in a ponytail, bounced behind her with each stroke of the pedal. Her muscular little body propelled the bike smoothly over the paved road. Another year or two and he wouldn't have to ride in the grass so that she could keep up.

Tasker's ten-year-old, Kelly, was in her weekend art class at the Kendall Community Center. He used the two-hour class time to take Emily on little adventures she liked, generally something athletic, in keeping with her attributes. Only having them every other weekend made each visit special. He took any minute he could to spend with the girls. Even if he couldn't live with them, he wanted them to remember all the fun they had when they did see him. Things like this would keep their mother from saying he was too focused on his job, that work was always his first priority. Real type-A personalities didn't find time to ride bikes with their daughters. Did they?

They tracked west on Coconut Palm Drive in the Redlands, having to deal with only the occasional car. Emily told him about school and gymnastics and her friends near his old house in West Palm Beach, about an hour and a half north of southern Dade County. Her permanent good mood was infectious, but Tasker was still troubled. He had tried to ask his youngest daughter about her mom's dating status. His ex-wife had come on strong while he was in the soup with the FBI but had cooled things off when he was cleared. She'd been vague about the reasons, but he knew one of them was a defense attorney named Nicky Goldman. Tasker knew him a little from his days working in West Palm, and he did seem like a nice enough guy, but that didn't lessen the pain of knowing his ex-wife was dating a lawyer. A defense lawyer at that. At least personal-injury attorneys didn't risk public safety to win a case. Tasker's uncle had been a lawyer until he'd become a judge in the mid-eighties. He was a man of integrity and had real disdain for most of the modern attorneys. Tasker respected his uncle's views and attitudes. Now, with televised trials and million-dollar jury awards, it seemed lawyers had mortgaged their souls for some success. All that was fine until he thought of one of them interacting with his daughters or, worse, interacting closely with Donna.

He pulled his bike onto the road for a minute, coasting next to Emily. Catching his breath, he asked, "How's your mom doing?"

"Fine."

That was a hard answer to follow up on. No useful information, but indicating that there was no real problem. Damn. He hit it another way.

"What's she doing this weekend, since you and Kelly are gone?"

"She said she was going to stay in bed all weekend."

"She sick?"

"No."

Damn. He pedaled back onto the grass.

"Daddy?"

"Yes, sweetheart."

"I'm tired. How far are we going?"

He smiled. "One more block and we'll turn around after a quick break. How's that?"

"Thanks, Daddy."

They turned north on the next block, but Tasker kept them pedaling for a few more houses. Then he saw it. The small, lime-green one-story with a carport and rotting shed next to it. The guy he'd arrested on South Beach, Gene, had given him the name of the man with the Stinger for sale. A little research had turned up this address.

"Let's take a quick break," he said, stopping the bike with Emily in front of him so he could see the house but make it look like he was talking to her. He memorized a few details: the location of the house numbers, the shape of the front bay window, the white chipped paint on the latticework by the front door. A pickup truck with a toolbox on the rear and side of the bed was parked on the grass. The door had a faded magnetic sign that had something about large pests written on it.

Then Emily said, "Let's head back. I need a drink."

Tasker nodded as he started off and took one more look over his shoulder at the house.

Derrick Sutter let the phone ring six times, then hung up. He hadn't talked to his friend Slayda "Mac" Nmir in a month. Only once, in fact, since the FBI had transferred Mac without comment to the Boston field division. It was like he had never existed. Mac had been a stand-up guy, and it was his quick thinking that had kept Sutter from being killed. He would have been more impressed with the FBI if it hadn't been for Tom Dooley of the FBI trying to kill him at the time. He set down his cheap portable phone.

Slouching down into his couch, Sutter looked around his crappy apartment. Sure, it was technically on South Beach, even if he couldn't see the water. But he couldn't care less. He didn't swim. Not after his childhood. He couldn't afford the prices on a Miami detective's salary. And the women weren't as impressed as they once were when he told them he lived on South Beach. He looked around again.

He really didn't have any regrets. He could always ask his folks for some cash if things got too tight. He let out a laugh. That would never happen.

He stood and stretched as he got ready to go meet Bill Tasker out at the ATF office for this new case. He liked to complain to the straitlaced state cop, but he really did enjoy working these big cases that took him all over the county. He loved Miami but was beginning to see there was a whole wide world out there.

The weekend had reenergized Tasker. The girls didn't want to go back the night before, which meant they had had a good time, and he'd slept well for a Sunday night. Now he took the few minutes before the briefing to chat with Camy Parks outside the ATF office. He sat on the rear steps that looked out onto a parking lot while she sorted through some raid clothes in a blue ATF duffel bag. He didn't mind watching her muscular arms lift and toss old shirts or see her smell socks to determine how dirty they were. It was crude and base, but as long as he didn't say anything he figured he was safe. He was, after all, a guy.

"You got all the background on this guy you need?" asked Camy. She always seemed to look right into whoever she was talking with. Tasker found the sensation agreeable.

"According to my snitch, Gene, the guy is Bernie Dashett from the Redlands. He has a history for dealing in stolen property and burglary. I took a look at his house this weekend in case we have to do a search warrant. Been some kind of exterminator for large pests the last few years."

"What's a large-pest exterminator?"

"It was in an ad for his business. I guess like rats and things like that." Tasker noticed a black Honda Accord cut into a low rider with silver rims roll into the lot. "Who's that?"

Camy smiled. "You'll see."

Tasker watched a white guy about thirty pop out of the low car and strut toward them. The man had on baggie pants that showed about six inches of his red boxers and a tank top covered by an unbuttoned collared shirt.

Camy said, "That's one of our partners."

"You're shittin' me."

"No, sir. That's Jimmy Lail, special agent of the Federal Bureau of Investigation."

Tasker just stared as Lail strutted up to them and said, "Hello, Princess, you lookin' dope."

Tasker, still sitting, calmly turned his head in case the man's blood flew that far. He saw Camy Parks ball her right fist and swing like Lennox Lewis right at Jimmy Lail's left eye. The fist connected with a sharp smack and Jimmy went to the ground. Tasker didn't know why she hated her nickname—Camilla Parker Bowles—but she did. It didn't really mean anything. It was just one of those stupid things a cop says, in this case, making fun of her real name, which was Camilla Parks. But someone had said it and the name had stuck, and it had evolved in turn to "Princess." Now others paid the price for using it.

Camy went back to zipping up her bag and said, "Bill Tasker, FDLE, meet Jimmy Lail, FBI."

For his part, Jimmy took it all in stride. He stood casually and offered his hand. "Yo, my dawg."

Tasker took his hand and just nodded.

Inside the office, Tasker kept his distance from the odd FBI man. He met Sutter at the door, hoping to warn him before he met Jimmy, but it wasn't possible. As soon as Sutter came through the briefing room door, Jimmy was up to greet him.

"Yo, my brother—Jim Lail, FBI."

Sutter shook his hand silently, eyeing Tasker for signs of a practical joke. He had to force the young FBI agent to shake in a standard way when he tried to add new modifications.

As Jimmy bopped back to the other side of the room, Sutter turned to Tasker. "What's that all about?"

"I guess he wants to be black."

Sutter said, "He's got a good start with that eye. You do that?"

"Nope. My beef with the Bureau is history."

Sutter unconsciously fingered the bullet hole on his upper chest under his silk shirt and said, "I've still got issues."

Tasker gave the overview of the case once everyone was seated. The only other significant addition to the group was an FBI agent named Sal Bolini. He worked in some special unit and was supposed to be an expert on terrorism. Tasker eyed the fifty-year-old, clean-cut man suspiciously. His experience with senior FBI men had been marginal at best. At least Lail didn't seem smart enough to screw him.

Tasker handed out his info sheets on Bernie Dashett and explained that he had a preliminary meeting scheduled with Dashett later in the day.

Camy added, "There won't be any cash or the missile, so we're gonna keep the surveillance light."

Bolini cut in. "I wanna see who shows up. I'm coming out."

Tasker immediately said, "We set the teams already. I'm undercover with the snitch. Camy and Derrick are cover."

Bolini didn't bother to look at Tasker. "Last I checked, the city has no jurisdiction down here, and the Bureau needs to be on any surveillance having to do with this case. After all, this is a federal case." He cut his eyes to Sutter, then Tasker. "I own this part of Dade. If something goes on here, I know it."

"I need people I can trust if I'm undercover, and I'm not depending on the FBI to get me out of a jam."

"You said it was just an introduction. You'll still have your playmates, but I'm coming, too. I want to know everyone involved. Understood?"

Tasker rose slowly. Camy put her soft hand on his arm and said quietly, "Let it go, Billy. He won't cause any trouble."

Tasker relaxed, but had to ask, "What's your problem, Bolini?"

"I told you, I own this end of the county. And I don't want some yokel to screw it up." He paused and said, "And I don't want you to make the Bureau look bad again."

Bernie Dashett let the armadillo squirm in his hand until it wore itself out. The extra-thick leather gloves protected him whenever he had to grab some critter like this. He turned from the laundry room where he'd grabbed the ten-pound armored rat.

An elderly lady jumped back. "How'd it get in there?"

He concentrated on the tiring armadillo and said, "Mrs. Vorse, you might have left the door ajar one night. Possums and such love to explore carports, and a room like that is awful inviting."

"Well, Bernie, thank you for coming over so quick. I'll tell your mama what a big help you are."

He stopped at the rear of his truck and slid the armadillo into a metal cage. "Thanks, Mrs. Vorse. It would have been easier if my trap was working, but I'm having it fixed." He secured the cage and headed for the driver's door. Hopping in, he said, "Call me if you have any other problem. I'll tell Mama you said hey."

The older woman waved as he backed out onto the road and headed toward the east. He was meeting Gene Antero over at the mall in Cutler Ridge and didn't want to be late.

He had bought and sold guns with Gene over the years and trusted him as much as he trusted anyone from New York. The guy usually paid up and always seemed to have cash on hand to buy whatever old piece-of-shit pistol Bernie could find. This was different. A whole new level, but he figured if Gene had connections and had come through before, why not now.

Gene had told him he'd bring along his buddy named Willie. He vouched for him and said he had plenty of cash. When Bernie asked him why this guy Willie needed a Stinger, 'cause he didn't want someone to kill a bunch of Americans with it, Gene told him that Willie was just a collector. That was good enough for Bernie. He was going to ask sixty-five hundred and would take five grand. That was pretty good profit for only paying two thousand in Tampa. The National Guardsman who'd sold it had wanted cash so Bernie had to sell off some of his fishing gear and an old pop-up camper. Now he'd be able to buy all new stuff.

As he came north on US 1, he saw the Sears a few blocks away. The mall had been a landmark in the Perrine and Cutler Ridge area since he was a boy. He'd figured it was as good a place as any to meet.

Gene had said they'd be in a brand-new Suburban and park back in the lot directly in front of the Sears. Bernie saw them sitting inside the big SUV alone in the rear of the almost empty lot.

They came out of the Suburban to greet him. Gene, in his usual shiny pants, talking quick, and the other guy, Willie, about six foot and pretty solid.

"Hey, Bernie, how's it going?" asked Gene, and then before he could answer, "This here is my pal Willie. He's the man with the cash."

Bernie shook the man's hand. He looked at his casual appearance and sandy hair, trying to get a feel for the guy. Nice-looking, early thirties, nothing about him looked like a cop. At least none of the cops who had locked him up in the past.

Willie said, "You ready to talk business, or do we have to waste time bullshittin' for a while?"

Bernie liked someone so direct who didn't sound like a New Yorker. He smiled and said, "What kind of business we talkin' about?"

Willie frowned and looked at Gene. "You didn't tell me we'd have to play games with this fella." He looked at Bernie, then at the driver's door of the Suburban. "Let's go."

Bernie was just trying to be mysterious, like they were in the movies. Now he said, "No, no wait."

Willie stopped and looked at him.

"We can talk about the missile. I know Gene, so I know you must be okay."

Willie nodded and Gene started to talk. Before he got out a full word, Willie held up his hand and said, "Shut up, Gene. Let Bernie talk."

Bernie smiled at the courtesy. "I was lookin' for about eight large for it." He thought, Why not go for it.

Willie thought about it and said, "Who manufactured it?"

Bernie just stared at him. "I guess the U.S. Army."

"That's who owned it. What company made it? It'll be on there somewhere."

Bernie said, "I honestly don't know."

Gene started to speak, but again Willie shut him down. Bernie had never seen anyone do that to Gene before.

Willie said, "Eight grand is a little high, especially if I don't know who made the damn thing."

"How much was you thinkin'?"

"If it is what you say it is, maybe sixty-five."

Bernie almost jumped up and down. That was exactly what he wanted for it. "We might could work that out."

"Where'd you get it?" asked Willie.

"Just came by it. You know, knew the right people." In fact, he'd only met the National Guardsman through a friend and didn't even know his last name. He had been very careful who he told about it.

"Where is it now?" asked Willie.

"It's safe. No kids or nothin' could get to it. I was savin' it for a collector like you."

For the first time, Willie smiled, showing white straight teeth. "Okay, Bernie, sounds like we can do some business."

"I'll go get it right now if you want."

"I need a day to get the cash. What about tomorrow, noon, right here? Won't take five minutes. I'll even take you to lunch after if you want."

Bernie smiled and said, "Count on it."

Willie let Gene say goodbye, and they were gone. Bernie was gonna have some cash soon. He felt like a million bucks, or at least sixty-five hundred.

four

"nice job on the setup, willie," said Camy Parks. "Nice middle-of-the-day deal, plenty of time to set it up and check out any leads on him. I like it."

Tasker smiled. He was happy with yesterday's meeting, too. He could've let Bernie Dashett run out and get the Stinger, but by putting him off until today he'd been able to get surveillance on him and plan things more carefully.

It was an hour before he was supposed to meet with Bernie, and everything was going well. The FBI had put a surveillance team on his house, the briefing was completed and everyone was ready to head out to the undercover location at the Cutler Ridge Mall. Although Tasker had seen FBI surveillance teams firsthand, he didn't think this good-old boy from the sticks would be able to pick them up.

Jimmy Lail bopped up and said, "Dawg, I got your back on this. Things slide shallow and I'll be in the shit."

As Tasker tried to decipher that comment, Sal Bolini, who hadn't said a word, approached them. "Well, kids, I'm outta here."

Camy asked, "You're not interested in a potential terror case?"

"Doesn't involve my informant. I checked with him and he never heard about any Stinger for sale, so you can call me if there is a problem."

Tasker asked, "Did your snitch know Dashett?"

"The FBI doesn't have snitches. We have informants or sources of information. I didn't even bother to ask my informant about your mope. This informant is too valuable to taint with this penny-ante shit."

"So you're done with the case?"

"If I need something else, I'll read Snoop Dogg's 302." He gave Jimmy Lail a look almost as condescending as he'd given the other agencies involved.

Tasker never understood why all the Feds referred to their reports by numbers. The FBI used 302, the DEA wrote a DEA-6. All Tasker ever wrote were investigative reports. Nothing fancy, but somehow he still managed to make arrests and solve cases.

Bolini patted Tasker on the back and said, "Good luck, kid. Don't decide to take the money and run."

Tasker flushed as the older FBI man walked away casually.

Bernie Dashett hadn't scheduled any work appointments for the morning so he wouldn't get tied up. The truth was that since more communities were being built in the area, the bigger animals that lived here had all moved west, away from encroaching civilization. Aside from possums, which were still as common as cats, he didn't get that many calls. He hadn't even seen a fox in months. Although most of his calls had to do with animals getting inside, like raccoons in the roof eaves or possums in a carport pantry, he had seen a big decline in sightings of wildlife all through Homestead and the Redlands. The one animal he saw more and more of was iguanas. They must mate like rabbits, 'cause they were everywhere. He liked it, too, because aside from the fifty dollars to trap them, he usually could sell them for another fifty. They scared the shit out of little old ladies, so they never bitched about the price to get rid of them. Bernie had even thought about planting some at certain houses. He might keep the next one he trapped and use it to generate a little extra business.

He dressed in his work shirt and headed out to his truck. He had stored the Stinger in a safe place the day after he'd bought it. With Ellie coming into the house all the time, he didn't want to risk her seeing it. Even though she acted like she was over the divorce, Bernie had heard too many stories of ex-wives causing trouble.

At eleven-thirty, he pulled out of his driveway and drove down toward Coconut Palm. He wasn't nervous, just a little excited. Maybe this could be a new line of work. International arms dealer. He liked it.

Bernie noticed a few cars on the normally quiet streets but didn't think about it again. He decided to make a quick stop at the shop where his possum trap was being repaired. Off Newton Road, he pulled behind the little house to the garage behind it. Hopping out of the truck, he saw Daniel Wells sitting at his workbench, fiddling with some contraption.

"You got it?" asked Bernie.

"Right here," said Wells.

FBI Special Agent Jim Cobb knew there was no way this hillbilly would burn their surveillance. The guy was the only car on the road, and he had that sign on the door. He could've followed him by himself. At first he thought the exterminator was going to drive directly to the meeting with the FDLE guy, but he'd made this stop and Cobb knew this might be a big chance for him.

Now, as the only one with an eye on the truck in the back of the house, Cobb saw Bernie Dashett walk into the garage and talk to a white male, about thirty. Cobb made a few notes and then saw the unidentified male walk out to the truck with Dashett and hand him a duffel bag with something in it. This was it. The source of the missile.

Cobb got on the radio. He couldn't wait to demonstrate how smart he was to the other agents. He only wished Agent Bolini was out here. That was where Cobb wanted to be: counterterrorism. Maybe if he helped make this case, he'd get his chance.

Cobb keyed his radio. "The subject just got the package from this house. I'll stay here while you follow the subject to the UC location. Copy?"

A female voice came back, "Okay, Jim, we'll be back when the deal is done. Don't do anything on your own."

"Got it. But I saw the exchange. This is definitely where the package came from." He didn't want any question about who had made this case.

Tasker was a little nervous. He made sure he could see Derrick Sutter sitting in his Buick Century about five rows over in a line of parked cars. Camy and Jimmy Lail were on the other side of him, about the same distance away. There were five other ATF agents strategically placed in the lot. He felt well protected.

Tasker was still pissed off over Bolini's comments. He'd beaten the allegations and exposed an FBI agent as the real bank robber, but some people just didn't want to believe it. Even now, two months later, there were people who thought Tasker had been partners with Tom Dooley. That was ridiculous. Tasker hadn't been able to stand that racist loudmouth even before he'd been framed by him. Bolini seemed like he came from the same mold. That FBI mentality of superiority died hard. His Nextel beeped. Camy Parks' voice floated through. "Billy, Dashett is a minute out."

Tasker waved to her and cut off the speaker on his phone. He rechecked his little Sig .380 hidden in the seat, and waited.

Bernie Dashett pulled into the lot and right to Tasker, like he had no doubts.

"Hey ya, Willie," he said, hopping out of his truck and walking over to Tasker.

"Bernie, it's too hot out here, let's jump in my Suburban to talk." Without a word, Bernie moved to the side of the Suburban, climbed in the high vehicle and settled into the cool seats.

"This is nice, Willie," he said, running his hands over the leather.

"Yeah, I like it." He paused and checked the mirror to see at least two cover cars in position. "What'd we decide on again?"

"You mean on a price?"

"Yeah." Tasker wanted Bernie to do most of the talking on the tape.

"You said sixty-five."

"That gets the whole thing?"

"There's only the one."

Tasker played stupid. "One what?"

"Stinger, or whatever you call it. I never checked the manufacturer like you wanted."

Tasker smiled. "That's okay. You got it with you, right?"

"Yeah. C'mon, have a look."

Tasker slid out of the high SUV and waited a second while Bernie went to his truck. Tasker wanted the cover surveillance to see him and realize the deal was close. He let Bernie root around in the bed of the truck and then walked over to it.

"Here she is," said Bernie, looking down at the five-foot missile in the bed of the truck.

Tasker stared at it for a minute. This had been the easiest case he'd ever put together. "Looks like we're good to go," said Tasker, as he stretched his arms over his head. He gave both the verbal and visual signals for the arrest team, then moved to the other side of the truck.

The team moved perfectly. Two cars were almost on top of Bernie Dashett before he even noticed them. Sutter calmly opened his door and pointed his Glock at Bernie.

"Police, don't move," he said, calmly and professionally.

One second later, Camy came out of her Crown Vic, and Jimmy Lail squealed the tires of his little black Honda, burst out of the door and started screaming, "On the ground, be-autch!" Holding his gun sideways, he shuffled up to Bernie, pointing the gun at his head, still sideways and said again, "On the ground, be-autch."

Be-autch? Oh, God, it was that gangsta talk again. Bitch. He meant bitch. Tasker shook his head.

After Bernie Dashett was cuffed and in the back of a car, Camy Parks came up to Tasker. "One of the FBI guys saw where he got the missile."

"No shit?"

"Saw the exchange plain as day. Over in Naranja, not far at all."

"Let's go," said Tasker, jumping into the Suburban.

five

jim cobb had been an FBI agent for nearly four years, the whole time stuck down here in Miami, following different suspects as part of the SOG, or Special Operations Group. What sounded like a great assignment had turned into the most monotonous, mind-numbing task ever invented. All he did, with a squad of other agents, was follow people. No arrests. No investigation. Just surveillance. Following people running errands, meeting other mopes and mainly going about their lives—while he wasted his. Now he was doing the same thing. Watching this guy who just gave a missile to the main suspect, Bernie Dashett, while everyone else got to kick ass and take names.

Cobb heard over the radio that the deal had just gone down. He knew the arrest team would be over here in the next few minutes and decided he needed to do something to make a name for himself. He could see the guy who'd handed off the missile, wandering in and out of a small, detached garage. If he pulled up nice and easy to the street, he could cut across the yard and get the drop on the man before he even knew anyone was on the property.

As Cobb watched the man move around, he couldn't resist the urge to jump in and make the arrest. His bosses might be so impressed they'd bump him over to counterterrorism or some other high-profile assignment. He'd have to come up with a reason why he'd acted alone. He thought about it and decided that he could always say it looked like the man was about to drive away. That's why he'd made the arrest without backup.

Cobb checked the black belly bag that held his Glock model 23. He unzipped it and checked the compact .40-caliber pistol. He pulled a set of handcuffs off the car's brake release, where he always stored two sets. Putting the car in drive, he eased off the curve and slowly headed right for the house. He could feel his heart rate climb. This was only his fourth actual arrest where the defendant hadn't surrendered at the U.S. Marshals' office at the courthouse.

He parked the car casually without squealing the tires or turning on his blue light. That was a little disappointing, but he knew he had to keep it calm. He stepped out of the car and then up the slight slope of the side yard to the carport. His hand was shaking as he unzipped his pouch and slowly drew his Glock. He kept his eyes on the door to the garage and started to creep toward it.

Just as he got to the door, he heard someone say, "Excuse me, can I help you?"

Cobb spun to see the man he had been watching standing at the rear of the garage. He must have walked out the other side while Cobb made his way over.

Cobb raised his gun and placed the sights at the center mass of the man, right at his chest. "FBI, on the ground." The man looked stunned, so Cobb added, "Now!"

The man complied, falling straight to the hard cement floor of the carport with his arms naturally splaying out. Cobb knew he just had to wait till the troops arrived. He was gonna be a star.

By the time Tasker and the others arrived at the house in Naranja, an FBI agent already had the homeowner in custody.

Tasker walked up to the little detached garage. "What's the scoop?" he asked the lone FBI man standing next to a cuffed man on the ground.

"I'm Cobb, FBI. Didn't want to risk this guy giving us the slip, so I nabbed him."

"You sure he gave Dashett the package?"

"Saw it myself. Into the bed of the truck."

Tasker nodded. He turned to the man on his stomach with his hands secured behind his back and asked, "What's your name?"

The man was obviously angry. "Daniel Wells."

"Okay, Dan . . ."

"The name is Daniel."

Tasker shrugged. "Okay, Daniel, you wanna tell us what's going on?"

"I think you need to tell me." His face changed different shades of red as he spoke.

Cobb said, "We don't have to tell you shit."

Veins popped out in the man's head. "I tell ya, I got nothing to do with this. You've got the wrong man."

Cobb snickered. "Yeah, I heard that before. But at least you admit something is goin' on."

Wells, in cuffs, twisted his head toward Tasker, apparently looking for a more reasonable person. "This is wrong. This man says I gave someone a missile. I've never even seen a missile."

Cobb answered before Tasker could say anything. "It doesn't matter if you ever saw a missile or not. I have. Today, about twenty minutes ago. You fucking gave it to the redneck in the exterminating truck."

"Bernie Dashett? I didn't give him a missile." His face was now into stages of purple and he looked close to the edge.

Now Tasker squatted next to the man. "Catch your breath there, Daniel." He patted him on the back. "Why was Bernie Dashett over here?"

Before he could explain, a blond woman with a little girl in her arms and a boy about six came out of the house.

"What's going on?" She looked to Wells on the ground.

Cobb, the FBI agent barked, "Shut up or you'll be in cuffs, too."

She stared at him.

He added, "And your kids will go to Child Services."

Tasker saw Camy and Sutter arriving. "Let's calm down and we'll sort this mess out."

Cobb said, "Nothing to sort out. I saw the exchange, and this guy"—he kicked Wells in the leg—"is listed as an associate to a domestic terror group."

Tasker nodded. If the man on the ground was a terrorist and they'd gotten a missile from him, they were doing all right.

Tasker asked the young FBI agent, "How do you know about the terror link?"

"I called the address into our office while I waited for the deal. They came up with his name and then a photo of him at some white supremacist summit at a restaurant."

Tasker looked at the FBI man, then down at the handcuffed prisoner. Cobb added, "Besides, he's under arrest. Let's get him to the Marshals and sort this out after we eat."

Jimmy Lail bopped up from his souped-up Honda and said, "All right, dawg." Camy gave Tasker a hug and he started to feel pretty good until he noticed the sobbing wife and kids by the back door, watching the still-protesting Wells being dragged to a waiting FBI vehicle.

six

the phone kept ringing even after Bill Tasker woke up, making him realize it wasn't a dream. He reached across to the nightstand and fumbled with the receiver.

"Hello." He sounded like an old frog with throat cancer.

"Long night?" asked a female.

"Kinda." He waited to identify the voice, then realized it had to be his ex-wife, Donna. "What's up? The girls okay?"

"Just making sure you remembered I was dropping them off about six."

"Can't wait."

"How's everything with you?"

Tasker wanted to make a comment about her recent reversal on their relationship, but let it slide. "Good, good. Made a big case yesterday. I bought an air-to-air missile."

Donna said, "Wow, that is big. I saw in the *Post* that the FBI bought one, too. Are there that many floating around?"

"Where'd the FBI do it?"

"Cutler Ridge."

The FBI had started their normal bullshit again.

Tasker joined Sutter in a booth at the Denny's on Thirty-sixth Street. Sutter always tried to eat in the city. It gave him a sense of security to be in his town, or at least that is what he said. Tasker just figured he liked the half-priced meals.

"You see the news?" asked Tasker.

Sutter, his eyes still at half-mast, said calmly, "Big deal. They stole the credit, what else is new?"

"Doesn't it piss you off?"

"Did they frame you for any crime?"

"No."

"Did any of them shoot me?"

"No."

"Then we're doing better than our last case with them." He sipped his coffee. "I'm more interested in that fine little ATF girl, Camilla Parker Bowles."

"I wouldn't call her that. She hates that nickname, and if you don't believe me, just look at Lail's eye. He only called her 'Princess.'"

"She could smack me any old time." Sutter laughed at his own comment and nodded his head like he was imagining the lovely Camy Parks punishing him.

"I know you're God's gift to ladies, but she might be interested in a different type." Tasker didn't want to go into it any further, but he didn't want his friend to waste his time, either.

"I know she's supposed to play in the all-girl league, but I think I could convert her." He paused, then slapped his friend on the back, apparently sensing the concern that was overtaking him about the FBI. "Cheer up, Billy. We're heroes, even if nobody knows it."

Tasker smiled at that thought until he pictured Wells' kids crying as they took him away yesterday.

39
shock wave

That evening, after a day of congratulations and paperwork at the office, Tasker relaxed at his Kendall town house, waiting for the girls to arrive. He planned to work only a couple of hours tomorrow, then spend the whole weekend with them. This teachers' planning day would give them time to just kick back before he took them to the little beach at Biscayne Bay, or maybe to the Monkey Jungle.

Without knocking, Donna popped her head in the front door, followed closely by the girls.

"You decent?"

Tasker avoided the obvious comeback.

After the hugs all around and settling the girls in their room, Tasker and Donna walked out onto the patio together.

"You look great," said Donna.

"Having a normal schedule and less stress helps."

"No more problems from that FBI case?"

"No, pretty much people act like it never happened, which is fine."

She paused and looked him in the eyes. "I'm sorry I've screwed with your emotions. I didn't mean to."

He gave her a flat stare. "You mean leading me to believe we were getting back together was an accident?"

"No. I mean yes." She gathered her thoughts. "You were just so down and I was in a different place."

"What place was that?"

"Billy, don't be like that. We have a good relationship now. Let's not blow that."

"We had a good relationship four years ago. Now we skirt all issues and hand the girls back and forth like a hot plate."

"What issues do we have now?"

"Your boyfriend."

She stared at him. "My feelings for Nicky don't really affect us."

"Unless you hate him, your feelings don't help us, either."

"I don't hate him, but I do have feelings for him. Everything'll work out, Billy. You're a good-looking guy and have a good job. You're a catch."

He smiled and nodded his head. "Thanks."

She leaned in and hugged him. "It really is good to see your life back on track. How're your folks?"

"Good. I'd send them a newspaper about this case if FDLE were even mentioned."

"I remember you being media-shy not too long ago."

He remembered how he'd been scrutinized by the press then, and suddenly felt better about not being in the papers now.

Bernie Dashett sat in one of the interview rooms of the Metropolitan Correction Center southwest of Miami, listening to this attorney his mama had hired for him. He wasn't sure there was much he could do, since he really was guilty of trying to sell the missile.

He looked across at the twenty-five-year-old Reynaldo Hirsh, as the young man ran his hand over his slicked-back hair for the sixth time in the last five minutes.

The tiny room had just a small table in the middle with two chairs. The guards for the Bureau of Prisons only allowed the attorney to bring a pad and pen and searched him thoroughly. Bernie wore his orange jumpsuit.

"What are we gonna do?" asked Bernie.

"You had first appearance, so now we figure out how to cut a deal quick. What about the other guy, Wells?"

"See, that's what's so funny. Daniel Wells didn't have nothin' to do with this. I just stopped there to pick up my possum trap."

"Your what?"

"Possum trap. For my exterminator business."

"So Wells didn't do anything?"

"Naw, nothin'. I was just waitin' for someone to ask, but the FBI fella just brung us here. Daniel and I never even got the chance to talk with each other."

The lawyer stood up. "Don't tell anyone this. If we tell them Wells wasn't involved, we got nothing to deal with. Some phantom National Guardsman from Tampa won't cut it. You keep your fucking mouth shut."

Tasker took a minute to make sure he had everything that wasn't necessary out of his pockets and stashed in the car. MCC Miami had good security and didn't waste time making state cops comfortable. He looked up at the high walls, with row after row of razor wire strung on top. He knew no one had ever made it out of the federal holding facility, but a couple had tried. The concrete compound had even held Manuel Noriega for a time.

Camy Parks pulled up next to him and sprang out of her old, beat-up issued Ford Crown Victoria. The big car made her look like a dwarf next to it. She had on tight slacks and a polo shirt with the ATF emblem on the left side of her impressive chest.

"Hey, Billy," she glanced at her watch and added, "Sorry, late night."

"Out partying?"

"Better. *In* partying." She let out a sly smile.

Tasker felt his face flush. He wanted to ask more questions but refrained. "Dashett's attorney just called me and said we couldn't talk to his client. Since Wells asked to see us, we're on good legal ground."

"Did the court appoint an attorney?"

"Not yet. Wells said he wanted the weekend to try and find one."

"Think he's got anything good?" She was emptying everything in her pockets, too.

"Don't know until we talk to him."

After they had gone through security and waited almost an hour for Wells to be brought down, a guard finally told Tasker and Camy they could go into one of the interview rooms. Tasker counted every minute as one more he could spend with his daughters, but knew he had to get this interview done before Wells changed his mind about talking to them.

Inside, Wells sat on one side of the small table. His eyes followed them into the room without giving away any hint of emotion.

Tasker said, "Daniel, you remember me?"

He just nodded.

"This is Agent Parks with the ATF." Tasker waited, then after no response, he went on. "We're here 'cause you said you wanted to talk."

"You got the wrong man."

Camy cut in. "How do you figure?"

"I don't know nothin' about any Stinger missile. As far as I know, Bernie Dashett is an exterminator."

"How do you explain an FBI agent seeing you give Dashett the Stinger just before he tried to sell it to us?" asked Camy.

"All I did was fix his possum trap."

"His what?"

"Possum trap. For his business." He looked at Tasker. "Look, mister, you seem pretty reasonable. You guys have made a mistake. That's all. I did not have anything to do with that missile."

Camy looked at Tasker and said, "You'd think these mopes would come up with a better story after surveillance saw the whole thing."

Wells cut in. "That's the problem. They didn't see it because it didn't happen. Listen, I got a friend, an associate, who could clear this up if you called him."

Camy cut him off. "You need to call a lawyer, Wells. If you don't want to help us, you're gonna need to hire one."

"But if you just call this friend of mine at—"

The ATF agent held up her hand. "We've wasted enough time." She turned to Tasker. "Let's go, Billy."

To keep the unity up, Tasker walked out, but not before considering what Wells had said. Maybe he could check a few things out real quick before he got home to the girls.

seven

at the atf impound lot, Bill Tasker looked over the old Chevy 1500 truck that Bernie Dashett used for his exterminator business and to deliver the Stinger missile. Camy had gone into her office and left him to look through the toolboxes that ran around the entire truck bed walls. The toolboxes had been unlocked, but nothing appeared missing from inside. Anything that had been loose in the truck bed had been thrown into the cab.

He opened the door and had to step back from the stench of tobacco and something else. He couldn't be sure what caused the musky odor, but felt confident it had to do with Bernie Dashett's occupation.

A metal cage with springs inside sat on the seat. Tasker lifted it and examined it closely. This had to be the cage Wells said he fixed. He set the large cage outside on the ground. The cab was still a mess. He couldn't tell if it was always like this or was the result of the search by impounding agents. An empty duffel bag lay crumpled on the floor in front of where the cage had sat. He found a lone sheet of paper that wasn't stained and wrinkled. An official receipt from Naranja Engineering, for forty dollars, for repairs and alterations on a possum trap. The receipt was dated two days earlier. The day of the arrest.

Inside the office, Tasker told Camy Parks and Jimmy Lail what he had found.

"So," said Jimmy, "the banger just slid word in with his story."

Tasker looked at him. "What?"

Camy interpreted. "He knew what happened and used it to fit his story."

Tasker said, "Was the possum cage in the bed of the truck?"

"We weren't sure what it was, so we left it in the cab but, yeah, I think it was in the back when we seized the truck."

"Did you guys seize anything of evidentiary value?"

Camy looked at a sheet on her desk and said, "Nope, just a precaution." She saw Tasker's expression and said, "Billy, don't worry, it's airtight. With his past connection the FBI has documented, he's all done."

Jimmy added, "Yo, my brother, we got that dawg in pound. For true."

Tasker stared at him, weighing the value in punching an FBI agent.

He made it home after five. The girls were ready to rumble, having been cooped up all day in his town house. His older neighbor, Mrs. Hernandez, who treated Tasker like a relative, always trying to feed him empanadas or some other outstanding Latin dish, watched the girls for him. She enjoyed the two girls and sometimes took them to her daughter's house to play with her three granddaughters.

Now the girls wanted to roughhouse with him, but he couldn't concentrate. He kept going back in his mind to see if Wells' story could be true. The key factors were the FBI agent seeing the exchange and the FBI intel report on Wells. But Tasker knew firsthand how FBI allegations could spiral out of control. If he hadn't jumped to his own defense, he'd be at MCC right now on charges the FBI had dreamed up based on worse info than this.

"Daddy, can we eat at Chili's?" asked Kelly, the oldest.

"Anything you angels want," he agreed without thinking.

On the drive over there, he ducked the usual questions about girls and boys and if he was dating. His girls had a good outlook on just about everything, and that included reconciliation with his wife. He'd held that hope for a while. Now he was less confident. He could trace where things had gone wrong. He was in Miami in the first place, instead of the West Palm Beach office where he'd started, because of a shooting incident up there involving a corrupt West Palm cop who had been his friend. For a while, some people had thought he was corrupt, too, maybe even killed the cop to hide his role in it, but that was crazy, and eventually everyone realized it. The case had garnered a good deal of publicity, though, and he had started to drink. More important, he'd changed. He changed from good-natured to gloomy, his marriage had broken up, he'd been transferred to Miami. It had only been the last year that he realized it had been all his fault.

Ironically, it was the recent ordeal with the FBI that had brought him and Donna back together. He now figured that if they were meant to be together, things would work out. Maybe he was going back to good-natured, but he wasn't sure.

After dinner, instead of heading back north toward his town house, Tasker headed east to US 1, then turned south.

"Where are we going, Daddy?" asked Emily, her bright eyes happy to take in whatever new landscape they passed.

"Just thought we'd drive around a little. You don't get to see much of this area. That's all gonna change. I don't intend to work as much as I have, so we can spend plenty of time together."

He cut through Pinecrest so the girls could see the nice houses.

"Why don't you live there, Daddy?" asked Emily.

"Costs way, way, way, way too much."

Kelly said, "Sarah Colgan at school says you're rich."

"How does she figure that?"

"She says no one ever found the money they said you took, and her dad says you still have it."

Tasker chuckled at that. "You can tell Sarah Colgan she is full of beans."

As they passed the mall at Cutler Ridge, Kelly asked, "Is that where you got the bad guy?"

He smiled. "Sure is. How'd you know?"

"Mom showed us the news story and said they got the FBI confused with FDLE, but that you were the one who stopped that bad man. She said we should be proud."

"Did she?" He smiled all the way down to Southwest 264th Street, where he turned right.

"Where are we?" asked Emily.

"They call it Naranja."

"You know someone here?"

"Sort of," said Tasker, as he drove past Daniel Wells' house. The lights were on in the living room and he thought about the kids whose dad wasn't there.

eight

early monday morning, after a good weekend with the girls and a pleasant conversation with his ex-wife when he dropped them off, Tasker found himself again in Naranja. He had already been by Wells' house twice. Once at six-thirty, then again at seven. Finally he saw movement about seven-fifteen. It was early, but he didn't have much time. He parked on the street and walked up to the front door over the long, narrow driveway.

A wiry boy about six with a buzz cut showing just a haze of blond hair answered the door. Tasker flashed back to his childhood summers of sunburnt heads from Mom's buzz cuts the day after school let out.

"I bet they call you Buzz," said Tasker, leaning over with a smile.

The kid slammed the door. Tasker heard him yell. "Mama, there's some weird guy at the door."

After a minute's wait and some peeking from behind the curtains, a surprisingly beautiful woman answered the door. She seemed different from the other day somehow, more striking. Her blue eyes and light complexion made her look Scandinavian, but her accent marked her as a southerner. Not Florida. Alabama maybe.

"Can I help you?"

Tasker showed his badge and identification. "I'm Bill Tasker."

"I remember you." Her tone wasn't harsh, just cautious.

"Mrs. Wells, I was wondering if I could talk to you for a minute."

"Daniel says he tried to explain at the jail, but you wouldn't listen. You don't understand. My Daniel is a good man. A smart man. He has three years of college. He only left the University of Florida to help his daddy when he got sick. He'd never do nothin' like you said."

"That's what I'm trying to find out." Even in a nightgown with the boy hanging on her leg, this girl exuded grace. The words "southern belle" came to mind. There was something else. Something that didn't fit with his image of a southern belle.

She looked at him. "What do you need?"

"I'd like to look at his workshop."

She shook her head, tentatively. "I don't think that's a good idea."

Tasker nodded. "I understand your reticence."

She gave him a quizzical look.

"I understand your reluctance," Tasker said. "But I need to check some information."

She thought about it. "I don't know," she started slowly. "I don't wanna get him in worse trouble somehow. You ain't got a warrant, do you?"

"No, nothing like that. I want to see if I can back up Daniel's story at all."

She looked up at his face, almost studying it. "That other fella just tried to trick me into saying stuff the other day."

"What other fella?"

"The FBI agent, Mr. Cobb. He told me all kinds of things, but he didn't want to help Daniel. If Daniel can't work, we'll lose this place. I don't think I should make it worse for him."

"Mrs. Wells, I am not with the FBI. I swear to God, all I want is the truth. The truth might be that Daniel tried to make some extra money and didn't tell you a thing about it. But if the truth is that he wasn't involved, then that's what I want to find out."

She assessed him carefully. Looking up into his eyes and taking a step closer, she asked, "You swear that's what you're doing?"

Tasker looked into her beautiful face and felt himself hesitate as he lost concentration. This girl had to know she had this kind of effect on men. She was better than a polygraph. She knew no mortal man could look into her eyes and lie.

Tasker said, "I swear to you I just want the truth."

She took a long moment, squeezed the boy at her side and then sent him into the house with a playful swat on the butt. She looked at Tasker again. "Okay, I'll open it up. I don't know why, but you look sincere. I don't think you're trying to hurt Daniel."

"I do just want the truth. We have enough to hold him now, anyway. But if I find anything, then *I'll* know we were right. And if I find something that helps *him* significantly, I'll let the prosecutor know before his bond hearing this afternoon. That's why I'm bothering you so early."

She nodded slowly, obviously still coming to grips with the bizarre fate of her husband. She led him through the carport to the detached one-car garage. An oversized van with faded signs that said NARANJA ENGINEERING was parked at the end of the driveway.

She stood on her toes in her bare feet to reach the keypad that opened the door. "Go ahead. I got to get my other two fed." She hurried past him toward the house without another word.

He nodded and proceeded to scan the top of the workbench. Nothing more than tools and some instructions for a welding torch. The garage as a whole was very neat and orderly. He knew the type. A place for everything and everything in its place. His father had run the dry cleaners in Boca like that.

He looked in a few containers, one with rusty roofing nails and one with a noxious smelling, gooey liquid. Then on a small, neat desk he found something that immediately caught his attention. A personal check. Bernie Dashett had written a check to Naranja Engineering for forty dollars. Giving an alibi was one thing. But this kind of detail was unheard-of. Tasker snatched up the check and headed back through the carport. As he neared the front door, Mrs. Wells stepped outside. Now in a sundress, she looked like the girl next door, if you lived next door to the set of *Baywatch*.

"Find anything?"

Tasker almost stuttered. "Maybe. We'll know by the hearing. What if we talk then?"

"You help Daniel and we'll talk any time you like." She smiled and Tasker knew it was time to get to the office.

He walked through the front doors of the new FDLE building off 107th Avenue and Twelfth Street at exactly nine o'clock. Before he could make the inner doors, the receptionist called to him from behind thick, clear Plexar.

"This was in the mail shoot for you when we opened." She held up an envelope a little larger than a sheet of paper. The word "Urgent" was written in red marker across the front with his name in the corner. The receptionist slid it under the glass.

He opened it as he took the elevator to the third floor. Walking down the hallway, he heard, but didn't acknowledge, greetings from everyone he passed. He slid out an eight-by-ten photo with a note on the back. The comment read: "Nazi summit, Dell Linley et al., August 4, 2002." There was an address and time marked on it as well. The "et al." was something cops and prosecutors used to say "everyone else involved." Sometimes it was to save time and sometimes it was just laziness. He turned over the photo and looked at two young men talking in the outside courtyard of a McDonald's. The photo was taken from across the street with a telephoto lens. Who the hell would send him something like this? Tasker looked at the scene again and didn't see the connection until he noticed the man inside the restaurant with two small children eating at a table. It was Daniel Wells.

All day he had wondered who had sent him the photo of the "Nazi summit." The piece of the puzzle that had led to Daniel Wells' immediate arrest.

It hadn't exactly been a summit, and more important, Wells had had nothing to do with it. So the question hit him again: Who had sent it to him? He toyed with the idea that it might have been the FBI agent who'd spotted the transfer of the Stinger, Jim Cobb. Maybe the guy realized he had screwed up and wanted to set things right. But it didn't add up. Cobb certainly didn't strike Tasker as the kind of cop that went back on a judgment, no matter how outlandish it was.

Now Tasker couldn't worry about it anymore. He had other problems. He tried to talk to the assistant U.S. attorney just as the hearing started, but traffic was brutal, and trying to run down where the photo had come from and what it meant had taken time. It seemed clear to him that the FBI intelligence that had helped land Daniel Wells in jail was shitty, if it was based on this photo. Who has a summit of white racists with only two rednecks talking outside a McDonald's? Wells wasn't even with them. He was just having lunch with his kids. Tasker had just driven down past the McDonald's in Goulds an hour ago and confirmed it was the closest one to the Wells house. They had the wrong fucking guy in jail.

The refurbished Magistrate's Courtroom, or "Mag Court" for short, was in the Federal Courthouse on Miami Avenue in downtown Miami. A large deputy U.S. Marshal in a suit stood next to each door, since there was a prisoner involved in the hearing. The high ceiling and the space between the formal-looking magistrate and lawyers gave the courtroom the feel of a big meeting hall. The room wasn't particularly crowded. A few old men from Miami Beach. They just liked hearing cases now and then. A few reporters and the guy who sketched the hearing. Federal courts, unlike state courts, didn't allow cameras of any sort in the courtroom.

Tasker fidgeted in the seat as the hearing got under way. He didn't want to just stop it, so he waited for a recess. They were going to look at Bernie Dashett first, anyway.

Tasker nodded to Camy, who was sitting up front. It took him a second to recognize Jimmy Lail in a nice blue business suit sitting next to her.

After a short opening statement, the portly assistant U.S. attorney called Jimmy to the stand to summarize what had happened the day of the arrests. Tasker thought this should be good for a laugh.

When asked to lay out the whole scenario, Jimmy began, "After identifying one subject, Bernard Harold Dashett of 21468 Hallow Road, an undercover sting operation was set up to interdict the Stinger missile Mr. Dashett had offered on the open market." He had a southern, possibly Texas, drawl.

Tasker was stunned. The idiot could talk. A casual observer would view him as an intelligent, professional law enforcement official. If they only knew.

Finally, at a five-minute recess, Tasker stepped up to Camy and said, "We gotta talk."

"What's up?"

"We grabbed the wrong guy. Daniel Wells handed him a possum trap, not a missile."

She smiled. "Stop fooling around."

"I'm serious." Tasker ran down all of his leads as Jimmy Lail walked over.

Jimmy jumped in. "No way, dawg. That gansta is righteous and going down."

Tasker stopped and looked at him. "Talk to me like you were on the stand."

Jimmy frowned, straightened his tie and said, "Mind your own fucking business, Tasker. Everyone knows you'd do whatever you could to tarnish the Bureau."

Tasker decided he liked the urban mode better, but simply turned and explained the entire situation to the assistant U.S. attorney. Five minutes later, the heavy little prosecutor stood and said to the magistrate, "Your honor, at this time, the government would have no objection to Mr. Wells being released on his own recognizance until further investigation is complete." There were murmurs throughout the small crowd.

Tasker looked up to see Camy and Jimmy Lail scowling at him.

When the magistrate asked what the reversal of request was based on, the AUSA said, "Agent Tasker of the FDLE has uncovered sufficient information as to cast doubt on Mr. Wells' role in this venture."

The magistrate banged her gavel and said, "Mr. Wells, you are released based on your word that you will return to this court if required. Do you agree?"

Wells stood and said, "Yes, Your Honor."

With that, Tasker felt Mrs. Wells' soft arms wrap around him and a voice too close to his ear say, "Thank you so much." Tasker looked over to see the *Miami Herald* reporter furiously scribbling notes and the independent sketch artist looking at him and the defendant's wife in an embrace. This was going to cause some shit.

It had seemed so simple. So necessary. He had done what he needed to do. They had made a mistake and he'd corrected it by doing what he was trained to do: investigate.

Not everyone agreed with that simple logic. Now, sitting in his supervisor's office, he was starting to feel the consequences.

"Billy, you made the right decision, no question," said the special agent supervisor, his gray eyes warm and friendly.

"But I'm effectively cut out of my own case?"

"No, you'll still testify if it goes to trial."

"I can't believe you caved to the Bureau like that."

"It wasn't a question of caving. The U.S. attorney said it was best for the case. They were happy that you saved them going after the wrong man, but you still got Bernie Dashett. He's the right man."

"That's the only reason?"

The supervisor paused. "That's the main reason."

"What are the other reasons?"

"The Bureau raised hell."

Tasker sat at his desk, doing the mundane paperwork that every cop complains about. After half an hour, he dialed Camy Parks' cell phone.

"Hello." Her bright voice cheered him immediately.

"Camy, it's Bill Tasker." Before he could say anything else, she hung up. He just stared at he phone. This was like breaking up with a girl.

He sat there, staring off into space, when a slap on the back brought him back to reality.

"Billy, why so down?" asked Frank Hutcheon, one of the senior squad members.

"Just case problems."

"Look on the bright side, at least you're not the target of the case." He chuckled, but when Tasker didn't laugh, the older agent added, "Are you?"

After a day during which his friends at the office really did try to make him feel better, with no effect, Tasker went home. Throwing together a salad for dinner, he had the local Channel 11 news on. They had led the charge against him in the media when he'd been suspected of the Alpha National Bank robbery, but he still tended to watch. They really did get the scoops most often.

As he half-listened, he heard the name of the local FBI assistant special agent in charge. His head snapped up and he saw the trim, well-dressed, Latin man talking on camera. Not behind a bank of microphones, like at a news conference, but one-on-one, as if they'd surprised him in public. What he said wasn't a surprise or off the cuff. The FBI ASAC had a well-prepared statement.

"We at the Federal Bureau of Investigation are a little concerned that FDLE Agent Tasker has allowed his personal feelings for the FBI to influence this investigation."

Tasker noticed that the administrative creep wouldn't even refer to him by his correct title, "special agent," because they felt only FBI agents should be called special agents. Aside from that, the ASAC never even hinted that anyone was worried about arresting the wrong guy based on some ambitious rookie's incorrect observation. Tasker looked at the TV and wondered who had sent him the photograph of the so-called Nazi summit. Then, as he saw file footage of himself, taken after the Alpha National Bank case against him had been dropped, he realized this was all too similar to his last experience with the FBI.

To gain perspective, Tasker took a drive down into Naranja, just to see the Wells' house. As he came down the road, he saw the oldest boy in the front yard, kicking a soccer ball. His blond hair was a little longer than his little brother's. He noticed Tasker and immediately ran inside. Daniel Wells hurried out and waved to Tasker as he walked to the car.

"What are you doing down here?"

Tasker smiled. "Don't really know. Guess I just wanted to make sure you were doing okay."

"Good. At least better than the weekend in jail. The news people won't leave us alone."

"I know the feeling."

Wells smiled. "Come on in. Alicia would love to see you."

"No, I couldn't."

"Are you kidding? Come on in." He turned and headed back up the driveway, obviously expecting Tasker to follow.

Inside it was a madhouse, with kids running around, a dog barking, the TV blaring and the lovely Alicia Wells scurrying around the kitchen in tight jean shorts and a tank top. Her hair was pulled into a ponytail, making Tasker realize she was even younger than he had first speculated. He guessed that the oldest boy was about Emily's age, seven or eight. Maybe the lithe and friendly woman was twenty-five, but he doubted it. More like twenty-three. That made Daniel Wells . . . That made Daniel Wells a criminal. At least it did a few years ago.

Tasker bumped into a suitcase, knocking it into another and then a third, like a row of dominoes. He bent over to pick up the canvas bags, mumbling an apology.

Wells said, "Don't worry about it."

Tasker looked at the five matching suitcases, then at Wells.

"Like I said, the news people been buggin' us, so I'm sending Alicia and the kids to some relatives tomorrow."

Tasker nodded, surprised at how sorry he was to see Mrs. Wells leave the county.

Wells said, "I've got family all over."

Tasker smiled. "Noticed you didn't have an accent like your wife."

"Had one when I was younger. Growing up in Ocala, you can develop a drawl, but my dad was strict about language, and a few years at UF knocked it out of me."

Tasker nodded. "I know what you mean. I had the opposite effect. Raised down here, I didn't hear a drawl until I went to FSU."

"You're a Seminole? You seemed so smart."

They both laughed at the familiar rival university jabs. The phone started ringing, adding to the atmosphere of total confusion. Wells made no effort to answer it. Instead he held up a finger to Tasker, indicating he'd be right back. Tasker figured sign language was used a lot in this house. When he jumped at a screeching cat zipping through the living room, he saw Alicia Wells come up to him, smiling.

"Don't pay no mind to all this. This is a quiet night." Without warning, she leaned into Tasker and stood on her tiptoes to kiss him square on the mouth. "That was to thank you for everything."

Completely flustered, he said, "Didn't do anything but straighten out a mistake." To quickly change the subject and get Alicia to move back a pace, he looked at the two wrestling boys in the family room and said, "They don't look too upset by the whole thing."

"They were. It was actually quiet here over the weekend. It's Daniel that likes the noise and confusion. He stirs it up more often than not."

Tasker felt relieved when her husband came back from the rear of the house. She immediately slid away from Tasker.

He had an odd feeling, like she was coming on to him. From his experience with rural families, he decided he was imagining it. His body wasn't, but he was.

Tasker and Wells moved to the small dining room and sat at the round table.

"I owe you a lot, Mr. Tasker. And one day I'll make it up to you."

"You don't owe me a thing." He paused and then said, "You know I had some help getting you off the hook."

"Really," was all Wells said.

"There was a photograph that was supposed to show you at a Nazi summit of some kind."

Wells laughed. "Nazis! I wouldn't hang out with them. Their idea of anarchy is blowing up an empty bus. And they're very unreliable in payin' bills. Just a bunch of dumb-asses, you ask me."

Tasker looked at him. He didn't know what that meant. Before he could ask, Alicia Wells came out in a short skirt with a new, sheer tank top. Her pink nipples clearly showed through the top as her long, smooth legs glided her toward the dining room.

Tasker stood. "Gotta go."

Alicia registered disappointment, but Daniel Wells pushed him along, thanking him again.

As he backed his Jeep out of the driveway, Tasker's headlights fell across the old step van next to the garage. The whole visit had left him somewhat uneasy. When he pulled out onto the road, he saw Daniel Wells watching him from the carport.

nine

"billy, you gotta get back on the horse what threw ya," said his supervisor, in his typical Long Island take on English.

"Sure, boss. Just take me a few days to get a handle on something decent."

"In the meantime, I got a lead request from our Pensacola office about some fugitive down here."

"What's he wanted for?"

"Selling some kind of homemade explosive. Got him as part of a RICO on dope smuggling as well as separate charges having to do with an incendiary device. Could be fun." He handed Tasker a folder with six sheets of paper and a photograph. The wide, dark-haired man had a surfer cut. He looked like he might be thick with broad shoulders and a perpetual five-o'clock shadow.

"I'll jump right on it. Do you mind if I let my buddy from the city tag along?"

"Free manpower, no problem."

"He just likes to get out once in a while, and I screwed up his chances on the Stinger case."

"Don't forget, he's on your badge outside the city. Keep a good eye on him."

"Believe me, boss, with Sutter you always keep an eye on him. If you don't, he'll have your woman, your money—and still be your friend." Tasker winked and headed out.

Derrick Sutter stood outside the Miami Police substation on Fifty-fourth Street, waiting for Tasker to pick him up. He tried to dress down, based on where they were headed. No one in Florida City would appreciate his imitation leather jacket or fine, almost real, jewelry. He'd even changed his shiny Thom McAns for a pair of hiking boots he never thought he'd wear.

He spotted Tasker's gold Monte Carlo a block away and moved to the street, looking from one apartment complex to the next. He jumped in, suddenly conscious that he didn't want anyone from this neighborhood seeing him with a white guy. Even a real decent white guy like Tasker. Was he a racist? He couldn't care less.

"Appreciate you taking the brother outta the city for a while," Sutter said with a smile.

"How'd you clear it with your boss?"

"He assigns me all over the place. I'm workin' with vice four times in the next three weeks. He don't know I'm not on the missile case. Hell, he probably didn't even see it on the news. Now what do we got?"

"Fugitive from the panhandle. Lives in Florida City. Shouldn't be a problem to find."

"I never been to Florida City."

"You're shittin' me."

"Furthest south I been is that tittie bar near Kendall."

"You love your topless joints," Tasker said.

"That a problem?" asked Sutter.

"Only if you're short of cash like me."

"If Florida City or Homestead don't have a notable titty bar, then I never been there. In fact, I think the Wells house is the furthest south I ever been and that was just last week."

"You had to pass Florida City to get to the Keys."

"Never been to the damn Keys. Hate the beach. That's why I only visit my folks on holidays."

"Your parents live on the ocean?"

"Don't sound so surprised. Haitians ain't the only black folk that came from waterfront property."

"I didn't mean that. I just figured they lived in the City."

"Hell, I don't even live in the City. And just because I live on Miami Beach don't mean I do it 'cause of the beach. I live there 'cause of the pussy."

"Where do your parents live?"

Sutter folded his arms. He usually avoided this type of conversation. It chipped away at his image as the urban defender of the people. Tasker was a friend. Probably his best friend. He wouldn't give him a hard time. "They live over on Hollywood Beach."

"For how long?"

"I dunno. Fifteen, eighteen years."

"So you lived there too? What, until you were eighteen?"

"Twenty-two."

Tasker broke out in a broad smile. Sutter had noticed that the FDLE agent didn't smile all that much, so he didn't mind if it was at his expense once in a while. He waited for the inevitable grilling about his childhood as he took in the scenery, heading south down US 1 after the interstate ended.

Tasker held off a minute and then asked, "Where were you born?"

"Miami."

"How old were you when you moved?"

"Two days."

Tasker just looked at him.

Sutter wanted to move this along. "I was born at Jackson Memorial because my mom was a nurse there and got a good discount. I grew up in Hallandale until I was twelve, when we moved to the condo on Hollywood Beach. Satisfied?"

"What'd your dad do?"

"Liquor store robber."

"Good money in that, huh?"

"You moron, he's an accountant."

Tasker slowed so he could look over at Sutter. "So Mr. badass, supercool Miami urban legend was raised on the ocean in Hollywood."

"Only since I was twelve."

"What about being from the street?"

"Ocean Avenue is a street. How do you think we drove home?"

Tasker kept staring at him. His mouth even dropped open.

Sutter said, "Now you can stop, you're giving me the creeps."

"So the urban-street stuff is all bullshit?"

"That's one way to look at it."

"Is there another way to look at it?"

Sutter gazed out at the Dadeland Mall as it sprawled, and simply said, "Not really."

Using some information on data sheets that Sutter had never seen as a City of Miami cop, they drove right up to a house that the fugitive, Anthony Mule, probably lived in. At least he'd paid the electric there in the past month. The small concrete-block house sat on the northern edge of Florida City. The place wasn't in bad shape, with a fairly new roof. Sutter thought about it and realized that every house in Florida City had a fairly new roof, at least since Hurricane Andrew.

"What's the plan?" asked Sutter.

"Let's ask a few neighbors, to see if he's around." Tasker surveyed the street. "You take this one and I'll go next door." He pointed at the two small houses sitting in front of them.

"You crazy? These rednecks'll think I'm here to do their lawn or that I'm a home invader. You ask, I'll wait."

"You're a racist. Give these people a chance. I've found that no one wants a criminal living next to them. They'll talk to us."

"Okay, Saint Bill, you follow me while I ask, we'll see who's crazy."

The house next door had a wraparound porch and a small putting green for a front yard. Sutter walked to the door while Tasker stood near the carport, where a three-year-old Buick LeSabre sat. In truth, Sutter really hadn't had much experience with neighborhoods like this. In the City, areas were bad or ritzy. Nothing in-between. The funny thing was that the bad areas only had a few bad people. Most everyone else treated him, and even the cops in general, pretty good. It was the rich people who were a pain in the ass, always demanding things and treating the cops like servants. This was like a foreign land to him in the south county, with all the trees and plants and pickup trucks.

An elderly lady, so small she may have been a midget, came to the screen door but didn't open it. Before Sutter could identify himself or ask anything, she said, "No, I have someone cut my grass already."

Sutter threw a look over to Tasker. He turned back to her. "No, ma'am"—he pulled out his badge—"I just wanted to ask you a few questions."

The woman gasped and stepped back. "I'm calling the police."

"I *am* the police."

"There is nothing here worth taking." She put her hand on her chest like she was feeling faint.

Sutter shook his head. "Lady, I'm not a criminal. Here, look." He motioned Tasker to the door. "I brought my own white man."

As soon as the old lady saw Tasker, she calmed down and stepped back to the door. She eyed them carefully.

Tasker said, "I'm Bill Tasker with the State Police. We were wondering if we could ask you a few questions."

The lady sighed and said, "Oh, why yes, of course. What do you want to know?"

Sutter said, "Well, first off, how come I show you a badge and you think I'm a robber, but he just says he's with the police and you believe him?"

"Because you're black."

Sutter was shocked, then a little amused. In this world of political correctness gone bad, this lady just told him the truth. That was better for his soul than all the lying store clerks and lawyers and politicians who said one thing and did another.

The old lady added, "I'm sorry, son. I just don't see many colored police officers down here. I was wrong."

Sutter could've kissed the old lady. She was honest and admitted she was wrong. Maybe these old, ignorant rednecks weren't so bad after all.

After a few minutes they learned all they needed about Mr. Anthony Mule. He pronounced it Mule-*lay,* with an accent on the *e.* He lived alone. Didn't talk to the neighbors much. Was up all night and quiet all day. She didn't think he left the house too much but he had a fair number of visitors. He had an old van and sometimes carried surfboards around in the van.

Armed with that information, Sutter and Tasker decided a quiet recon was the way to go. They split up and eased around the outside of Mule's home, peeking in windows where possible and looking for signs of life.

Sutter noticed one window-mounted air conditioner running in the rear bedroom. Tasker found a beat-up Ford van with two surfboards crammed inside behind the house. They concluded it was a good bet the fugitive was asleep in the back bedroom.

Sutter said, "What's your policy say? Call in SWAT, alert the locals, write up a plan, call the media and wait for the guy to come out?"

"Funny. I'd usually knock, but this guy won't come to the door."

"Let's try the kitchen door. If he ain't home, we lock it back up and come back another time."

Tasker nodded his head in agreement.

The rickety old door popped out at the bottom and was missing a couple of jalousies in the middle. The handle was unlocked, but a bolt held it near the top of the door. Without hesitation, Sutter popped out a spring-loaded knife and slid it up the crack of the door jamb. In less than three seconds, the door was open and they were inside the hot, musty old house. The smell of cheap homegrown pot hung in every inch of the house. All the interior doors were open but one. The one with an air conditioner.

Sutter thought that once inside the house, it didn't look all that different from a house in Liberty City. A cheesy felt painting of a matador hung on the living room wall, an old TV with rabbit-ear antennas sat in front of an old sofa. People were people.

They crept down the hall to the closed door. At the door, Tasker tried the handle quietly. When he was about to go in, they heard a toilet flush and looked at each other. It didn't sound like it came from inside the room. Behind them a wide man with dark hair, wearing only a pair of gym shorts, opened a bathroom door and stepped into the hallway. His eyes were half closed and hair stuck out in wild designs, even the thick hair on his back. He looked up, opened his bloodshot eyes and without warning darted down the hallway toward the rear door. On his way, he hopped up and yanked on a string hanging from the ceiling. A set of attic stairs swung to the floor, blocking the entire hallway.

Too late, Tasker yelled, "Police! Don't move!" The two cops rushed down the hallway, Sutter throwing his weight into the stairs to get them up and Tasker scrambling below them. By the time they reached the kitchen, Mule was out the back and streaking across the sandy yard to a detached garage.

Tasker repeated, "Police! Don't move!"

Sutter added, "You're dead meat, redneck."

Instinctively they both paused at the garage, not wanting to rush into a waiting gun. As they stood on either side of the door with pistols drawn, Sutter reached over and shoved it hard so it would swing open, giving them a clear view of the interior. When the door reached the end of its arc, Sutter heard a click, and then his world became a confused tapestry of sound and dirt.

The single window blew out with an orange haze of fire behind it and the door swung closed so hard it splintered. Tasker flew back into the yard and Sutter was knocked off his feet. It took five seconds of clearing smoke and settling debris for him to realize they had set off an explosive booby trap.

Tasker was up quick. "You okay? You okay?"

Sutter nodded, pushing himself up slowly. Tasker was off around the back. When Sutter slowly made it to the side of the garage, his ears ringing, he could see his partner chasing the still-shirtless Mule across the wide-open field. Trees lined the end of the field where the next road cut in. Tasker was going to have to pick it up if he expected to catch that guy.

Bill Tasker gasped for breath as he closed the gap on the fleeing fugitive. He always seemed to get winded in a foot chase, no matter how much he trained, but this time he attributed a lot of it to the fact that the explosion had scared the living shit out of him. Making matters worse was the uneven ground on the weed-ridden field. He yelled at Mule a couple of times and even thought about firing a shot into the ground to scare him, but then decided to rely on his own aerobic ability to wear the fugitive down.

Tasker was careful as he closed the gap, because he saw that Mule now had an army green bag with a shoulder strap slung over his hairy shoulder. Had this moron picked up a gun? The question was answered when Mule, without breaking stride, pulled something from the bag, fiddled with it and threw it straight up in the air. Tasker slowed and watched the small cylinder hit the ground. A loud, gut-jarring explosion blew up weeds and sand where the object had hit.

"Holy shit," Tasker said aloud, dropping to the ground. He watched as the running man headed for the tree line. Now Tasker was mad enough to take a potshot at this asshole. He got up and started to sprint when another explosion cracked behind the running man. The guy didn't even know if anyone was chasing him, that one was just a precaution.

As Mule made the trees, Tasker was fifty yards behind him with his ears stuffed from the explosions. He tried shouting, but it just reverberated in his head. The man darted through the trees and out of sight.

Before Tasker reached the trees, he heard a thump and three of the loud explosions almost simultaneously. He paused at the trees, taking cover as he looked onto the road. He was surprised at the sight of his car—stopped, Mule on the ground in front of it, his bag torn to shreds and smoking on the ground. Sutter leaned on the hood with his arms folded. "I don't like snakes. Hope you don't mind me borrowing your car?"

"I had the keys. How . . ." Tasker stopped when he saw the look Sutter gave him. He hoped his friend hadn't damaged the steering column too much.

It took about ten minutes to clean up the slightly dinged fugitive. Sutter claimed he had run him down by accident and intended to stick with that story. Tasker noted the lack of skid marks and the satisfied tone in Sutter's voice, but decided to let the matter rest.

Tasker sat in the backseat next to the handcuffed man. The pot smell even emanated from his pores. Mule had cuts above his eyes, his upper lip was still bleeding and he had road rash on his left arm, back and hip. He had a dazed look that had as much to do with the "accident" as it did with the fact that three explosive devices had gone off within ten feet of his head and he had smoked an ounce of marijuana the night before.

Tasker said, "What were those things?"

"Huh?" asked Mule.

Tasker raised his voice. "The bomb things, what were they?"

"Oh those. Little nonfragmenting hand grenades I made. Pretty cool, huh?"

Tasker noted the lack of twang and asked, "Where you from?"

"New Smyrna Beach."

A surfer. That explained it. Tasker knew the Central Florida town because his ex-wife's family still lived there. This guy must have been some kind of genetic freak to be from the small beach town and still smart enough to put these things together.

"You ever know Donna Andrus?"

"Yeah, I did her once."

Tasker narrowed his eyes at the slightly younger man. "I married her once."

Mule cringed and added. "Only kidding, man. I knew her in high school, that's all."

"Really, you did know her?"

He nodded. "Sure. Blond chick. Nice titties."

Tasker didn't acknowledge the description but thought it was pretty accurate.

"I guess I only did her in my imagination." He wiggled his eyebrows and grinned.

Tasker turned professional and changed the subject, saying, "You're under arrest on a warrant from Pensacola, and we'll have to come up with charges on these things, too."

"Man, can you cut me a break?"

"You almost killed me."

"No, dude, those things don't fragment. Just noise and a flash."

"What's in 'em?"

"Little black powder, few other things. I make one with pepper that will burn your eyes for a whole day. It's way cool."

Tasker had to laugh at the shirtless man. This is the kinda guy that lives at home until he's thirty-five and then raises kids that live at home until they're forty. "You got anything else dangerous at the house?"

Mule looked at him. "I don't want to . . . what's the word? Incriminate myself."

Tasker thought that was fair. "I'll tell you what. You let us back in and point out the dangerous stuff and we'll give you a pass on it. We just don't want kids or somebody stumbling into it. Then you might be hit with serious charges."

Mule thought about it. "Okay, if you don't charge me with the poppers I set off today."

"Poppers? That what you call those things?"

"Yeah, or flashers. Depends on the relative mix of materials."

"Let's see how helpful you are, then we'll decide."

Mule evaluated him for a few moments. "I don't know why, but you seem pretty honest. I'll trust you on this. Besides, I got some stuff that might help me."

In the house, Tasker flushed the last of the pot they found as Mule pleaded.

"Please, man, not my Mexican tap dance. That shit is the best. You can dump the shit I grew behind the garage, but that Mexican shit cost mucho, man."

Tasker paused for a minute, playing with Mule for making the comment about Donna, then when his hopes rose, Tasker dumped the rest into the toilet. "You sure you never did her?"

The hairy man shrugged and nodded. "Okay, you owed me."

Sutter was carefully setting the last package of black powder into an empty Corona twelve-pack box. Mule had pointed out everything he could think of, including a water bottle filled with a liquid he called TATP. He told them it was a little nasty, so the two cops should be careful.

Tasker remembered Camy telling him about the cruise ship bombing and how the bomber had used TATP. Had he stumbled onto the bomber by accident? Stranger things had happened.

Tasker said, "All right, Anthony, you've been pretty good about pointing shit out. Got anything to seal the deal?" Maybe he'd slip up and say something.

He smiled, revealing standard surfer's chipped front teeth. "I got something, but I want some help on the warrant charges, too."

"Can't agree to that until we see what you got."

"Can't show you what I got until you agree to help."

With that, Sutter came over to the table where Tasker and Mule were sitting.

He started, "Tell you what, slick. You give us what you got or you can go for a jog in the road again until I catch you in the car. Got it?"

Mule hesitated, then said, "In the drawer under the phone is a three-page list."

Sutter said, "That's better. What's on the list?"

"Everyone I ever sold an explosive to. What kind of explosive. When and how much."

Tasker was up and to the phone before he finished talking.

Mule continued. "I never heard of nobody doing anything wrong with my shit. Rednecks buy them to scare birds away from the crops. The Miccosukee Indians use it as part of their shows for tourists. Kids buy them for fun, and the Cubans, or at least the Alpha 66, buy them for God knows what. But they pay real good and are easy to deal with."

Tasker looked over the list. No one had bought a single huge amount of anything, but the intel guys at FDLE might work something up on the list. Then on the last page he brushed over a name and had to go back. Daniel Wells. Thirty ounces of TATP he bought three years ago. Tasker looked up at Mule. "This guy Daniel Wells. You remember him?"

Mule thought and said, "Yeah, sure. The engineer from up in Naranja or the Redlands. What about him?"

"Why would he need an explosive?"

"Didn't ask."

"What exactly is TATP?"

"Triacetone triperoxide. Bad shit, man. Especially the way I make it. It could blow a hole in granite."

Tasker's stomach continued to tighten as he put it all together. Clues he'd seen and didn't register. The suitcases he'd knocked over while visiting Wells—he could see them vividly in his mind. They had been red. And they had been Samsonites. No way, it couldn't be. He gathered his thoughts and looked at Mule. "You got any of this batch of TATP left?"

"Yeah, your buddy just loaded it in the water bottle."

Tasker wanted to be sure. His stomach was already flip-flopping. "What did Wells look like?"

"Late twenties. Good shape. Dark, short hair. He had a couple of kids with him. Think he was a single father or something."

Tasker thought about the lovely Alicia for a second.

"How bad is TATP, I mean what will it do?"

"Little unstable, but like I said, has a good punch. He bought enough to blow the shit out of a few things."

"Could you make a bomb in a suitcase with it?"

"Easy."

Tasker thought about what this meant and mumbled, "Oh shit, what have I done."

ten

daniel wells jerked the old parachute off his Toyota Corolla. When he climbed into the car, he realized the silk chute hadn't kept out much water. The mildew smell made him feel like fungus was growing in his sinuses. He had spent the morning cleaning things up around the shop. Trashing old containers he didn't need anymore. Keeping track of old accounts payable to collect. He just had a feeling his life was about to change, and the media calling him had not stopped, so he thought it was best to send Alicia and the kids away for a little while.

He had plans that had to be set in motion. Big plans. It was really all he could think about anymore. Even while he sat in jail over the weekend, his mind worked out the details that would make him a success. He'd put on a show that everyone would remember. That's what he lived for anymore—putting on the shows. Although he had been setting small fires and playing pranks since he was five, the real urge, the feeling that kept him sane, had kicked in during his senior year in high school. After filling a milk carton with black powder and then leaving it at the table the jocks took every day, whether someone was sitting at it or not, Wells used an old garage-door opener to detonate the device. The noise and smoke were enough to give him shudders of delight. The fact that two of the star football players suffered permanent black powder marks and scars on their faces only gave him a sweet reminder every time he passed them in the halls. And he had never told a soul. He learned that when you tell someone, you get caught.

Then a year later, the same trick at the Tri Delta house at the University of Florida. This time it had detonated prematurely and set a small fire, which the sprinkler system took care of. He read in the paper about a "prank" gone bad and the subsequent editorials about how someone could have been killed. That's when it hit him. What if someone died during one of his shows? At first it concerned him, then it excited him. The thought never really left his head.

Too bad his attempt to set off a quarter-stick of dynamite under the visiting Florida State bench a year and a half later had gotten him thrown out of school. Old Bobby Bowden would've shit in his pants if that baby had gone off. His story—that he came home to help his sick dad—still held up to this day. Unless he was talking to someone who was at the game that day.

Considering all the shows he had either put on or helped others put on during the years, it was amazing that the baggage handler on the cruise ship was the first person ever killed. At least that Wells knew of. He had built remote bomb devices for a couple of people and didn't know what had happened those times. The local Nazis, the ones that called themselves the American Aryan Movement, had a pretty good plan to blow up a Metrorail People Mover bus. The problem was they didn't want anyone in it when it happened. Wells had built them a nice, clock-operated, dynamite-based, flammable bomb, but the cheap bastards had stiffed him on the thousand-dollar payment. That was just plain uncool. He'd gotten them back, but still figured they owed him some cash. That was something he'd see to as soon as he had the time.

Now he had to get serious about his new idea. This one would get some attention, and he might even brag about it, but only after he was out of the area.

Bill Tasker and Derrick Sutter booked Anthony Mule into the Dade County jail after promising they would talk to the prosecutor about his assistance. Tasker was much more interested in verifying that information. As soon as he had the hairy surfer in the can, he had jumped in his Monte Carlo and raced back toward Naranja. Sutter had a previous commitment and was skeptical about the bomb-maker's information. He had argued, probably correctly, that it could easily wait until tomorrow. After all, the crime had been committed almost two years ago. But Tasker couldn't wait.

He still hadn't decided what to do as he neared the house. Should he talk to Wells? Should he arrest him? Would he be cutting in on Camy Parks' case? He decided that just making sure Wells was still at the house would satisfy him for now. Then he'd get ahold of Camy Parks and see where to go from there.

He turned onto Wells' street and saw that there were still vehicles in the driveway. The step van was back toward the garage, and the station wagon was by the house. When Tasker turned onto the street that ran on the side to the rear of Wells' lot, he saw a third car. One he had not noticed before. Behind the garage was an old Toyota Corolla with damage across the front roof section. It seemed familiar, too; then he remembered the photos in Camy's file. He couldn't tell if it was the same car, but it was one hell of a coincidence.

Three blocks away from the house, his hands shaking, Tasker pulled off the side of the road and picked up his Nextel. He hit the speed dial with Camy's cell-phone number.

"Hello," said Camy.

"Camy, it's Bill." Immediately he lost the connection. Or did she hang up? He tried again. This time there was no answer.

This was unlike any surveillance Tasker had ever been on. He was in a car—that was not unusual. In Miami, watching an office building—that was still normal. But watching another law enforcement office, waiting for a fellow cop to come out—*that* was new to him. He sat across Fifty-eighth Street, looking at Camy Parks' issued Ford Crown Vic. Unlike at some of the Federal agencies, the ATF agents tended to put in some long hours. Along with investigative responsibilities, they handled some regulatory duties with gun dealers. The agency was traditionally grossly understaffed. He wasn't surprised she was still at the office near seven o'clock, but he had to see her. She hadn't returned his calls and the secretary wasn't taking messages from him anymore. Finally he saw her at the side door to the building, dressed in workout clothes. Even from this distance he could make out the muscles on her legs.

As he pulled closer, he saw her shorts and sweaty T-shirt. The ATF could use her as a recruiting poster, as long as they didn't include too many details about her personal life. He pulled his car directly behind her parked Crown Vic. She looked up as she came closer, taking a second to register who had blocked her in.

He stepped out of his Monte Carlo and met her at his hood. "You're tough to track down."

"I'm pretty sure our case is done. At least half of it."

"I know you're pissed but I gotta talk to you."

"Billy, I'm not really mad. I did feel like you stabbed us in the back, but after reflecting on it, I suppose you had 7your reasons. I saw her, too. She is a hell of a reason."

Tasker looked at her. "*Who* is a hell of a reason?"

"Wells' wife. She could tempt anyone."

"Please tell me that's not what you think. I couldn't live with grabbing the wrong guy. That's it. I had no other motive."

"But the FBI agent, Cobb, said he saw the handoff."

"He saw the possum cage handed off. The missile was already in the truck."

She looked like she was considering it, then said, "Why does it matter? I can't work with you again anyway."

"What? Why not?"

"Because my bosses think you're unstable. The FBI bosses spent a few hours over here yesterday making sure everyone had the same opinion. You are not to be involved in another FBI or ATF case ever again."

"That's a lot of administrative effort spent on one guy. If they concentrated that energy on crime, I wouldn't have to lock my door."

She looked at him sharply. "Billy, the way our bosses feel about you now, you won't ever have to shower again. No one will ever be close enough to smell you."

That hurt Tasker. He wouldn't admit it to her or anyone else, but it stung to have someone say they weren't interested in working with him. He waited, then said, "I have something that might change your mind."

"I doubt that. Billy, do you realize that the FBI wants to *indict* you for this? They're convinced you did it to make them look bad."

"That's ridiculous. They do enough on their own. They don't need others making them look bad."

"I'm serious."

"So am I." He took a few steps back, leaned into his car and retrieved a small vial of the noxious liquid that the Homestead bomb-maker claimed was TATP.

Camy asked, "What's that?"

"It may be the explosive used in your Krans-Festival cruise ship bombing."

She smiled a little. "Jokes won't win me over, either."

"No joke. A guy we picked up made it. Says it's TATP and he sold some to Daniel Wells a couple of years ago."

Her light eyes took in the vial as Tasker held it up. "*Our* Daniel Wells? What's he got to do with it?"

"He may have made that bomb."

"Because he bought an explosive?"

"Other things, too. I need to check them out. But the explosives-maker, Anthony Mule, is certain it was our Wells that bought it from him."

"Did he sell only to Wells?"

"No, he had a pretty long list."

"So even if it tested positive, we can't say that Wells did it. Could've been anyone on the list, or the guy who made it."

"Wells has got a Toyota Corolla stashed behind his house and a matching set of red Samsonite luggage."

She looked at him, obviously intrigued. "If all that is true, why aren't you over there right now?"

"Because I'm not in it for glory. I want to do it right. He has no idea about the information we have. He'll be there for a while. I intend to get an airtight search warrant and build the case right. That is, with your help. I don't jump other people's cases."

She smiled. "You don't help them, either." She took the vial and held it up to the halogen streetlight. "You know what this means to me. I lived this case for nearly two years."

"That's why I came to you."

She gave him a skeptical look.

He continued unfazed. "Test it. If it's not a match, nothing happens. If it is, then we need to hit Daniel Wells quick and hard."

She held the vial with no sign of giving it back to Tasker. Looking at it, she said, "As tempting as that sounds, Billy, I was told, just this afternoon, not to have any contact with you. I just can't work with you right now. Especially not on Wells. I mean, you're the one who let him out. The Bureau would have me skinned alive."

"Since when does ATF worry about what the FBI thinks?"

"Since we moved to the Department of Justice and they work with us on everything." She paused and looked at him. "I'm sorry, Billy, but I just need them more than I need you."

Tasker nodded.

She kept the vial and said, "But I'll drop this off at the lab right now.

We'll see what they say. If it checks out—I'll thank you later for cracking my case."

"I don't care who stops him, as long as he's stopped now."

"I promise to run it up the chain and see what the bosses say."

"Sounds fair."

She turned and started back to the building. Tasker didn't mind seeing her walk away.

Daniel Wells dried the tears in his daughter's eyes. "It's all right, Lettye. Daddy will come and get you in a few days. Don't cry, sweetheart." He looked in the backseat of his wife's old Ford station wagon. His two boys were quiet, sitting side by side, waiting to leave. "You two be good, you hear?"

"Yes, sir," they said in unison.

This wasn't the first time they'd gone to relatives for an extended time. He'd packed them off to his uncle's twice, Aunt Sara's house three times and his cousin in Tennessee for a whole summer. This time he had Alicia driving them to his uncle Tom in Plant City on the west coast of Florida. No matter what he got involved in, he always made sure the kids were safe. They shouldn't have to pay for his problems. His uncle had taken them when he was afraid those Arabs might come back on him. His cousin in Tennessee when he was afraid someone might link him to the damn cruise ship. Now he was just generally worried. That state cop, Tasker, was sharp. Twice as sharp as the other cops he'd dealt with. He just thought it'd be best if the kids weren't around while he finished up some business and tried to satisfy his own needs.

He raised his voice, calling over his shoulder, "Alicia, you coming?" That woman would be the death of him. He'd said that about several other women, too, and it was never true. With one of them, the reverse was true. It was really an accident that she had opened the bottle in his workshop, but the fumes had killed her just as sure as if he'd shot her in the head, which was what he had been thinking of when fate had stepped in. He'd found the biggest problem was just getting rid of the body. She was a stout girl, and it had taken all his strength just to load her in the van. Luckily he'd been doing some welding for Mid-Stream Septic Tanks and just planted her under the foundation for a new tank. They'd never been legally married and she had no family. By then the kids were used to running off women, so no one ever asked where she'd gone. He didn't think the kids even remembered her name.

He heard his wife trotting up behind him.

She wrapped her arms around him. "Sorry, honey. Had some last-minute things to pack."

"You stay with them, okay?"

Her pouty lips turned lower. "Can't I take a little break? Your uncle won't mind. He loves seeing them."

"Why do you need a break?"

"C'mon, Daniel, I've treated them like my own for near two years now. Just want a little time away."

"Done good, too. They even call you mama and everything. Never did that with Melanie. Hell, Lettye didn't even know her real mama. She ran off when Lettye was only a few months old." He knew it had more to do with him than the kids.

"I won't run off. Just wanna get away a little."

Wells looked at her. Good-looking women were a pain in the ass. He wished he could be satisfied with an ugly girl. Just like he wished he could be satisfied with a little excitement instead of spectacular shows. If wishes were baby back ribs, he'd weigh five hundred pounds.

Alicia squeezed him and laid a long, deep kiss on him until his mind melted. He could only wave as the car pulled away, carrying his own little agents of anarchy off to safety. At least for a while.

Camy Parks stretched her legs and arms like she was Supergirl. A naked Supergirl with massage oil on her back. She felt her body let go as she willed the tension out of her toes and fingers. Hands worked her trapezius muscles and then her neck. She couldn't control her sigh.

She kept explaining her day. "Then I took the little bottle from Billy Tasker and turned it into the lab. But it looks like it's not going to make a hell of a lot of difference, at least for me. The SAC told me point-blank to my face that he doesn't care if Wells blows up the *Queen Mary 2* right in front of me—I can't touch the guy. The Justice lawyers expect a major media-grabbing lawsuit filed by Wells any day, and they say this will look like a vendetta."

"So *Tasker* gets to run with your case? After all that?"

"Yeah, if our lab makes a match."

She sighed. Enough. She enjoyed massages, but wasn't keen on talking about work after hours. She barely wanted to talk cases at the office gym. Too bad only other ATF agents worked out there. Work was all she seemed to have in common with any of them. Her dad had worked for Jack Daniel's for years and she never once heard him mention the office or other Jack Daniel's employees the whole time she was growing up. When he was home, it was to be with her and her five brothers. It was a good lesson to learn.

She rolled over, allowing her back rub to move to the front. She loved the light oil splashed over her breasts, pleased that they were real and everyone noticed. She said, "You got to hand it to Billy, though. He certainly kept at it."

"Yeah," came the reply. "Some people don't know when to quit."

Wells slowly padded back up the slight slope to the front door after he watched his family drive away. Often he'd lock himself in the shop and catch up on work when the kids were gone. Or, better, work on his own special projects. That was his one fear: one of the kids might be hurt inadvertently by something he did or was working on. He didn't think they would just wander into the garage and find something. He'd trained them too well.

He thought about what might happen if a timer went bad or some of that unstable shit just decided to blow. That was why he had fire alarms and smoke detectors all over the garage and house.

He wandered through the quiet house. It unnerved him. He needed noise and confusion. The only order he liked was in the shop. That gave him his baseline for the rest of his life. There was nothing more orderly than the little detached garage where he affected other people's lives. And it was getting to be more and more people every time.

The phone's single ring cut through the silence, making him jump.

"Hello," he said, half-expecting it to be Alicia saying she couldn't go with the kids.

"Daniel, you okay?"

He recognized the voice.

"No thanks to you. Were you just gonna let me rot in jail?"

"Don't you worry, I had it well in hand."

"Hope so. That Tasker fella is smart. I don't want him figuring anything out."

"That's why I'm calling."

Daniel Wells listened, glad he'd already sent the kids away.

eleven

bill tasker stared at the red numbers on the alarm clock next to his rumpled bed, making a game of trying to guess how far they'd advanced every time he opened his eyes. When he was a student at Florida State, he'd been a subject of a psychology grad student's test of internal clocks. At the time he'd done it for extra credit; now he found it interesting, if for no other reason than it took his mind off how he'd let Daniel Wells walk. All he could think about was getting to the ATF lab and finding out what the results showed. He looked at the clock again: 4:43. Shit. He decided to make use of the early hours and go for a run.

Thirty minutes later, with no hint of the sun arriving any time soon, Tasker picked up his pace, cutting through the Kendall neighborhood he knew so well. No women in bikinis like at Haulover Beach or calm water like at Biscayne Bay—just some simple, efficient exercise to get him in the right mind-set for the day. He went through the details he might have to put into the search warrant for the Wells house. He could already provide an accurate description, and he knew the layout for tactical considerations. In comparison to some drug warrants, it was easy. He didn't have to rely on some informant with no eye for what cops needed to know when they came through the door. Tasker had been inside the small house a couple of times. His main concern was the kids and Alicia. If Wells was a mad-dog bomber, would he be calm when they knocked on the door? Tasker still had a hard time believing the whole thing. Daniel Wells appeared to be a normal, decent guy. There was nothing about him to indicate he was capable of something like trying to blow up a cruise ship. Why? What would drive a man to do something like that? Had he been paid by someone else? Had he been pissed at someone in the cruise industry? Tasker was going to have to do some digging on this one.

He was showered, shaved and had finished eating just as the sun started to peek over the house across the street. He used the early hour for a quick drive by Daniel Wells' house. It was as quiet as every other house in the south Dade neighborhood. He just made a few quick notes about the placement of street numbers and colors in case he needed to put it all in a search warrant.

Near noon, Tasker was finally able to get Sutter to meet him. As usual, part of the inducement was food. They met at the La Carreta near the International Mall, off 107th Avenue.

Sutter glowered at his half-eaten Cuban sandwich. "I don't know why I let you talk me into these places. I hate foreign food." He held up the sandwich and then tossed it back on the plate. "I like hamburgers and pizza. Shit like that. I should boycott foreign food. Then maybe every white guy I know wouldn't drag me to places like this all the damn time."

"How many white guys do you eat with?" asked Tasker.

"Counting you? One. And I don't want no more foreign food."

Tasker had been raised in South Florida and never considered Cuban food as foreign. It was more just a different local flavor, like barbecue. He kept picking at his chicken fricassee while Sutter bitched. It was actually relaxing hearing the Miami cop complain about everything from food to television shows. To Tasker it meant the world wasn't too far off its axis. He was still free and able to work. No one was going to indict him, even if the FBI wanted to. But he had to do everything he could to arrest Daniel Wells if he was guilty of the Krans-Festival cruise-ship bombing. If Tasker did nothing and Wells struck again, he wouldn't be able to live with himself.

Sutter looked at his friend. "What are you so bent out of shape about?"

"Wells killed a guy and could kill someone else if we don't do something."

"So could I. Doesn't mean I will. If that good ole boy did set the bomb on the ship, then we'll be able to pin it on him. Those kinds of techno-freaks don't strike every day. Look at the guy the FBI chased for so long."

"Ted Kaczynski?"

"No, man, the crazy guy, lived in a cabin."

"Theodore Kaczynski."

Sutter couldn't hide his irritation. "No, the Unabomber. Took him months to set up another attack. Only killed two or three people. Shit, we got crackheads kill more than that on a weekend."

Tasker shook his head. "I think Wells could be a real menace."

"But he didn't sell the Stinger."

Tasker smiled. That put it into perspective. He still couldn't separate the act from the man. He had set this nut loose in South Florida. Then he said, "I appreciate what you're saying, but I gotta forget the philosophy and ethical standards I may have met and get him off the streets. I may have followed my conscience and the law getting him released, but I'd do anything now to get him back inside."

"What'd you have in mind?"

"A search warrant, for starters."

"When?"

"Our legal counsel is reviewing it now. I need some info on the explosive from ATF and maybe I'll have it signed by this evening. We can hit the house first thing in the morning."

"And ATF won't be involved?"

"I asked, they declined. I'll see Camy this afternoon when I get the lab results."

"If you're gonna see the princess, then I'm going, too."

"No comments, okay?"

"Me? Please, I'm a professional."

"Good. I don't need the ATF feeling about me like the FBI does."

"You kiddin'? They should kiss your ass for even telling them about this. They should be sittin' on Wells' house right now for us."

"Once we have him, they'll come to their senses."

"You don't think it's politics?"

"How do you mean?"

"They don't want to piss off the FBI. They're worried about a lawsuit for Wells' false arrest. That sort of politics."

Tasker considered this and said, "That's over my pay grade, brother. We just arrest them. The bosses can work out who's upset and who's happy."

Sutter smiled. "Amen."

Daniel Wells was thirty years old and had only been into the heart of Miami a few times. Once as a kid when his family visited the Miami Seaquarium on Key Biscayne and his dad wanted to show the family what Hell was really like. Once when he worked a welding job at the port terminal. The day he drove to the port to have his suitcase loaded on Krans-Festival's *Sea Maiden.* And today. Every time, he saw prostitutes near Biscayne Boulevard. The big park, Bayfront, was immediately east of him. I-95 was to the west.

Now he was alone in his little nine-year-old Toyota Corolla. The rear seat was out, and a sketchpad sat on the passenger seat next to him. He was a few blocks north of the federal courthouse and a little west of where the Miami Heat played. The main streets were all four-laned, but the side streets, the ones running east and west that ended at I-95, were all narrow, two-laned theaters. That's how he liked to think of areas: theaters. How many spectators could fit in an area, then react to the demonstration? The ultimate interactive performance art. And what a charge he got from the interaction. The rush of seeing people panic. The turmoil caused by people running willy-nilly had actually given him an erection on several occasions.

This place might work if he had the right show planned. It'd have to be big and loud. People from the high-rise offices to the south would be able to see it and then who knows what the media might do to drive it. He had most of his plan mapped out, but he still needed a way to move his traveling show to this area. Maybe a problem on I-95 would divert the cops' attention. Then he had an idea. Maybe a brilliant idea. He let out a yelp of excitement.

A homeless man approached the little car. The black man's gray-streaked hair hung over a scarf into his face. His eyes looked surprisingly alert, but as he walked up to Wells' car his body odor radiated out in front of him. He silently held out a small tin can with the label worn off.

Wells nodded and said, "No thanks, I'm not thirsty." He drove on west to the interstate. Time to get back to his own kind of neighborhood. As he drove away, he looked in the rearview mirror and noticed the bum staring at his Corolla.

Tasker and Sutter waited in the small lobby of the ATF building. The receptionist behind the thick bulletproof glass had called Camy Parks ten minutes ago. Tasker hadn't had the nerve to tell the Miami cop he'd had to stalk Camy just to give her the explosive to test. He was embarrassed enough that she was making them both wait in the lobby for so long. The receptionist didn't care. From the looks she kept shooting Tasker, she was aware of the entire situation. With a lot of agencies Tasker wouldn't have cared, but he respected ATF. They were one of the most kickass agencies in the federal government. They were able to tack on real charges to almost any violent crime involving a gun and they weren't afraid to come out on anything. Now they thought he was an asshole.

After more than twenty minutes, Camy Parks came to the main door. She opened it halfway and stayed in the secure area, blocking their way like she was talking to a vacuum-cleaner salesman at her house and didn't want to be bothered.

She nodded professionally. "Gentlemen, how are you?"

Sutter spoke up. "Right now I'm a little pissed off you left us pullin' our puds out here."

"Sorry, but I'm real busy." Her gaze shifted to the main door and she smiled.

Tasker turned to see FBI agent Jimmy Lail bop into the lobby, his jeans hanging low and his shirt opened to reveal a white tank top undershirt. He saw Sutter and brightened immediately. "My brother." He reached out to touch fists with Sutter.

Sutter nodded silently and forced the young man to shake hands instead.

Jimmy looked at Camy. "Yo, beautiful, whazz up?"

He glared at Tasker, squeezing past without a word.

Tasker said to Sutter, "There's one positive thing out of this mess."

The Miami cop snickered.

Camy, ignoring the childish behavior of the non-federal agents, turned to Tasker without another glance at Sutter. "The tests on that liquid won't be done for at least ten days."

Tasker frowned. "Can they tell us anything? Aren't you interested in this case? You started it."

She softened slightly. "Bill, I've been ordered not to get involved. My bosses think this is some kind of stunt by you to make up for what you did on the Stinger case. We're waiting for a major lawsuit from Mr. Wells and this will look like some kind of harassment. So even if it was an exact match, I doubt I'd do much other than note in our case file that you suspect Mr. Wells of the bombing."

Tasker looked stricken. "You mean the ATF actually thinks that I'm making this up? That I fabricated evidence?"

"We're not willing to state that publicly, but, yes, that's about the size of it."

Sutter broke in: "Bullshit! You don't want to admit that you guys couldn't solve the case. If that explosive matches exactly, you'll have to shit or get off the shitter. You'll either jump in the case or have to investigate how Billy made it up."

"That remains to be seen. I'm sure the ATF will do what's right."

"It's right to help us now. Not hide behind some political motive." Sutter's voice had grown louder since he started to speak.

She ignored him, keeping both eyes on Tasker. "The preliminary results indicate that it is similar to the explosive used in the cruise-ship bombing. I don't know if that will help, but it's all we have."

Tasker nodded. "Thanks, it might give me enough for a warrant."

Sutter leaned in between them. "Listen, Princess, when you get off your high-fucking-horse and see my man here didn't do nothin' wrong, you're gonna sing a different tune. You should save us all some time and accept it now."

She smiled. Not a dainty, radiant smile like Tasker had seen so many times, but an evil, almost threatening smile that some street predators let out before they slash your throat. "First," she started slowly, "you call me Princess again and you'll be picking some of that gold in your mouth out of your shit." Her eyes cut into him like a laser. "Second, I am not on any kind of horse, and I don't have to explain anything to you. And third, I know all about you, Mr. I-can-have-any-woman-I-am-so-cool-and-smart-and-slick. So you can save the lectures for one of your little hoes on South Beach."

Sutter said, "Heard I couldn't get you."

"Not on your best day."

He added, "Unless I didn't have a dick."

She turned, letting the door swing shut and lock automatically.

Sutter stared at her perfect ass as it disappeared behind the door and said out loud, "That is some kind of great genetic code."

Camy Parks waited in the ladies' room for more than five minutes as her heart rate slowed to near normal. She sat on the second toilet, practicing the breathing exercises she learned in yoga. It worked eventually and she checked herself in the lone, cheap, industrial mirror. She could still look at herself in the mirror. But if Tasker was right and she didn't help with Wells, she might not be able to look at herself for long. This was one part of being an agent with the Bureau of Alcohol, Tobacco and Firearms that she didn't appreciate. Smaller than other agencies and often in danger of being disbanded or merged into another department, they didn't have the capacity to butt heads very often. Fortunately, they did such a good job and worked with so many cops that it wasn't necessary to exert influence often. Now she would have liked to have her bosses stand up to the damn FBI and say they would work on this case because it was right. Instead they came up with excuses like Tasker was just trying to make himself look good. If they knew the state cop, they'd know he wasn't capable of something like that. She'd have to explain it one more time.

She came out of the bathroom and through her squad bay, ignoring Jimmy Lail as he sat at an extra desk, reading a hip-hop magazine. She marched down the long corridor through the administrative area to the secretary in front of the special agent in charge's office. The SAC of any federal investigative agency was the final word. They ruled their empire as they saw fit.

"Does the boss have a minute for me?" Camy asked the lovely young Latin secretary.

The girl, whose English was questionable, just smiled and nodded.

Camy stepped up and knocked on the frame of the open front door. "Do you have a second, sir?"

The large man with a ruddy face and graying temples looked up from part of the mountain of reports littering his desk. "Sure, come in," he said, motioning her to a chair in front of his wide oak desk. "As long as it doesn't have to do with that FDLE agent, Tasker. That's a dead issue."

She didn't even bother to sit down.

twelve

The sun had just popped up over the Naranja neighborhood about ten minutes south of Bill Tasker's town house in Kendall. He sat in his state-issued Monte Carlo, Derrick Sutter nodding off next to him. Three FDLE agents were at the rear of the house and three more in a car behind him. When they pulled in front of the Wells residence, all the agents would converge at once on the small house. He'd finished the search warrant about six the night before. By ten, after the FDLE legal counsel and assistant state attorney had reviewed it, the duty judge for the Dade Circuit Court had signed it. He hoped he wasn't too late. His boss waited in his big Crown Vic, probably smoking a cigarette and thinking of everything that could go wrong. That was his job. The former NYPD detective was a good guy and let his agents run their own cases. That's all anyone could wish for.

Tasker didn't see the big step van Wells used for work. He noticed the old Toyota was not next to the garage, either. This was a dilemma every cop faced at some point: Do I go in or wait till he's home?

Tasker nudged Sutter awake. "What do you think? Should we wait till there's a car here?"

Sutter blinked hard. "Just cause there's no car don't mean nobody's home."

"House is dark and quiet."

"All of them are. It's only six."

"No cars."

"That's true, but when will he be back? Could be waiting a long time. We'll get burned before eight o'clock. Every redneck down here will think we're looking for a grow house or chop shop. Shit, not one of these crackers got a job."

Tasker smiled. Sutter sounded just like a racist carrying on about black residents of Liberty City. He picked up his Nextel and called his supervisor. He could tell he was awake by the smoke pouring out of the cracked window. "Boss, you out there?"

"I'm here."

"We were discussing what to do. Looks like no one's home. You wanna wait?"

"Nah, let's hit it. If your man's not there, we'll grab him later. If there is anything you need for your case in there, it don't matter if anyone's home or not."

"Ten-four." Tasker set down the Nextel on his seat and looked at Sutter. "Looks like we go."

"He sounded just like a boss at Miami PD. If you wait, it may cost overtime."

Tasker nodded and then picked up the car radio to broadcast to the other agents. "We're gonna go in a minute. We'll do like we briefed, slow and easy. Don't enter the garage. If no one's home, we'll get the Metro bomb techs just in case. The team at the front door is going to knock nice and polite, then see what happens. There may be kids inside." He heard the acknowledgments from the others, then turned to Sutter and said, "Showtime."

At the front door, Tasker, his supervisor and Sutter fanned to either side of the door. Tasker knocked hard, then shouted, "Daniel, it's Bill Tasker. Come to the door." Nothing.

Sutter stepped back and lifted his leg to kick when Tasker held up his hand to stop him. He tried the handle, and the unlocked door opened easily. Tasker signaled to the others to move up.

Drawing their pistols, the three cops entered the house. Two more agents came up to the front and started leapfrogging from one room to the next while Tasker's supervisor covered them. The house was empty, neat and open.

Once the house was secure and they had the lights on, Sutter said, "It's almost like he was expecting us and didn't want us to damage the house getting in."

Tasker had had the same feeling. Before he could prepare to search, his supervisor started flinging open drawers and poking around in cabinets. This happened at most search warrants the boss was on. He still did things the old New York way. His methods worked, but they were expected to follow a different set of rules nowadays in Florida. Tasker subtly tried to distract the portly supervisor, finally giving up, saying, "Boss, stop!" When the older man turned to look at him, he added, meekly, "I need you to arrange for the Metro bomb squad."

After the supervisor had stepped outside, Tasker said, "Let's do a quick look through the house. Grab personal phone books and things that might point to where Wells is if he's in the wind." He sat down at the same dining table where he'd watched Alicia Wells glide out in that sheer top. If Wells was gone for good, how did he know to leave? This was a troubling consideration for Tasker as he waited for the bomb techs to get into the garage.

Three hours later, after the search of the house and the garage was done, Tasker placed a copy of the warrant on the dining room table. He also left a short note. Something he'd never done on a search warrant before. It just said, "Daniel, you said you owed me. Prove it. Call me." He signed it and left his cell number at the bottom of the page.

The garage had been cleaned out. Only a few of the larger power tools and some papers were left. Tasker approached one of the uniform bomb squad officers. His German shepherd sat next to him on a leather leash.

"Can you guys tell me anything?"

The muscular Metro-Dade cop said, "Bandit alerted on the workbench, the rear storage area and on the side of the garage. Looks like this guy worked with all kinds of explosives."

"Anything worth taking?"

"Your guys grabbed two empty containers. May be some residue."

Tasker thanked the Metro cops and headed back to his car, where his supervisor and Sutter were talking.

His boss said, "Billy, you done a good job. I don't want you beating yourself up over this thing. Take a day or two. Make it a long weekend. Monday we'll kick it hard and find this mope. These hicks don't go far from where they know. He'll turn up. I just don't want you getting so worn-out you get in trouble."

Tasker looked at him and said, "Again."

"I didn't say that."

"You didn't have to."

His supervisor stood tall and looked right at him. This was a guy who didn't say that much, so when he did, people usually listened. "You can have a chip on your shoulder if you want, but I never figured you for that type. I'm tellin' you there's more to life than this shit. This is a job, not a crusade."

Tasker nodded. "You're right, boss. Donna asked me if I could come up and spend the night with the kids while she went away for a couple of days. That way they don't miss school on Friday. Maybe I'll do it."

"Where's she going? Some kind of teachers' conference?"

Tasker slumped slightly. "Nope, she's going away with her boyfriend."

"And you'll watch the kids?" Tasker could see this veteran of three marriages wouldn't do something like that.

"It's not for her, it's to see the kids."

"You're a better fucking man than me. That shit makes this shit look good."

Tasker wasn't sure what he was looking forward to less: waiting to chase Daniel Wells or seeing Donna leave with the defense attorney.

By noon, Daniel Wells had heard that cops had been inside his house. Now everything he had feared had been confirmed. Everything had changed. Was he wanted? He knew the cops at least wanted to talk to him, but was there an actual warrant? He knew who to call to find out. Wells didn't think that relationship had changed too much. This wasn't news to everyone in law enforcement.

His mind wandered as he darted down East Palm Drive near the Homestead Racetrack. His little Toyota's engine whined as he headed west, away from Turkey Point. He had a good stash site near the power plant. Before the security checkpoint, there were two worn-out limestone roads that cut south to the canals that fed the nuclear cooling towers of the power plant. Years before, while he was working with those two crazy Jordanians out this way, he'd found a metal footlocker still in good shape. One day, months after the Jordanians had gone to jail, while the boys were with him, he'd let them dig a hole around the box to keep them occupied while he went fishing. They were little then, maybe four and six. Before he knew it, the tiny hellions had managed to sink the box even with the ground. Over time he'd added a liner and some weatherproofing, and now he had a secure, watertight secret hiding place that only he and the kids knew about. The boys had probably forgotten by now, but he still used it. He'd just stored his remaining TATP and some quarter- and half-sticks of homemade dynamite the gentleman in Florida City had sold him a few years back. There was no shit left at his house for anyone to find.

He didn't know exactly what the charge was for the bombing. He thought they might try to stick a murder charge in there. He realized someone had died because of the bomb he'd made and planted. The problem was that the wrong person had died. If someone was going to get killed on that ship, a lone baggage handler didn't do much to add to the terror.

Wells shrugged. You live and you learn. He was just glad he was using his engineering classes. Maybe things would have been different if he'd graduated, but maybe not. He'd still have his urge. He'd still need to scratch that itch to see people's lives thrown into disorder. At least living in Naranja, fixing people's little engineering problems allowed him to keep a low profile. Maybe he'd survived a little longer because of it. He kept daydreaming as the long, empty road slowly showed signs of civilization, or at least the city of Homestead.

As the racetrack came into view, Wells saw a police car parked on the corner of the track property next to the road. Too late, he realized the uniformed Homestead police officer had a radar gun in his hand. Wells dropped his eyes to the speedometer of the old Corolla. Eighty-one—shit! The cop noted his speed, too. The cruiser was onto the road and behind Wells before he'd driven a few hundred yards.

There was nothing in the car except the Ruger Mark II .22 automatic pistol he kept hidden beneath his seat. Strapped in a leather holster, the gun was a quick bend-and-snatch away from his hand. If all he got was a speeding ticket, no problem, but if he had a warrant connected with the search of his house, he might have to use the gun to gain a little time. He had no desire to shoot a policeman. Where was the thrill in that? But he couldn't let the plan that would make him a legend go down the tubes because he was doing eighty-one in a fifty-five zone. No way.

The blue lights flashed on in Daniel Wells' rearview mirror. The big white car with a blue stripe pulled in tight behind him. Wells knew he'd never outrun him in this Toyota. He slowed and pulled onto the shoulder of the road almost even with the press box for the track. No cars in either direction. Perfect.

He waited as the short cop slowly stepped out of his car, adjusted his gun belt and slowly strolled up to the Toyota, showing off his stride and official status.

Wells cranked down the window as far as it would go, leaving about three inches of glass still up. "Howdy, officer, looks like you got me goin' a little quick."

The cop didn't acknowledge him. "License and registration."

Wells looked over his shoulder at the cop with his hands on his gun belt. A small metal tag had the name DRISCOLL on it. Wells calculated the odds of reaching the pistol and getting off aimed shots at the cop's head before he reacted. He couldn't go for the body because the cop obviously had on a bulletproof vest. Besides, he had a little beef on him, mostly muscle, and the .22 might not penetrate.

The cop repeated, "License and registration."

Wells used all his nerve to stay calm and to retrieve his driver's license from his wallet and grab his messy paperwork from the car glove compartment. He handed them over and noticed a tremor in his grip. The cop was probably used to people being nervous when they were stopped.

The cop stood next to the window as he studied the paperwork and filled out a ticket in a metal ticket case. He was extremely efficient. He stepped back and spoke into the radio mike on his shoulder. Wells didn't hear what he said, but didn't want to hear the reply. He flexed his hands as the cop stepped back to the window.

The cop said, "Mr. Wells, this is a simple citation for speeding. Please sign the bottom. It is not an admission of guilt, just an acknowledgment of the citation." It sounded like a script the way he said it. He had a funny northern accent.

Wells signed and handed it back to the cop. He still hadn't heard a response from the cop's call into the dispatcher. He couldn't risk it. His hand seemed to have a mind of its own as it slowly crept toward the gun in the holster under his seat. "No problem, officer," Wells said, leaning forward. As he was about to dart the extra five inches to grip the gun, the cop's radio came to life.

A female voice, showing little stress, said: "All units near turnpike exit one and US 1—two troopers are in pursuit of a signal-ten, southbound, headed into Homestead."

Wells didn't hear the rest because the cop tossed the ticket on his lap and raced back to his car without another thought of Daniel Wells.

thirteen

"let me guess, your life depends on this, too?" asked the sixty-year-old man from behind his thick, dark glasses. Computer screens glowed behind him, giving him an electronic halo, like an angel. To Tasker, Jerry Ristin *had* been an angel when he'd helped him piece together the identity of a man who'd been part of the bank-robbery scheme. If Ristin hadn't contributed his incredible skills as a crime analyst, Tasker might be in jail right now.

"No, Jerry, it's not life and death, just normal urgent."

The older man chuckled. "Whatcha need?"

"Sort through the phone books we took from Wells and see if there are any interesting links or contacts. Crooks, foreign spies, Al-Qaeda terrorists, that sort of thing." He winked.

"Billy, for you, anything." He took the three small personal phone books, flipped through the pages and added, "How about something by end of next week?"

Tasker controlled his anxiety about waiting, but knew the analyst would do it right. "Jerry, you're the best." Before he could say anything else,

Tasker heard his supervisor bellow from the other side of the squad bay: "I thought you was off today?"

Tasker shook his head. "No, sir, tomorrow. I'm headed up to West Palm right now to meet my kids as they get home from school. I even have my P-car outside." Tasker still used the old federal term for personal car as opposed to an official government vehicle, or G-car.

"I want you to step back from this case," said his boss, as he walked closer, "but I'm not sure baby-sitting so your wife can get laid is the right choice."

Tasker nodded thoughtfully. "I didn't look at it like that, but it's too late. I already committed."

"You do more shit like that and you *will* be committed."

Tasker smiled and headed out the door.

Derrick Sutter sat in the rear of the group of fifteen Miami police officers. He was helping out Vice on one of their giant combined operations—first they'd hit a bunch of search warrants, then execute arrest warrants for local people who had been videotaped selling crack to undercover cops over the past three months. Sutter liked hanging out with some of the troops, but he didn't like the "big net" theory of scooping everyone up at once. He knew it had to be done, but sometimes it looked like it was put on more for show than for trying to clean up a neighborhood.

The whole assignment was a big change from his work with Bill Tasker over at FDLE. This was lots of action for little return. No one really cared what happened once you cleared these guys off the street. The cases he'd worked with Tasker had some impact. That was obvious from the way everyone got so bent out of shape when things didn't work out right.

Sutter looked around the group as the sun set into twilight. This was a good time, because they usually caught the dealers at their houses and sometimes picked up extra buyers who were on their way home from work. Each cop wore a simple black Miami Police T-shirt under his black ballistic vest and jeans or black fatigues, depending on which unit they worked on a regular basis. The narcotics guys liked to look tough, so they wore fatigues. Sutter, officially assigned to crimes/person, or what was commonly called robbery, just wore plain jeans. Tonight he actually had on running shoes. He liked a little rubber between his feet and some of the nasty floors of the buildings in the area. His Bruno Magli knockoffs had awfully thin soles.

The big sergeant with the kind of rough complexion you got from acne as a kid finished his briefing, saying, "We got six cops on each site. If people run, it's up to you. If you think you can grab them easy, do it. We don't have enough manpower to have a whole squad chase one rabbit." He looked over the group to make sure everyone was paying attention. "We got a couple of guys sitting at each location. We're hitting three of the eight apartments over on Sixth Court. Two downstairs and one up. That's where the shit will happen." He went over more details and assignments, then sent them off to meet a block away from their assigned locations.

Sutter was one of the cops going to the notorious apartment on Sixth Court. Everyone knew the building. Seemed like half the drug sales and a third of the shootings in the whole city occurred at that run-down concrete-block apartment house.

After a quick gear check at the rally point, Sutter found himself in the lead car with three Vice cops he knew from the substation. They were going to enter the downstairs apartment at the far end of the building. They slowed as they approached the address and let one car stop first so that the cops assigned to the apartment upstairs had a little time to climb the crumbling cement stairs.

"Now," said the driver, as he listened for a signal on the radio. In one motion, all four of the cops opened the doors just as the car stopped and popped out into the small lot in front of the apartments. Two more cops, who had been sitting in a car across the street, joined them as they approached the door to the apartment, each man drawing his sidearm. Sutter held the barrel of his Glock toward the ground until they were at the door. He could hear the team upstairs start to bang on the door and yell, "Police! Search warrant!" The first man on his team repeated the same phrase as he pounded on the door and immediately tried the door handle. It turned, but the door was caught by a chain when he tried to open it. Inside, the sounds of people moving started to grow. The first man raised his long leg and kicked the door wide open, then stepped to the side as the other cops poured into the first room.

Sutter was the second cop in the door and saw that two women were already being held at gunpoint by the cop who had come in first. Sutter and the others immediately flowed into the next small room, the whole time shouting, "Police! Down! Police! Get down!" Their shouts were mingled with the cry of a woman and the shouted obscenities of several men inside. The combination of the noise and the musty smell of crack and cigarette smoke made Sutter's head spin slightly as he tried to focus on any threats in his field of vision.

Sutter, his Glock still in front of him, headed down the hallway just as he saw a dark figure dart toward the rear window and dive straight out the screenless opening. Sutter took two quick steps and peered out to see the man running with a small gray package in his hand.

"Shit, I got a runner. I'm going," he yelled over his shoulder. As he climbed through the window, he heard the cop behind him say, "Not more than two blocks."

Sutter grunted in acknowledgment as he hit the ground and went to one knee, then was up and closing the distance on the fleeing man in a matter of seconds. He wasn't going to yell and let this asshole know he was chasing him. When the time was right, he'd say something. Sutter noticed the guy's hands were already empty. That package was somewhere close.

The man ran west through a couple of yards and a parking lot until he was out on Seventh Avenue, the main north-south artery in this section of town. He looked like he was slowing down, until he turned his head and saw Sutter still loping toward him. Then the afterburners kicked in and he flew across the four busy lanes of traffic without looking. Sutter was right behind him. Just as he was about to make the curb, a low-rider Dodge screeched its brakes and knocked the running man onto the sidewalk. He landed with a grunt, his hand spreading a blood jelly across the rough concrete.

Sutter was about to ridicule the man for getting what he deserved when the same Dodge, still moving, swerved slightly and hit Sutter, throwing him onto the trunk of a stopped Chevy.

"Motherfucker," said Sutter, sliding back onto his feet from the trunk. Before he could yell at the Dodge's driver, he realized his man was up and running, although this time with a slight limp, north on the sidewalk. Sutter started after him.

After a block, the man darted into the Church's Fried Chicken.

Sutter drew his pistol as he approached the restaurant and rushed in the door. Everyone stared at him, and one small girl just pointed toward the swinging door to the kitchen. Sutter pushed through it.

The man, yammering loudly in Spanish, held a five-inch paring knife to the throat of a young female Church's manager. She was silent as tears ran down her face.

But as soon as Sutter raised his pistol and took aim at the man's face, he dropped the knife and backed away with his hands up. The manager rushed from the kitchen.

Sutter advanced on the man, saying, "Get on the ground, now." He repeated it, but the man started circling the large food preparations table with a giant pan of fried chicken legs on it. Sutter stopped and so did the man, his hands still in the air. Sutter took a step and so did he.

Then the man edged back toward the swinging door, reached down and grabbed several chicken legs and started flinging them at Sutter, who dodged two and flinched at another, until he remembered they were only chicken legs. He took two fast steps, surprising the man with his speed, and swung his pistol in a short arc, clipping the man in the head.

The man fell to one knee, dazed, as Sutter holstered his pistol, drew some handcuffs, grabbed the man by the arm and spun him down in one motion, then cuffed him cleanly with his hands behind his back.

Sutter leaned in close to the man's face and yelled, "You're under arrest." He kneed him in the side and added, "Asshole."

The man said, "Why'd you do that?" With no accent.

"You speak English, too," yelled Sutter.

"Yeah. I was born in Kendall."

Sutter kneed him again.

After taking a few minutes to gather his breath and call into the command post that he was fine and had one in custody, Sutter yanked the man to his feet and shoved him though the swinging door. The place had emptied out, with only one teenage worker still there.

"Where's the manager?"

"Tracey? She left."

"When will she be back?"

"Won't. That was the third time she was threatened here. She quit. Said she wouldn't ever come back."

"Shit," mumbled Sutter. Now he'd have to track her down later for a statement. He looked at his prisoner. "You happy now? The girl quit, I'm pissed and we gotta walk back to the processing scene."

The prisoner asked, "Why we gotta walk?" as they left the Church's Fried Chicken.

"We need the gray package you had when you ran."

"What gray package?"

"The one that if we don't find I'm gonna shoot you for trying to escape. That one."

The man didn't miss a beat. "Oh, the package I threw in the bushes over off Sixth."

Bill Tasker always used the commute time from Miami to his old house in West Palm Beach to hash out problems while he listened to sports talk shows on AM 560. At first, using the shorter ride from the West Palm Beach office, it was the whole shooting incident and the cloud from that. Then it was Donna throwing him out of the house. After that it was the impending divorce. More recently it was his troubles with the FBI. Now he tried to look at his Daniel Wells problem from the outside. Although he had wanted to find evidence at the Wells house to build his case, his first concern was simply locating the man. The problem was that he had no idea where the man was staying. He obviously wasn't at the house, and it didn't look like he was coming back. Tasker remembered him saying something about relatives in Tennessee. For all Tasker knew, he could still be in Naranja. If Wells was in Florida, Tasker had the resources to track him. Outside the state, it got trickier. Who could he call for help? The FBI was his obvious choice, but they weren't too friendly lately. Jimmy Lail showed it in his attitude. What about the counterterrorism guy, Sal Bolini? He'd call him on Monday.

Tasker's other worry, more of a vague anxiety, was: Had Wells known about the search warrant ahead of time? Or was he just lucky? Was he part of some terrorist group? What drove him? These questions haunted him almost every hour of the day.

Tasker pulled into the driveway of his old house. The two-door garage was closed and Donna's tan Nissan van sat on the spot closest to the house. Tasker's stomach completed a three-sixty as he hopped out of his Jeep and headed for the front door.

She had the door open before he could ring the bell. "Thank you so much, Billy," she said, giving him a quick hug. "The girls are over at Morgan's. As soon as they see your Jeep, they'll race back."

He just nodded, noticing how she looked like a Dolphins cheerleader in the light sundress, her blond hair in a ponytail.

"Nicky is picking me up in about ten minutes." She looked at him and froze. "You're all right with this, aren't you?"

He shrugged. "Would it make a difference?"

"It would as far as who baby-sat for me."

In his head, he said, Bitch! Out loud, he said, "No, it's fine."

"You're the best," she said, and she leaned over and kissed him as he got comfortable on the couch.

He watched her scoot around and finish little chores for a few minutes until the doorbell chimed. He stood and opened it to see a short guy, about thirty-five with perfectly arranged, short-cropped brown hair, wearing shorts and a loud Hawaiian shirt.

The man said, "Hey, Bill, remember me?" He stuck out his hand, "Nicky Goldman."

"Yeah, Nick, I remember you." He let him in the house. The guy had the class not to kiss Donna in front of Tasker. To his credit, he went to her and asked what he could do to help. They seemed to have a pretty good connection, moving around the house like coworkers as they loaded the suitcases in his Expedition.

Tasker had almost made it—until Donna took a few extra minutes in the bathroom, which left him alone with her new boyfriend. They avoided eye contact and made small talk for a few minutes, until Goldman said, "That was a pretty wild case you got involved in with the bank."

"You mean the one I was accused of robbing?"

"Yeah, I saw the news reports and Donna has filled in the blanks. Who was your attorney?"

"I retained Clayton Troub, but never needed him. The situation cleared itself up."

"So I heard. Pretty incredible, huh? I never heard of a frame-up in real life before, only in the movies." Nicky smiled like they were talking about a football game.

Tasker nodded, thinking, What does this guy want me to say?

"I have to deal with the cops piling on the charges all the time. I know how you must have felt."

"What?" Tasker stood, hoping he hadn't heard this moron correctly.

Goldman stood, too. "I didn't mean it that way."

"Bullshit. This had nothing to do with legal charges. I was intentionally set up by an FBI agent. I guarantee none of the lowlifes you represent were ever set up like this. And cops don't pile on charges unless the criminal committed multiple crimes."

Nicky Goldman held up his hands in surrender and started to back away.

"You fucking grave-robbing attorneys complain when your clients are charged, hoping for some sympathy. Let me tell you something, Counselor, you don't help the downtrodden, you hurt them. Every day. By helping those predators get back into those neighborhoods." Tasker started to go into his remedy for attorneys when Donna emerged from the rear bedroom.

"You boys getting along okay?"

Tasker cleared his throat and Nicky turned his flushed face. Both mumbled, "Yes."

She kissed Tasker on the cheek, again saying, "We have to move on. At some point we have to meet each other's new friends."

Then Tasker realized that his ex-wife's change in attitude in the last month may have been prompted by something other than fear of commitment. Maybe she was just afraid to recommit to him. He froze, wanting to apologize to the still-silent lawyer. He didn't need this now.

After Derrick Sutter's little adventure, he realized just how much he missed working on the bigger cases with FDLE, and missed his partner, Bill Tasker. They had fun together, and even though Tasker wasn't the most cheerful guy, considering what had happened to him the past few years he seemed to maintain pretty well.

The Vice unit was finishing the sweep. They hardly made anything of Sutter's efforts to run down the dope dealer earlier. Pretty common stuff for these tough veteran cops.

Sutter had placed the guy he had chased in line with all the other suspects, sitting on a curb, waiting to be processed. He had given the gray plastic package he'd recovered to the sergeant, who had opened it to find a load of cash.

Sutter liked helping out, even though he was still assigned to robbery. This gave him a chance to roam Liberty City and help clear out some of the dickheads that made it hard for the ordinary residents of the area to live and raise families. It also felt good to run after someone once in a while. At least the brothers here didn't throw little sticks of dynamite at him or cook up all kinds of nasty explosives in their bathtubs. He decided that he preferred to have chicken thrown at him anytime.

Now, as his shift started to wind down, he was filling out an arrest form on one of the dozens of prisoners. With the other cops in a straight line, sitting at long, portable tables with folding chairs, it looked like a recruiting drive, with people filling out employment applications.

Sutter looked across at the young black woman, her hands secured behind her back with plastic flex cuffs. He recognized her from the neighborhood over the years but had never spoken to her. She was pretty, with a full-framed gold front tooth and funky, slicked-down hair. He didn't like it when they just swept up everyone in a big net like this, but he knew it had to be done. Crack sales were killing neighborhoods all over the country. The regular people who lived here had to put up with it every day, and that was definitely not right.

As Sutter filled out the top part of the form, the woman said, "I gettin' out tonight?"

"Doubt it. You'll see a judge tomorrow."

"He just let us out then. Why bother with this tonight?" She wasn't nasty, just exasperated.

"'Cause this is my job." Now he really started to miss Tasker and the big cases. He came to the prisoner-information section on the form. Looking up at the woman, he asked, "Last name?"

"Williams."

Sutter wrote in block letters and asked, "First?"

"Sha-theed."

He started to write, then said, "Spell it."

"S-H-I-T-H-E-A-D."

Sutter wrote it in, then stared at the name until it made sense. "Funny. Now what's your first name?"

"That *is* my first name. Look at my ID." She nodded toward the small plastic evidence bag containing her personal property.

Sutter retrieved the official Florida identification card, usually issued if you couldn't get a license for some reason, and found that the young woman's name was, in fact, Shithead Williams. Sutter let a smile slide across his face and said, "I bet you have a nickname." He was about to write "Shitty" before she even answered.

The woman said, "Yeah, my brothers call me Anita."

Sutter stopped writing and looked up at her again. "Anita, where's that come from?"

She shrugged.

"Is that what you use everywhere?"

"No, I likes to be called Sha-theed. It's prettier."

Sutter was about to explain the mean joke her parents had played on her when a big sergeant walked over, rotated his head on his massive shoulders and said, "Sutter, can you run down to the Gables and see if that guy is staying at the address he just gave us?" He pointed to the small, dark, Latin-looking man at the end of the row who Sutter had caught earlier. His head drooped down and shoulders hunched.

Sutter said, "No problem, Sarge."

The big man said, "That package you found had eight grand cash in it and we need to know who he is for sure. He may be a good link to something else. Figured you caught him, you'd want to do the follow-up. I know you been kicking around in south county with your FDLE buddy. I send one of my guys out of the city, he's liable to end up in Tampa."

Sutter laughed. "I hear ya. I'll call when I find anything out."

"If it looks like he lives there, see if we need to get a search warrant for the house."

"How do you want me to do that?" Sutter asked.

The sergeant just looked at him. "You'll know what to do."

Sutter nodded and handed the lovely Shithead, or Sha-theed, off to another cop and found his issued Buick parked around the corner. There was a good-sized crowd on the street watching the cops complete the search and haul away the prisoners.

Half an hour later, Sutter had determined that the address provided by the suspect was a Publix shopping center. He cruised the lot and asked a few questions about the man in case he was homeless and really did live here. The Publix produce manager explained that Coral Gables didn't have any homeless people and assured Sutter that he had never heard of the suspect.

After Sutter reported this info back to the Vice sergeant and was told to head home for the night, he found himself driving south on US 1. Since his adventures in the southern Dade area, he'd found he liked the idea of there being such a diverse and different place only a few miles from the city that he loved. He would've liked to have Tasker with him now, but his friend had agreed to watch his girls so his wife could get away for the weekend. That made Tasker either one of the greatest guys he'd ever met or a sucker. He'd seen the FDLE agent's ex-wife and figured she could've turned *him* into a sucker, too, if she wanted to.

Sutter noticed a bar attached to the end of a little strip mall in what Sutter believed was South Miami, a separate little town just south of the Gables. He was about to pass it when he saw it was a nude bar. His favorite kind.

The bar had no visible name until he entered and saw it was called the Tittie Shack. Probably not a name the landlord of the shopping center wanted outside the club. He paused, looking past the sign, and the doorman demanded a ten-dollar cover. The vibe the big man threw Sutter's way wasn't positive, but Sutter ignored him. The small façade hid a good-sized place with two stages. He thought, What the hell, and handed the giant bouncer a ten-dollar bill. There were only five customers and at least ten girls, most sitting around in skimpy outfits, looking bored. A pretty Latin girl with too much makeup smiled and patted the empty space next to her on a bench by the rear wall. No one else seemed interested, so he strutted over, letting the girls look him over, and took a seat on the padded bench. As he sat, he realized that the table had hidden the girl's substantial lower body, but to Sutter that was a plus. She introduced herself as "Diamond," and Sutter said his name was "Gold." She accepted it just as he had accepted her stage name. Half an hour and two drinks later, Sutter felt his groove coming on. He thought this girl might be good for a party. As he worked his mind around how to ask if she'd like to see his South Beach apartment, he noticed the blond dancer on the far stage. She had a body but not many moves. Still there was something familiar about her. He stared at the light-skinned dancer until his Latina flicked his ear. The rest of the night was a blur.

Daniel Wells cringed as he squished the last cone under the wheels of the big tractor-trailer. Counting the two garbage cans before he'd even entered the course, he had hit twenty-two objects. He didn't figure that to be a passing score. He looked over to the fifty-year-old heavyset instructor.

The older man said, "Mr. Westerly, that was god-awful."

"Don't pass yet, huh?"

"I'm not sure you should be allowed to drive a *car.*"

"I just need to get a feel for the distance from the driver's seat to the bumper." The big Freightliner Coronado made him feel like he was driving from the second floor of a building.

"No offense, but I seen fellas drunk on moonshine calculate distances better than you. Once, for a prank photo, we put a monkey behind the wheel. I believe he did a better job than you."

"Need more practice, that's all."

"Mr. Westerly, I don't usually say this, 'cause the school needs students and the income, but you been coming for lessons a long time and you ain't ready to drive a pickup, let alone a semi."

Wells nodded. The only thing he'd done right at this school was use a fake name and answer to it when someone addressed him. "Just let me work on cornering and some narrow lanes and I'll be happy."

The big driving instructor hesitated.

"I'll pay the full tuition again. Start from scratch."

The instructor shrugged. "Okay. I think you'd do better finding other work, but we can try again."

Wells slapped him on the shoulder. "Thank you. This is all part of my dream."

fourteen

bill tasker threaded his Monte Carlo through the typical Kendall-north-to-Miami traffic with his mind never once registering what he was doing. A hundred other things seemed to press in on him as he tried to get control of his life. He needed to figure out exactly what he wanted. What would it take to be happy? The answer kept coming back to his girls. He needed to spend more time with them and less time worrying about the million things a police job can throw at you.

Pulling onto the 836 expressway headed toward the office, he barely noticed other cars as they whipped past him or slammed on the brakes. He just wrapped his head around the thought of raising his girls right. He'd start today. After a short day at the office, he'd surprise them with a quick trip to the house in West Palm Beach. Maybe take them out to dinner. He immediately felt the change in his mood as he became more determined to complete this simple act by the end of the day. By the time he pulled into the front lot of the FDLE Miami Regional Operations center, he actually had a smile on his face.

Five minutes later, Tasker sat next to the criminal-intelligence analyst in his squad bay. He looked down at the pile of paper which contained all kinds of information on Daniel Wells. He had past addresses, even one from Gainesville when Wells had attended the University of Florida. The printouts also showed that Wells might have been married once before Alicia. There was so much information it was daunting, but still nothing pointed to where the former engineering student had disappeared to so completely.

The analyst, Jerry Ristin, looked up from his computer screen, his thick, tinted glasses obscuring his eyes. "Well, kiddo, you got a lot to work with, but nothing that jumps out. He had a lot of jobs."

"I thought he owned his own business."

"He did. Looks like he contracted out as part of his business."

"Anything interesting?"

"He worked at the Port of Miami for three weeks about two and half years ago."

"Yeah, I knew that. When I have time, I'll check it out. I'm planning on canvassing his old neighborhood today, see if anyone has anything to add. We didn't do it the day of the warrant because we were hoping he'd come back."

Ristin asked, "The couple of times you talked with Wells, did he ever say anything that might tip off where he'd go? I know you had to think of this, but I'm seeing if I can jog your memory."

Tasker had gone over that question in his head a thousand times. "I remember him saying something about sending the kids away, and maybe Tennessee. Shit, he could be anywhere."

"True, but you can look anywhere."

Tasker smiled at the older man's confidence. He'd been around a long time and had cracked a lot of cases that other people got credit for over the years. "Got any suggestions?"

"I knew you'd ask."

"I'm ready, let's hear 'em."

"Call someone over at the FBI. See if they have anything on him. See if they can contact agents in Tennessee to follow up the lead there."

Tasker frowned.

"I knew you wouldn't like it, but it needs doing."

Tasker said, "You're right, but I've already been thinking about it. I just need to decide who to call. I'm not sure the Great White Hope will talk to me."

"Who's that?"

"Jimmy Lail—just some young agent who was born in the wrong culture."

Ristin shrugged. "Do what you need to do. I know you want this guy. I'll check his phone books and see if they lead us anywhere."

Tasker sat for a minute, looking at the printouts and watching the analyst attack his computer. Ristin had saved him once with that thing. Tasker hoped he could do it again.

Tasker was eager to finish talking to the people in Wells' neighborhood, so he could start his ride to West Palm and the girls. He'd even decided he'd ask Donna to go to dinner, too. Screw Nicky Goldman.

The afternoon sun kept the temperature a little over ninety as Tasker stood in front of the small wooden duplex next door to Daniel Wells' house. He had spoken to two neighbors so far, and neither had any useful information. They agreed that he was a good family man, always roughhousing with his boys out front. The only problem seemed to be that the kids were a little wild. The family had lived there about a year and a half, and Alicia didn't say much to the neighbors.

The warped door squeaked open and a man of about forty, in shorts and a Marlins T-shirt, assessed Tasker. "Help you?" asked the man in a clipped Florida-cracker drawl. His thin neck and protruding Adam's apple marked him as at least third-generation redneck from the area.

Tasker produced his badge and said, "I need to ask a few questions about your neighbors next door, the Wellses."

"Saw you guys going through the house last week. What'd he do?"

"We're looking into a couple of things. No big deal." He'd learned to keep things low-key and not give out more information than he got.

"I saw you arrested him for the wrong thing a few weeks ago. You just sore he beat the charges?"

"No, sir. Just need to find him. Mainly to ask him a few questions. Got any idea where he might be?"

"Nope."

"Know anything might help me find him?"

"Nope."

Tasker looked over the slim man's shoulder into a fairly clean house. "You know Mr. Wells at all?"

"Talked to him once in a while. He fixed my lawn mower after one of his boys set off a big-ass firecracker under it."

"That's it?"

"I know he had a serious piece of ass for a wife."

That was something Tasker was already aware of. "When's the last time you saw him?"

The man thought about it, then said, "Probably the night before you guys searched the house."

"Is there anything you can think of that might help me?"

"Naw. Daniel, he's a pretty good guy. Smart as a whip, too. Can fix anything. Learning to drive a big rig. Does all kinds of stuff."

"Learning to be a truck driver? Where?"

"No idea."

"Why?"

"Well, Mr. State Policeman, I didn't go to no police academy, but I guess so he could drive a big truck."

Tasker laughed out loud. The redneck was probably right.

Daniel Wells loved making little things like this. In the tiny trailer he rented for four-fifty a month, he'd arranged a pulley system to provide a surprise for anyone who tried to get in the front door unexpectedly. This was his true gift—engineering the unusual out of the usual. If the door handle was turned so it faced down past eighty degrees, it would start one spring working with another, ending with a length of wire pulling a safety off a device hidden on the porch. Following that course of events, a scene of bedlam would develop that would surely ruin someone's day.

He liked this musty trailer west of Homestead but didn't completely trust the floor in the bedroom. He went as far as the bathroom in the hallway most of the time. He set the old thermostat to seventy and settled onto the soft couch in the main room, chuckling about his booby trap as he picked up his *Popular Mechanics*.

The sun was starting to drop to the west as Tasker maneuvered his Monte Carlo through rush-hour traffic. He had avoided the motionless vehicles on the interstate and was now in sight of his destination.

Sutter, in the seat next to him, had been happy to work in the city with Tasker, because he could show him all the wondrous sights and tell him the funny stories about working with Vice the night before.

"Stay in this lane," snapped Sutter. "People turn toward the arena from the left."

Tasker obeyed. "I wanna get there before five to talk to the management."

"Shit, the damn port runs all day and night. If it's not the cruise lines, the freighters are always coming in."

"You been there much?"

Sutter shrugged. "Once in a while."

They drove over the wide bridge that led to the Port of Miami and then through the security checkpoint. Three different uniformed security men had to verify their identification.

No one at the personnel office remembered Daniel Wells, but they had a file and a W-4. Tasker already knew all of the information on the form. Wells hadn't even listed Alicia, just his address and phone. As a contract employee, he hadn't received any benefits. His occupation was listed as "welder."

Sutter looked at Tasker as they handed in the file. "What now?"

"Let's go down to the terminal and see if anyone remembers him. We're here anyway."

Sutter hesitated. "Yeah, but the restaurants are over there." He pointed toward Bayside.

Tasker nodded, realizing he was getting hungry as well. "It'll only take a few minutes."

The terminal was slow, with only one cruise ship in port and no one boarding. They asked a couple of the terminal custodians and service people about Wells, but no one had a clue.

Tasker walked up to a thin man in his mid-thirties and said, "Excuse me."

The man turned and smiled, then said something Tasker didn't understand.

Sutter stepped up and said, "I'll handle this." He faced the man and said, *"Hola, mi amigo. Yo soy policía. Quiero hacerme lustrar los zapatos."*

The man stared at Sutter with an open mouth.

Tasker looked at his partner. "Good Spanish there, Derrick. Too bad he's Italian."

"How do you know?"

"His name tag says 'Dominic,' with 'Salerno' underneath."

Sutter just nodded.

Tasker added, "And you told him you're the police and you need your shoes shined."

Sutter looked at his shiny Bruno Magli knockoffs. "Those assholes in Vice told me it meant 'I need to ask you some questions.' "

Tasker couldn't help but laugh at his partner for falling for the oldest joke ever.

Dominic seemed willing to help, keeping a smile on his face and looking for a translator. He led Sutter by the arm to a similarly dressed man near the opened loading hole.

That man spoke Italian and French, but not much English either.

Once Tasker and Sutter had broken away from their newfound friends and walked halfway back to the car, Tasker stopped and looked back at the big ship.

"What would a suitcase bomb do to a ship that size?"

"Not much. Maybe scare some people, stir up the crew, cause a lot of confusion."

Tasker nodded, then slapped a hand to his head.

Sutter asked, "What? What's wrong?"

"I was gonna have dinner with my daughters tonight in West Palm."

"You need to call them?"

"They didn't know. It was going to be a surprise."

"Then they won't be mad."

Tasker started to feel guilty again as he nodded his agreement to his partner.

Sutter said, "Let's go. This was a waste of time."

"No it wasn't."

"How do you figure that?"

"We just met the kind of guy Wells killed in the bombing. Dominic could've been the victim just as easily as anyone."

Sutter looked up at the ship.

Tasker said, "Now I'm pissed off *and* worried."

fifteen

the small round table had nicks in its Formica top. The sleek, twenty-something waitress clearly resented having to work in her family's small restaurant near the Orange Bowl and showed her dissatisfaction with every gesture of her delicate hands and every expression on her flawless face. Tasker sat, mesmerized by this striking girl, as she tossed plates onto the marred table and ignored empty water glasses. She was one of the reasons he loved coming here. The look on FBI agent Sal Bolini's face was the main reason Tasker had asked him to meet him in such an out-of-the-way restaurant.

A thin film of sweat started to form across Bolini's tall forehead. The heat from the kitchen, as well as the owner's sparing use of the air conditioning, had had the effect Tasker wanted.

Tasker said, "You could take off your coat. No one'll complain." He smiled, comfortably cool in his polo shirt and khakis.

"I like the coat concealing my gun," Bolini said, using a napkin to mop his face.

"A belly bag conceals pistols and keeps you cooler." Tasker leaned back and patted his black bag. In truth it didn't hide the fact that you were armed, it only hid what type of pistol you had. No one ever asked, but if you wore a belly bag in Miami and weren't just off a flight from Stuttgart, you were carrying a gun.

"The bags go against the idea of being in plainclothes. If I were to wear a bag, everyone would know I was a cop."

"What about an untucked shirt? Wouldn't that accomplish the same thing, and you'd stay a hell of a lot cooler?"

"While I normally would enjoy a discussion on fashion, I can end this by saying that we at the FBI have . . . a certain image."

Tasker nodded. "I see."

"An image you tried to tarnish."

Tasker flushed. "Tell me, Agent Bolini, what was I supposed to do? Take the fall on a false charge so the Bureau looked clean? It was your own agent who took the money and framed me. Should I have kept my mouth shut?"

Bolini remained silent for a few seconds and then said, "It was your attitude. That cop attitude that the Bureau is a bunch of fuck-ups and we were all against you. That wasn't the case. Tom Dooley was an anomaly. Never happened before and won't happen again."

"Never happened before? What about that spy, Hanson? Or the agent indicted in the Midwest for murder? I'd say it happens more than you admit."

Bolini's face darkened. "This is why you called me? To nitpick? Get to the fucking point."

Tasker cursed silently. He needed a favor, not another pissed-off FBI agent. He took a deep breath. "You're right, I'm sorry. I need to run something past you. Something you may be interested in."

"I'm listening."

"You heard about arresting the wrong guy, Daniel Wells, on the Stinger deal."

Bolini couldn't hide his smile. "Yeah, I heard."

"I know you've got some good contacts in the south county and access to some decent databases." He paused.

"Yeah, go on."

"This guy Wells is in the wind and I need help finding him."

"If he was the wrong man and you got him turned loose, why do you need to find him?"

"I think he's the guy who set the bomb on the cruise ship a couple of years ago."

Bolini sat motionless and silent, staring at Tasker. Neither man spoke as Bolini seemed to gather his thoughts. "The *Sea Maiden*? What are you saying?"

"That Daniel Wells is responsible for the cruise-ship bombing."

"The same Daniel Wells that you had released?"

Tasker kept it professional, even though he felt the mocking sting in every word Bolini uttered. "That's correct, " he said slowly.

"You got a warrant for him?"

"Not yet, but I will."

Bolini started to laugh, silently at first, then in big gasps, rocking his firm, six-foot frame. "This is precious. We make the arrest, you get him off and now you want us back on the case. That is just fucking hysterical." He wiped his eyes. "Tell me, Mr. Hot-shot FDLE Superagent, why aren't Melissa Etheridge and Ice-T helping you on this?"

Tasker stayed calm, somehow. "If you mean Camy Parks and Jimmy Lail, they've opted out."

"I thought the princess was all over the cruise ship."

"Not with me."

"I see. So ATF jumped onboard with the FBI in thinking you're a mistake waiting to happen. Smart move on their part."

"How do you figure?"

"Legally, they can't be associated with you. They also can't go after a guy they just arrested, then had to let go. You managed to insulate this guy Wells perfectly if he is involved in anything else."

"I got evidence he was involved in the *Sea Maiden* bombing."

"Does Camy Parks agree with your theory?"

"She hasn't looked at it closely."

"How can that be?" Then he paused, running his hand over his perfectly trimmed hair. "I see. No matter what you find, she's been told to lay off. That's rough."

Tasker kept watching the man. He seemed sincere, for the moment.

Bolini asked, "When are you looking at getting a warrant?"

"Maybe today."

Bolini's eyes opened wide. "That's crazy. What's the rush? Shouldn't you find him first?"

"Why wait? I've got enough."

"Like when you arrested him for the Stinger?"

Tasker scooted back from the table, drawing looks from a couple of the other diners. He said, "That was based on what one of your agents saw. An FBI agent."

"So now it's the Bureau's fault again. Isn't it time you found a different scapegoat? Couldn't you be wrong about the cruise ship?"

"I've got evidence."

"Like what?"

"Wells is on a list of buyers for TATP, the explosive used in the bombing. The stuff he bought is a chemical match for the explosive, and the explosives-maker can positively ID Wells. And he's gone. Out of the house. No info. Just disappeared."

"What about family?"

"Gone."

Bolini considered all that and said, "Outta sight, outta mind. It's an ATF case, I'd drop it."

"Can't do it. I'm the one who let him out on the street."

"So what—he's no threat now."

"How do you know that?"

"A redneck like that. You got him running. He hasn't the time to cause any trouble. Shit, you probably scared him straight. He's probably deciding where to move so no one ever bothers him again about a prank at the port."

"A prank? Someone got killed because of that prank."

"Hey, don't get so hot. I'll tell you what. If you want to hand over all your stuff to me, I'll take a look at it. Maybe that'll help."

"Work with the FBI on this?"

"Oh, hell no. The Bureau would never touch you again. I mean I might take a look at it myself, then decide if it's worth pursuing."

"No way. At least I know I'm making an effort to find him. If you guys won't help, then you can go to hell."

"Whoa, is that why you asked me to lunch? To tell me to take a hike? What are you looking for from me?"

"I need to at least find Wells. That's why I called you. He's got relatives in Tennessee and a few other places out of state. He's in your intel base. Could you check around and see if you can find him?"

"Sorry, slick. You got into this mess, you can get out. If my bosses knew I helped you, I'd be on airport-security detail, checking for bombs shoved up people's asses." He took the last bite of his Cuban sandwich and added, "You're on your own."

Tasker thought, What else is new?

In the woods on the side of the trailer he'd rented, Daniel Wells pulled down his mask again and applied the flame to the wire weld. The heat inside his van varied from miserable to unbearable, but he kept at it.

He'd been lucky to find this place west of Homestead, so close to his own house but out far enough that no one would bother looking for him. He'd even been back to the house twice without anyone the wiser. He'd read the search warrant the cops had left and knew that they had made the surfer from Florida City talk. He'd have known anyway, from his friend. But this just made it seem more official. He kept the note from Bill Tasker. He did owe the guy, but his special feeling was bigger than his debt to a state cop. He might call him just for laughs. The effort they had put into linking him to the two-year-old bombing actually made him feel better, more satisfied.

It showed that what he had accomplished did matter. It had wreaked havoc on the ship and with the cruise lines for a while. He'd done some welding work for them and knew that the bookings would drop and cause more and more people to worry. It was like making the mood last longer than just the bang. Unfortunately, the cruise lines had gotten back on track pretty quickly and he needed something else to satisfy him.

He knew that his next move would have to be big. Even if he'd tried something smaller so he could enjoy Alicia and kids a while longer, that had all changed now. Now he needed to make a statement and show people what one man can do if he set his mind to it. The dang Muslims bragged about everything they did, but it always took a whole bunch of the little buggers to pull something off. They caused terror, there was no doubt of that, but they had to plan for years, use all kinds of confederates, and then die in the act. Wells hoped to show those little bastards that one smart, determined American could pull off an equally spectacular plan with only a little planning and no extra people who could blab. The most important point was that it would be one man . . . who survived . . . and didn't get caught.

He took a break, sitting in the van with the side door open. He turned off the torch and took off the welding mask. This was a great place. Cash rent, a landlady who didn't even know his last name. Plenty of room, too. Wells didn't even know where the property line ran, with all the pine trees and scrub brush clogging the yard. He had the Toyota behind the double-wide and the van in the cleared driveway, where he could work on it. The thick pad of pine needles made it easy on his knees when he had to stoop down outside the old van.

He looked at the crease across the top of the Toyota parked fifty feet away and thought about the piece of rebar he'd blown across the field that day. That was a good experiment, and it led directly to the device he had loaded on the *Sea Maiden.* That had been a good plan. Pack the suitcase with some TATP, two bottles of lighter fluid to make sure something burned, and lots of old rags. He'd just placed it with a stack of luggage a family from New York had set on the dock to be loaded and it went right up the plank. He had a timer that would've made it blow as it was headed out to sea but before it reached a cabin. At least that was what he thought. The damn baggage handlers must have thrown it so hard it detonated. That's why the handler had been killed. With Wells, it wasn't a numbers game. He couldn't care less as long as it caused confusion. Confusion and terror for the passengers and crew. He imagined it had, but he was sorry the explosion hadn't been on a higher deck with a more visible result. He would have been happy with the big bang and people scurrying about like mice, but the killing had spooked people. The death had added another element to his feeling, his urge. Made the story last a little longer, too. But now, he didn't care. He might want some numbers this time. After this, he'd be a damn folk hero. This was definitely a big plan, and he loved that he was the only one involved. No one to betray him to the police.

When it was all over, he'd have to go deep underground. Get the kids and Alicia and head out to the Northwest maybe. When people saw what he'd done, he could pick and choose where he laid low. Every fanatical crackpot group would want to hide him and the family from the authorities. Where would he go? He had to think of the kids. He couldn't go with the white supremacists. They had good accommodations, but he didn't want the kids affected by all that negativity. Besides, most of those guys were pretty stupid. And the local group, the American Aryan Movement, still owed him a thousand bucks for building a bomb. That simple fact stuck in his head and pissed him off every time he thought about it. He wanted the kids around smarter people, folks who would set good examples.

Maybe the tax protestors? He didn't really care about them much. He'd never paid much in taxes anyway, but it was something to consider. He'd find someone. Keeping Alicia in line would be the biggest problem. She'd been pretty good, but his uncle said she'd left last week, and even though she'd paged him, it sounded like from a bar when he called back, and she hadn't seen the kids since she left. That worried Wells a little bit. He could always let her go. She didn't know too much. Hell, even if she did, she didn't know what any of it meant. But, man, could she shake it.

He picked up his mask and set it in place on his head, then used his striker to light the torch. He turned and started to weld the two metal surfaces again, melting the rod to form a perfect seam. The sparks kicked past him as he worked closer to the open door. He didn't even notice the smoldering pine needles as he crawled into the van to work the seal closer to the other side. The small patch of ground popped into a low but spreading flame. Wells concentrated on his work, still marveling at how much he was accomplishing on his own.

About twenty minutes after starting back to work, Wells felt a tug on his boot. He jumped out of his skin, turning to see a fireman, in full protective uniform with his helmet under his arm, standing next to the van. Behind him, two more firemen hosed down a patch of blackened pine needles.

Wells shut off the torch, raised his clear visor and scooted out to talk to the fireman. He quickly stood between the fireman and the van in an effort to block the man's view. He looked over his shoulder at the other men scurrying excitedly to ensure the fire hadn't spread. Wells now realized how much smoke the needles had put into the air and wasn't surprised someone had called the fire department. In a small way, this little scene of turmoil caused Wells to feel his special feeling of satisfaction.

The fireman said, "You didn't even notice you almost burned down your trailer?"

"Don't get mad, Officer," said Wells evenly. "I'm sorry, I was working in a lot of smoke and didn't see this. I accept responsibility."

The tall fireman pulled out his notebook, still pissed off. "You scared the shit out of your neighbors."

"I said I was sorry. Isn't it your job to do things like this? If none of us made mistakes, we wouldn't need the fire department, would we?"

That softened the man. "I need a little information."

"Sure." Wells shifted to hide his work.

"Name?"

"Westerly. Dave Westerly."

"What's your address way out here?"

"Don't know. It's on the trailer." Wells looked at the other firefighters cleaning up their equipment. "What's this for?"

"Just goes in our records, that's all."

Wells led the taller man toward the trailer as the fireman took a few more notes. He walked with the fireman as he circled the trailer and the Toyota making notes and checking for any remaining embers.

The fireman finally said, "Looks all clear here, Mr. Westerly. Use a little more care with that torch, will ya?"

"You bet, Officer," said Wells, watching the man walk over to his waiting friends on the big truck. He turned to the van, wondering if the fireman would have wanted to know why he was welding a big gas tank inside the cabin of his van.

Bill Tasker left the welding supply store in Florida City and slowly started driving around the streets of the small town on Florida's southern continental mass. He liked the community feel of the town and how it flowed into Homestead as he drove north on Krome Avenue. He didn't have a real plan, other than to grab something to eat at his favorite Mexican restaurant in Cutler Ridge while he reviewed some reports. He was about to find one of the roads that cut east from Krome to US 1, when he saw a pillar of smoke rising from inside one of the rural neighborhoods. He could hear sirens and caught a glimpse of the fire engine turning down the street half a mile ahead in the direction of the fire. He never saw any actual flames.

About ninety minutes later, just as it was starting to get dark, after he had eaten his fill of refried beans and a fish taco, Tasker gathered his stack of reports concerning the profiles of bombers like Wells and headed north toward his house. Pretty much everyone agreed that bombers were almost always white males between twenty-five and forty. Wells certainly fit that broad guideline. Thinking of the failed engineer from Naranja, Tasker took an impulsive turn and headed west, then south, toward the neighborhood where the Wells house was located.

He drove past slowly, hoping he'd see something that might point him in the right direction. Some piece of info he'd missed the other times he'd been at the house. He could picture the heavenly Alicia Wells in her sheer tank top coming out to talk with him, and wondered where she and the kids were now. If he answered that question, he might be able to find Daniel Wells.

Sutter checked his watch, a nice Rolex knockoff that fooled most of the players in the city. It was past ten and he knew the second shift of dancers would be out soon. Even though he enjoyed the topless bars—what normal male wouldn't like looking at good-looking naked girls trying to dance to every song ever written—he was at this particular place looking for someone. He'd heard country ballads, hard rock, pop, and now was watching the slightly heavy, stretch-marked Latina friend he'd made on his last visit, shaking it to Eminem. White rappers—what was the world coming to?

Last time he'd been here, he'd seen a girl who looked familiar. He couldn't place her at the time, but he'd sure thought about her. A nice blond girl with blue eyes and a pretty face. The kind of girl you'd take to your mama, if your mama liked white girls. He couldn't figure how he'd know someone all the way down here in South Miami, but he felt like she was familiar.

When the second set of dancers came out, he didn't see her. He'd been quiet, sitting by himself away from the stage. He was dressed in a Joseph Abboud imitation that looked sharp on him for a quarter the price of a real Joseph Abboud, so no one would make him for a cop. He stood up and approached the doorman.

"Excuse me, my man." He waited for the behemoth to turn and acknowledge him. Now he tapped him on the arm. "Hey, buddy, can you hear me?"

The giant uncrossed his arms, which looked like thighs, and slowly rotated his melon head in Sutter's direction. "What?" was all that came from the bottom of the big man's diaphragm.

Even with the pounding music, the man's deep voice and direct delivery unnerved Sutter. He regrouped. "I was here a week ago and saw a girl. Blond girl with blue eyes. Real sweet. When does she usually work?"

The man just stared.

Sutter said, "You know, they say always be nice to the customers."

The doorman said, "You know what I say?"

"Fee, fi, fo, fum?"

The doorman stared at Sutter. "No, smart-ass, I say I don't got time for stupid questions. Go back and finish your drink before I mess that cheap suit."

Sutter had been a cop eight years. In the actual City of Miami, no one would talk to him like that. He didn't think he needed to take this kind of shit out in the sticks. "Look here, my man." Sutter held up his left wrist like he was showing him his watch.

"So?"

"You know how much this watch cost?"

The man squinted and leaned a little closer. "Maybe a hundred bucks."

"For a Rolex?"

"Ain't no Rolex."

"What are you talkin' about?" Sutter slowly moved to his right.

"The second hand don't move right."

Sutter moved a little more and lowered his wrist. "You're full of shit. Look in the light." He moved his arm so an overhead high-hat light illuminated the dial. "Look close."

The man now leaned lower with his head near the edge of the bar. Without warning, Sutter slammed the big man's shaved head into the bar and at almost the same time drove his knee into the side of his leg, striking the common peroneal nerve. The man shuddered from the knee spike and grabbed his head as blood started to pour from a gash Sutter had opened near his temple. Without anyone else noticing, Sutter shoved him hard out the front door, where the man tumbled down the three short stairs leading into the bar.

Once on the lime-and-gravel driveway, Sutter calmly walked over to the man writhing on the ground and said, "I tried it the nice way and you insulted my clothes. Now I'm gonna do it the easy way. Easy for me, at least." He stepped on the man's right hand, catching his ring finger curled underneath.

The man yelped, twisting his head to get a better look at Sutter, or to see if anyone else was around.

"Just you and me, Asshole the Giant." He put more pressure on the hand.

The man cried out.

Sutter said, "I was asking about a girl. I could tell by your face you knew who I meant. Now give me a name."

The man had given up any false heroics. "Her name is Champagne."

"Oh, please, I'm supposed to buy that? Not her stage name, doofus, her real name."

The man didn't answer. Sutter stepped harder on the hand, feeling one of the small bones snap under his foot. "In about three seconds, you're never gonna jack off with this hand again."

The man gasped. "Alicia."

Sutter froze. "What?"

"Alicia. Her name is Alicia Wells."

That was where Sutter knew her from. The Wells arrest. Now he had to find her. She might be able to lead them right to her husband. "When's she come in?" He moved his foot so the man would feel some relief.

"Who knows? These chicks keep their own schedule." He curled into the fetal position, whimpering like a sick dog.

"You better make a good guess, unless you want a matching cast on your other hand."

He stuck both his hands between his legs so Sutter couldn't get to them. "I'm for real. She usually comes in second shift, but I know she works a club in the city, too."

"Which one?"

"Don't know, man."

"Guess there's no way you won't tell her I was asking about her?"

The man just stared at him, tears still in his eyes.

"Next time you be polite to customers. We all know you're big. You don't have to scare us. Understand?"

The man nodded furiously as Sutter slowly strutted back to his car. Tasker was never gonna believe this.

sixteen

tasker had driven to work before traffic started to build. Inside the office, he found his reliable criminal-intelligence analyst, Jerry Ristin, staring at his computer screen through the thick, brown-tinted glasses that seemed permanently affixed to his head.

"Got anything for me, Jerry?"

"Hi, Billy, I'm fine."

Tasker felt embarrassed for not greeting the older man properly. "Sorry, Jerry."

"There's more to life than work, Billy."

"Yes, sir," Tasker said slowly, like a kid talking to an adult.

"Now, what I have that you'd be interested in is simple—two flags on the license plates for your good friend Mr. Daniel Wells of Dade County."

"Two hits, no shit?"

"Yes, shit," said Ristin in a professional monotone. "One was in Homestead. And one was in the city."

"Miami PD?"

"Yup."

"That must've been Sutter running him for some reason. He's working the case with me."

"Regardless of Detective Sutter's work, I can make a few calls and give you an idea of what you may or may not want to follow up on."

"Jerry, you're the best."

"Please, tell me something I don't know." The older man smiled and winked, as Tasker jumped up to see what else he could find out.

After a little work on the computer and a few phone calls, Tasker had headed down to Homestead to speak with Officer Mike Driscoll. The diligent Officer Driscoll had apparently stopped Wells last week and ticketed him for speeding. This was the kind of break that blew a case wide open.

Inside the neat, professional police department, Tasker sat in a conference room with Driscoll. The cop's blue shirt had every possible insignia in precise rows and perfectly spaced.

"You got some lapel pins there, don't you?" said Tasker, trying to loosen the mood.

"Why have 'em if you don't show 'em?" He had a slight Boston accent.

"You look like you know your way around a uniform."

"Four years in the U.S. Marines and two as a Connecticut state trooper. No room for errors."

Was this guy for real? Tasker looked at the young man. His broad shoulders filled out the uniform well. "You were a state cop in Connecticut? How'd you end up here?"

"Sir, you ever been to Hartford in February?"

"No, can't say that I've ever been in Connecticut."

"If you had, you'd know why I'm here."

Tasker nodded, "I see." He looked at the officer for any sign of a joke. He decided to get to the point. "You remember writing this man a ticket last week?" He held up a photo of Daniel Wells.

"Sure, got him doing eighty near the speedway. Happens all the time. Straight road, sight of the track. People go crazy."

"Notice anything unusual about him?"

"Like what?"

"Don't know. Anything stick out?"

"Just a redneck in a crappy Toyota. We didn't chat. I had to jump in a chase down the turnpike."

"He's the key to an investigation we got goin' on. Could you keep your eyes open for him or the car?"

"Sure. You want me to grab him if I see him?"

"Could be dangerous. Just try and figure where he lives."

"I doubt if any of these local good old boys could cause me much harm, but if all you want is his address, I'll try and get it for you."

"Thanks," said Tasker, feeling pretty confident that Daniel Wells was still in the area.

"You think Tasker is on to something?" asked Jimmy Lail, as he placed the thirty-pound dumbbells back on the old iron rack. He used his ratty FUBU T-shirt to wipe the sweat from his face.

Camy Parks looked up from her hamstring stretch. "You heard what he said the day he was here. They did the search warrant but didn't find anything."

"You sorry you're not down with the locals on this caper?"

She looked at him the way she had to do so often. "Yeah, I wish the bosses weren't so afraid. I think Billy is trying to do what's right."

"That dawg's got some drama playing out in south county. He's close to a sting sheet."

Camy stood up, adjusting her tight shorts. "A *what*?"

"An arrest warrant."

"Why didn't you say 'warrant'? Besides, I haven't heard that."

"I got scoop. The FBI makes it their business to know what's going on."

"Please, Jimmy, it's me. The Bureau is no closer to knowing what's happening than you are to being a black man."

He ignored the comment. People always resented his effort to know other cultures. He liked hip-hop and rap. He actually ate collards. He identified with the African-American experience. Why did people have to judge him? He made sure he slipped back into his original voice and accent from Laredo and asked, "We may need to decide if we have to take this case back."

"What do you mean, *we*?"

"I'm only good for certain cases, but not the big ones?"

"Jimmy, you're not even good on regular cases, but you do what you're told. That makes you useful." She shot a blinding smile at him as she walked into the ladies' locker room.

Jimmy Lail shrugged. He'd heard worse over at his own office. He smiled at the sight of her perfectly formed, firm butt disappearing behind the door. Maybe that was one thing in which he wasn't down with the African-American community: he liked small butts, and on that he could not lie.

"So how is Nicky?" asked Tasker, looking into the sea-blue eyes of his former wife.

She smiled. "Nicky is fine, why?"

"Just curious how the good counselor is feeling. I'd hate for him to catch a virus like cancer, or maybe Lou Gehrig's disease."

"Although we haven't discussed his last checkup, he looks fine and seems to be getting by all right for a thirty-eight-year-old man."

"He's that old? Wow, and it doesn't embarrass you to be out with him?"

"I hadn't really thought of five years being that big a deal, but since you asked, I'm not embarrassed to be seen out with him."

Tasker smiled. "I didn't mean because of the age difference, I meant because he's an attorney."

Donna laughed at that. He knew that she had no more use for attorneys than he did, so he'd already figured out that Nicky Goldman had to be a pretty good guy to overcome that stigma. He also should have backed off, because she was doing him a favor by bringing the girls all the way down to his town house. He'd been hesitant to ask, but he was so tied up trying to find Daniel Wells that he needed the help so he could spend a few days with the girls uninterrupted.

Donna said, "Can you get them back by six on Sunday? Emily needs some time to settle down for school."

"Whatever you want." He smiled.

"Billy, I'm not sure I'm comfortable with the nice act. What's going on?"

"No act. I appreciate you bringing them down, and I'll be happy to get them back when you want."

Her face straightened. "Okay, what do you want?"

"I have no idea what you're talking about."

"Billy, if you don't tell me, without any bull, in the next ten seconds, I don't want to hear it."

Man, did she know him. "Okay, okay. I need you to use your contacts and see if some kids are registered in school anywhere north of here."

"What kids?"

"Their name is Wells and their dad is a fugitive."

She frowned. "You really don't change. It's always job first, isn't it?"

"I'd love to debate this with you yet again, but I don't have time. Donna, please, look for these kids." He handed her a sheet of paper with all the identifying information on it. "It's important."

She took the paper. "I won't know until Wednesday or so. You know I'm still expected to teach occasionally."

He hugged her. "You're a champ. This is such a help to me I'll let you have sex with me real quick while the girls settle in."

She giggled. "Believe it or not, that's tempting. But I gotta go."

"Your loss."

"You wish."

She really was the most exciting girl he'd ever known.

Sutter waited in the lobby of the headquarters of the City of Miami Police Department. He usually worked out of the substation on Sixty-second Street, but he liked coming to the main building. The sense of history and tradition in the department was one of the few things that made him sentimental. He was proud to be a Miami cop because, overall, the Miami cops had done a great job in a tough place. There were a few high-profile incidents, but the day-to-day life of a cop in this city could be pretty satisfying.

He'd told Tasker to meet him here so they could talk to an undercover cop Sutter knew. Johnny Tatum worked the streets like no one else. He got down and dirty and blended in like a building or tree. Sutter didn't think he'd ever been burned, the way he dressed like a street person and wouldn't shower for a few days at a time. When the FDLE had found out that Daniel Wells' car tag had been run by Miami PD, and that the FCIC terminal was in the Street Crimes Unit, Sutter found out that it was Tatum who had run the tag.

Sutter decided this would be a good time to tell Tasker about his sighting of the beautiful, and naked, Alicia Wells. He knew his state partner would say he was wrong and that she wouldn't do something like that, so he'd have to convince Tasker.

Sutter spoke for a few minutes with the old communications sergeant who ran the front desk, until he saw Tasker coming through the front doors. So many people passed through the doors, it seemed more like a mall than a police department.

Sutter was so comfortable with this FDLE agent he hardly even greeted him anymore. He just cocked his head in a direction and Tasker followed in behind.

"You talk to this guy yet?" asked Tasker.

"Nope. Just confirmed he ran the tag. I do have some other info to go over with you."

"What's that?" Tasker said, quickening his step to keep up with the long-legged Sutter.

"I think I located Alicia Wells."

Tasker stopped, holding the slightly taller Sutter by the shoulder. "No shit? Where? With the kids?"

"I saw her in South Miami, but I think she might be in the city some nights. She definitely didn't have the kids with her."

"That's weird. I thought she was with the kids."

Sutter shrugged.

"Well, where'd you see her?"

"In a bar."

"Which bar?"

"The Tittie Shack."

"What? Why would she go in there?"

"For cash, it looked like."

"Alicia Wells was dancing? She wouldn't do that."

"I knew you'd say that. Sometimes you're clueless."

"She just didn't strike me as the type, that's all. Why didn't you snatch her up so we could talk to her?"

"It didn't hit who she was until a few days later. I went back and spoke to the doorman." He looked down at his cut knuckles on his right hand. "He told me she danced in the city, too. Give me a few days and we'll find her."

Tasker seemed to accept that as they headed back down the hallway and turned into the little squad bay that housed the Street Crimes Unit. Tatum was stretched out, leaning back on a hard wooden chair. He was so dark-complected that his nickname was the "Black Hole." He laughed at the name and played it up in crowds. His long dreadlocks hung loose around his face, which looked every bit of his fifty-one years. The gray streaks through his eyebrows and hair made him look more like a street person than the ratty T-shirt that said "Salvation Army" or his shredded jean shorts. His smell was unique. Sutter thought he had the same smell as a raccoon he'd once seen after it had been run over by a four-wheeler near the beach where his parents lived.

Sutter extended his hand as Tatum stood up. "Johnny, I'd like you to meet Bill Tasker from FDLE."

Tatum took Tasker's hand and smiled, revealing two gold teeth on either side of his front teeth. "You're a folk hero around here."

Tasker blushed. "Why's that?"

"Sticking it to those FBI pricks. I swear those guys have tried to make more cases on cops here than on crime lords."

Tasker just nodded.

Sutter said, "Billy is working on the guy I talked to you about. The one you ran last week."

Tatum nodded. "I was north of here about eight blocks. I remember 'cause I'd just walked from here. Been trying to find these creeps been hassling the homeless people. You know, smacking them around and taking their change they beg off the corners."

Tasker asked, "Wells bother you?"

"No, but he said something funny. That's why I remember him."

"What's that?"

"When I held up my begging cup, to see if he might try and take it, he said, 'No, thanks, I'm not thirsty.' "

They all chuckled at that. Then Tasker asked if Tatum had seen anything unusual about him.

Tatum shook his head. "Nope, he was in a little old Toyota and just looking around. At first I thought he was just looking for pussy, but there was enough around he woulda stopped for it. He just drove up and down the block."

"Would you mind taking me down to where you saw him?"

"Sure, but you gotta put me in the back of a car so it looks like you and Sutter just arrested me."

Sutter liked his style and dedication to stay in character. That's why he said, "Johnny, would you mind walking down there? You smell like you got a dead cat in your shirt."

Tatum gave a good hoot at that. "Close, my slim, well-dressed friend. A possum."

"A what?"

"I found a dead possum this morning and had to carry him a few blocks till I found a dumpster."

"You carried a dead possum to a dumpster?"

"I didn't want it scaring any kids that saw it. It was right near that little day care."

Ten minutes later, Tatum was in the back of Tasker's car, since Sutter refused to transport him, showing them how and where Wells was driving when he saw him.

Tasker stopped the car a couple of times and looked around. This was a little business district. Narrow streets, windowless buildings.

Tasker asked, "What am I missing? Why would he come down here?" He stopped the car and stood as Sutter joined him from the passenger side of the car.

Sutter shook his head. "I don't see it either. Ninety-five is close. So is Biscayne Boulevard, but that's it."

Sutter watched Tasker scan the area, and for the first time realized just how hard and personally Tasker was taking this whole thing.

seventeen

donna tasker looked at the computer screen in the main office. She had checked the entire district, trying to see if any of the names that Billy had given her were registered. There were a lot of Wellses, but when she looked deeper, none came close to the ones he was looking for. It was six in the evening. Between phone calls to her friend in Broward County, and then to another friend in Martin County, she had blown three hours on this.

It really didn't bother her; in fact, quite the opposite. Billy had never asked her for help before. She had to admit she felt a little thrill helping him put together a case, even though she had no idea what the case was about. But if he thought it was important enough to ask for help, it was important enough for her to do. She hadn't done that when they were married, and she regretted it. She'd got so wrapped up in her own problems and worried about so many little things that she'd missed his attempts to get help.

After he'd shot his friend, the corrupt West Palm Beach cop, things had just unraveled. Billy had done what he had to do, but it had still haunted her ex-husband. He'd drift off sometimes, and she just knew what he was thinking about. Maybe someday she could make it up to him. Set things right. He was such a good guy, she hated to see him unhappy.

She made one last check of the system, then grabbed her cell phone and hit the first speed dial.

"Hello."

She recognized his voice and smiled.

"Billy, it's me."

"Hey, everything all right?"

"Yeah, why?"

"You don't usually call out of the blue like this."

She smiled to herself, feeling like a teenager with a crush. "I wanted to see if you'd recognize my voice if I just said, 'It's me.' "

"Promise I'll never forget. How's that?"

"Great." She paused for a second. "I wanted to tell you that I couldn't find Wells' kids listed anywhere in Palm Beach County."

"Damn."

"And I checked Broward and Martin, too."

"You did all that for me?"

"Of course."

"I'm touched."

"Don't be a dork." She smiled again and said, "I gotta go."

"Thanks, Donna. You saved me a lot of time."

After she hung up, she found herself thinking about her ex-husband for another five minutes.

Wells was exhausted. The late-night planning and work he'd done around his trailer were catching up with him. It was only noon but he needed some sleep.

He almost crawled up the low, shaky steps and then pushed his flimsy front door open. He immediately turned back to the door and looped the small wire that activated his front-door security system. He ran his fingers along the wires to the pulleys, making sure everything lined up and would work if someone tried to surprise him.

Satisfied he was secure from the front, and not real worried about the back, Wells stretched out on the soft couch left in the trailer by some previous tenant. The stained flower design and slight smell of urine didn't really bother him as he quickly drifted off to sleep.

Tasker had swung by Sutter's apartment on South Beach to speed up his partner. This was the break he'd been waiting for. The Homestead cop he'd spoken to, Mike Driscoll, had apparently stumbled across Wells living in the western part of the town. Now Tasker intended to use the information immediately.

Sutter came out of the historic old apartment building still buttoning his shirt, his Glock with silver-painted handles exposed on his hip, and opened the car door. "Yo, what the hell, man? What's goin' on? You tell me on the phone to be ready in fifteen minutes and that's it? No explanation? Can't I take a day off once in a while?"

"We found Wells."

Sutter froze, then in a more subdued tone said, "Where? How?"

"Homestead. The cop that I talked to down there, the one that wrote him the ticket, was at a firehouse mooching food and saw a report about a minor fire at a trailer. The firefighter was sharp enough to write down the vehicle tags. Just for his report—he didn't run them. Anyway, this cop, Driscoll, is pretty sharp himself, and he asks a few questions. He'd been on the lookout since our talk."

"So your patrolman put this all together?"

"Sure did." Tasker accelerated west over the Julia Tuttle Causeway, swerving through traffic like a grand prix racer.

Sutter calmly strapped on his seat belt. "Does Wells have any idea we know?"

"No way."

"Then slow this vehicle down before I have to write *you*."

Homestead patrolman Mike Driscoll didn't want anyone else coming on the arrest. He made his point that three cops should be able to grab a guy from a trailer.

Tasker hesitated. "I can call for some agents from Miami."

Driscoll leaned in from the edge of his chair. "I'm tellin' you that the place isn't that big. We slip in quiet and snatch his ass up before he knows we're there."

Sutter added, "He's got a point. More men, more noise."

Tasker kept thinking about it. "It's still a probable-cause arrest. I didn't get a warrant yet."

Sutter said, "No problem. This guy was a pussycat last time. The three of us are plenty."

Tasker nodded and they headed out, all crammed into Tasker's state-issued Monte Carlo.

Daniel Wells couldn't get used to taking naps during the day. When the kids were around, he never tried to sleep. Always afraid he might miss some segment of chaos they'd create. They loved it as much as he did. He worked a lot at night, when it was cooler, finishing his van and getting everything ready. He wasn't going to pass the big rig test, but he knew how to get around it. He only needed to drive the thing twice, and after the second time he'd never go near a big truck again.

He picked up his *Popular Mechanics* and laid his head back on the soft pillow of his sofa. The old material felt like corduroy. He didn't know if they used that on couches back in the sixties, when this thing was made. All the furniture was old but comfortable, and he couldn't beat the price. Free with the trailer. This wasn't too bad, as long as his money held out.

He wasn't comfortable with the silence of this place at times. In one respect it was new and different, so he didn't mind experiencing it, but it was not his natural element. He'd never been around peace and quiet. When he was a kid, if it was peaceful he and his brothers would change all that. No wonder his dad was deaf now. He and his brothers set off thousands of firecrackers and cherry bombs. Then, as Wells got more experience, he'd make his own kind of fireworks. Often he'd slice open firecrackers for their tiny amount of black powder. Storing up jarfuls. Then he'd make his own explosive devices. Float model ships filled with powder, then detonate them with a long waterproof fuse in the pond near his childhood home. When that got dull, he'd set things where others would see them and react. His best was a giant firecracker he'd been able to secure inside a plastic jar. He'd glued a clear plastic tube down the middle so the firecracker and fuse wouldn't get wet, then filled the rest of the jar with a mixture of milk of magnesia, red food coloring and red raspberry syrup. He placed the jar on the newspaper box of the busiest convenience store in Ocala and waited across the street. The fuse smoked more than he thought it would, but nobody took the time to look for the source of the smoke. When that thing went off, his red sauce splattered eight people. They looked like slasher victims. They ran around in a panic, holding their nonexistent wounds to stem the bleeding. Then the fire department and cops showed up. It was on that day, when he was eleven years old, that he realized what was really important. At least to him. He also realized that the fact that it was fake didn't matter to him. He could have put nails in that jar and really hurt people and would have felt the same way. This wasn't a joke or a phase, this was a drive.

All these thoughts rushed through his head as he dozed off again on the flowered couch near the bay window of his rented trailer. Then something woke him. He didn't know what. A noise out of place, something man-made.

He sat up and looked out onto his wide front yard with the winding lime driveway. He could see all the way to the gate, and it was all in order. The gate was closed and nothing moved. Then he froze. On the edge of the driveway closer to the road, he saw a line of disturbed pine needles. The thick carpet of needles had ruts through it and was patchy in places where he'd walked, and then there was the giant burnt swath. But they always had a certain look when newly turned over. The black on the bottom had a different color until the sun baked it for a few hours. That was what caught Wells' eye as he looked outside. Then, while he was still motionless behind the tinted window, he saw movement. Someone had entered his yard and was crouching on the far side, slowly making his way toward the house. He looked around. The gun was under the seat of the Toyota. He had two cheap nine-millimeters in the van, but they were in pieces right now, waiting to be cleaned. He slid off the couch and into his kitchen, reaching up onto the counter and snatching his keys as he slid along the cheap linoleum.

Whoever was coming would get a surprise at the front door. He looked over his shoulder at the cable that ran from inside the house out to the roof and into the canisters in the dead hanging plants lining the porch. He cursed himself for not having anything as spectacular in the back.

He could run now or wait to see the bedlam. He slipped out the rear door and settled into the bushes. Then he worked his way around in the bushes and scrub pines until he could see the porch. There were three men. He was too far away to recognize any of them, but one was in a blue uniform. They were crouched behind his van, surveying the house. They had no idea he was already outside. He started to tingle inside. This was always the best time. The expectation. This was going to be great.

"Bullshit. I don't want to go 'round back. The redneck probably has a dog or something," said Sutter in a harsh whisper.

"Did you hear any dogs?" asked Tasker, confused as to why his normally kickass partner was hesitant.

"I'll go in the front with you guys. This place is so far out west he can't run nowhere. We go in fast enough and it won't matter."

Tasker didn't like having this sort of discussion at the scene of an arrest.

The Homestead cop, Driscoll, kept a former Marine's eye on the trailer, unconcerned about the spat between partners.

Tasker leaned into Sutter and said quietly, "I don't see why you can't cover the back. You're still on the arrest."

Sutter replied even quieter, "Snakes."

"What?"

"Too many woods. I can't handle the idea of snakes."

Tasker just stared and decided not to pursue the issue. He spoke a little louder so the Homestead cop could hear now. "We don't have the warrant yet, so we gotta see him or get him to come out."

Now Sutter looked shocked. "You tellin' me that if he don't answer, you're leaving without him?"

Tasker knew his partner was right.

The three men low-crawled to the end of the van and waited. Tasker casually looked in the small rear windows and saw the van was empty except for a box in the rear. He looked closer at the welded box and saw that it was a gas tank of some kind. He forced himself to concentrate on the trailer for now and shifted his attention back to the task at hand. After waiting a few minutes, the three men walked quickly at an angle to the edge of the trailer. Tasker had been careful to find an approach with no windows in direct line. They paused at the edge of the metal steps that led to the porch which covered twenty feet of the front of the trailer.

Tasker cringed as their weight on the porch made the trailer shake. They fanned out, with Driscoll covering the bay window and Sutter and Tasker on either side of the door.

Tasker knocked once. He looked at Sutter.

Sutter said, "We gotta move."

Tasker tightened his hand around the lever that operated the front door. He cranked it down and felt something click on the other side of the door. Before he could determine if it was the handle or not, he heard a sound above them and saw three separate flashes above the hanging plants. Then the deafening boom. He was on the ground with Sutter when the burning sensation ate its way up his face and over his eyes. Even with his ears ringing from the explosion, he could hear the other two men screaming.

Wells stood slowly and surveyed his trap. All three men were down and yelling obscenities and gurgled coughs. This was technically perfect. It'd had the exact consequence he had intended.

He opened the door to his old Toyota and retrieved his Ruger .22, then strolled over to his van and dug out his keys from his pocket and started it, not worrying about the men in agony on the porch.

He drove down his driveway, stopped at the gate, opened it and drove through like he did almost everyday. The only difference was he didn't bother closing it this time.

As he turned onto the unpaved road, he saw the gold Monte Carlo by itself near the corner of his property. He pulled up next to it and couldn't resist leaving another little package for anyone who opened the door.

Stepping out of the van, he found he didn't even need his slim-jim to pick the lock because the trusting cops had left the doors unlocked.

He took a plastic jar filled with a milky fluid out of the rear of the van and set it on the console between the front seats. He connected a thin piece of monofilament fishing line to a ring on the small detonator on the lid of the jar, then roped it through the passenger door. He took the other end and ran it out the driver's door past the lock. He looped the line once and then shut the door, tightening the fishing line.

Unless they looked closely before they opened the door—and nobody ever did—they'd be in for another surprise.

He smiled, jumping back into the van and rumbling toward Homestead. He needed another place to stay for a few days until he was ready to make his move to *The Guinness Book of Records* for "Most Shit Caused by a Single Man."

It took thirty seconds of screaming and rolling on the porch for Tasker to assess how badly they'd been disfigured. He opened his eyes past the intense burning and saw Sutter next to him, also holding his face. He also noticed that Sutter didn't have a mark on him. He sat up, trying to check his chest and arms for wounds, but he was just damp.

He looked over to Driscoll, who was now trying to stand. He didn't have a mark on him.

Tasker shouted, "It's okay, you're not cut. No blood."

Sutter paused his wailing to examine himself more closely. Then after feeling the film of liquid on him, he started to yell, "Acid! Acid!"

Tasker stumbled off the steps and down to the side of the trailer, looking for a garden hose. He felt along the tin walls, occasionally snatching views with his eyes—every time they opened, it was like a fire on his cornea. He found the nub of a short hose and followed it back to the faucet. He twisted the knob and let the water splash up onto his face. There was instant relief. It still burned, but much less than during the initial contact.

"Here. Come down here to the water. This helps."

The other two cops bumped their way to Tasker and shared the hose. Soon they had a system where any two of them could be washed at a time.

After three or four minutes, Tasker felt well enough to step back and consider what happened. He cautiously crept back onto the porch. He had seen the van leave, so he wasn't worried about the inside anymore. The hanging pots were all cracked on the ground. He found in one a ripped plastic container that had held the chemical.

"Looks like it was CS. Old-fashioned Mace."

Sutter barely looked up.

Over half an hour later, they had regained their composure enough to look in all the windows. They opened the rear door with a rope so no one was in danger and entered the double-wide.

Tasker, still red-eyed and blotchy around his face, walked through each room.

Sutter, his Glock in his hand, waited at the kitchen unless needed.

They still hadn't called for backup. No one had mentioned it.

Sutter opened the subject. "Okay, it was Mace. We're not gonna die. But the question is, Do we need to tell anyone?"

Driscoll was quick to answer. "Hell, no. My guys would never let me hear the end of this shit. Caught in an ambush and letting a fugitive escape. Fuck me, we can't ever tell anyone. In fact, you can drop me at home and I'll clean up before I go back to the PD."

Tasker turned and looked at Sutter, who said, "I couldn't agree more."

They searched the house for any information that might help locate Wells. Twenty minutes later, they walked through the yard, then back to Tasker's car. He was just starting to feel normal, except that his clothes were still soaking wet from his rinsing.

Sutter started yacking about how he wasn't worried on the porch and that now he had a personal stake in Wells, too.

Tasker looked up and down the street, which was deserted. Something didn't feel right.

At the same time, Tasker and Sutter opened their door and heard another bang. Tasker felt a fresh burning from the new booby trap.

He didn't panic this time as the Mace burned his eyes and nose again.

As he stumbled back toward the hose near the trailer, all he heard was Sutter scream, "Fuck!"

eighteen

bill tasker blinked hard, still clearing the CS from his eyes. CS was older and not used as much as the modern pepper spray, but not because it didn't work. Police had moved to pepper spray because it was safer. CS was effective, lingered and was a bitch to clean up. Eight hours and five showers had cleared most of the irritant from his face, but every few minutes he'd feel a burning sensation and blink. It was probably as much psychological as it was physical. But the gallon of snot that had poured out of his head wasn't psychological, just gross. Driving his personal Cherokee, because the CS had also made his issued car unusable for the foreseeable future, he turned off Pines Boulevard in western Hollywood into the new set of housing developments. The miles of new, similar houses caused the native Floridian in him to flash in anger. The houses were needed for New Yorkers escaping the cold and people escaping Dade County. It didn't change the fact that the land had been a marshland next to the Everglades just a few years ago, and now it was a wasteland.

Camy Parks was a perfect example of a former Dade resident now living on what should have been a wildlife preserve. Tasker had been able to get her address in about five seconds on the Internet and was on his way to set her ass straight about this case. It was her investigation, and ATF needed to be involved. Tasker sure could use the help.

He found the cream-colored, two-story, zero-lot-line abomination of a home with no trouble. Camy's ATF-issued Ford Crown Vic sat in the driveway next to a Saab that Tasker assumed was hers. There were several cars on the street near the house. No lights were on in front. It was only about nine, so Tasker wasn't worried about waking her. He rapped on the front door, then rang the doorbell to be sure she knew she had a visitor. He had thought about bringing along Sutter, but after their little confrontation at the ATF office and Sutter's lingering misery from the CS he'd decided to leave his partner out of this plan. Besides, after dark all he'd be interested in was getting the lovely lesbian ATF agent in bed.

Tasker heard Camy call through the door. "Who is it?"

"Bill Tasker."

She opened the frosted glass door a crack, then said, "Billy, what are you doing here?"

"I need to talk to you."

She opened the door wider and looked at him. "What happened? Have you been crying?"

"Yeah. Most of the day, as a matter of fact. Can I come in?"

She hesitated.

"It's important."

Camy sighed and opened the door for him. She had on a terrycloth robe and her hair was loose around her shoulders. She looked almost wild like this.

"Thanks," he said, stepping into the open room with high ceilings.

"First, tell me why you were crying."

He explained the event at Wells' trailer in decent detail, only leaving out that he and Sutter had fallen for the second trap in his car. He could see she was at least slightly amused by the story once she knew no one was seriously hurt.

Camy said, "I'm sorry, Billy, but just because this guy Maced you, I can't rejoin the case."

"What are you talking about? It's an ATF case. He is the guy who bombed that cruise ship. I know it. I also think he's got something else planned."

"Like what?"

"I don't know, but this afternoon in his van I saw he had a big metal tank welded in the back. Unless he's driving across the Kalahari, I don't think the tank is good for anything but blowing up."

Camy considered this.

"Are you gonna let a disagreement get in the way of saving people's lives?" Tasker looked hard into her eyes.

He jumped when he heard a male voice say "Letting Wells out wasn't a disagreement, dawg. It was a double-cross."

Tasker snapped his head in the direction of the man and was shocked to see Jimmy Lail in a silk, flowered dressing robe standing near the entrance to the bedrooms.

Tasker stared, speechless, then turned to Camy. Without thinking, he blurted, "I thought you were a lesbian."

She froze, then smiled. "I never said I was. That rumor started and it was no one's business, so I ignored it."

Tasker looked back at Jimmy Lail, saying, "Or were you just ashamed of your culturally challenged boyfriend?"

Camy didn't answer, but Jimmy crossed the room toward Tasker, his bathrobe flapping open slightly. "Listen, dawg. Don't try an' dis me." He moved past the couch and kept coming at Tasker.

In a smooth motion, Tasker wrapped his right hand around the handle of his ASP expandable baton in his back pocket and pulled it, not snapping it open but holding it in his palm like a eight-inch stick. He held up his hand and applied a little forward thrust as Jimmy came to him. The weight of Jimmy's body running into the point of the closed ASP aimed right at his solar plexus knocked the wind out of his sails and then the man off his feet. He stayed on the ground, gasping for air.

Tasker calmly turned his attention back to Camy like nothing had happened. "So what about it? Help me stop this guy."

"If I ignore orders, it could be the last case I ever work."

"Seems like it's that way with every case for me." He smiled.

"Can we do it quietly? Keep a low profile?"

"Everything I do is low-profile."

Camy looked at her pissed-off boyfriend and then at Tasker and simply said, "Okay, we'll help."

Daniel Wells still chuckled at the thought of the three cops rolling around on his porch that afternoon. But now the realities of life had squeezed out his mild euphoria over confusing the cops so well. Now he stopped the little Honda he had stolen and parked it a block away from the house he was about to visit. It was more a compound than a plain old house, with three separate structures and two full carports. He left the Honda with the broken window right on the street. That way, when the cops found it they would be able to return it to the kid who had parked it at the Wal-Mart in Homestead. Wells had simply broken the window, then cracked the steering column. Nothing fancy, but it got him where he was going.

As he walked up the long driveway to the main house, he noticed an old blue Ford Ranger pickup truck and two Dodge Diplomats. He smiled, remembering that these guys sometimes liked to pretend they were cops.

The compound was operated by the American Aryan Movement, but everyone just called them "the Nazis." The compound was owned by one of the members' parents who, Wells was sure, had no clue what was going on at the house. He didn't really care what was going on, he just needed some cash to help him get a decent vehicle before all his plans had to be scrapped because of something simple like no wheels.

He walked to the front door, amused that the supposedly vigilant master race had not even noticed an intruder walk through their yard. Before he knocked, he felt the handle of the Ruger .22 he had stuffed in his waistband under his loose shirt. Then he pulled out a small clear plastic tube containing six balls. This was a little surprise he'd cooked up with a mixture of TNT he'd gotten from one of his old employers, who'd used it to clear obstructions like tree trunks at construction sites. He slid the tube back into his front pocket. He didn't want trouble this time. He wanted to fly under the radar, but he needed money to get a car, and these guys owed him. He pounded and waited. Then pounded again until he heard someone inside say, "Okay, okay, hold your horses."

A thin, blond man about twenty-five named Dell Linley came to the screen door and said, "Hey, Daniel. Where you been?" then opened the door for him.

Walking in, Wells said, "Been busy."

Dell led him into a living room where four other young men sat watching TV.

On seeing Wells, several of them turned and one said, "Look what the cat dragged in. What's new, Daniel?"

Wells shrugged. "Oh, nothing. Just came for the thousand bucks you guys owed me for the bomb I made you."

They all laughed at once. Dell, the blond guy, said, "If we had the thousand, you think we'd be watching *Gilligan's Island* on Nick at Nite?"

"I got another idea. What about giving me that old truck in the driveway and we'll call it even?" Wells smiled to reassure the men.

The oldest and largest of the men stood up from the couch and said, "I got another idea. Why don't you get lost and forget about the thousand bucks? Joe and Pete got arrested for that thing, and no one noticed, anyway. I think we're already even."

Wells backed toward the kitchen, reaching into his pocket as he did. All five men slowly started to follow him. Wells said, calmly, "No, I need some transportation. I want the truck."

The big man said, "You must be crazy. What makes you think we're gonna give you a truck?"

Wells pulled his hand from his pocket holding the clear plastic tube the size of a roll of quarters. He let them see the tube with the claylike balls in it. "*These* make me think you'll let me take it." He wanted to keep things quiet, but felt his urge, mixed with anger, start to build in him.

"What're those?" asked one of the men.

"I like to call them 'super blast balls.' Just Silly Putty with a kick." He let a ball drop into his right hand, then, without hesitation, threw it at the refrigerator. It exploded on contact, blowing a six-inch hole in the refrigerator with a deafening blast. In the ensuing commotion, Wells drew his pistol and blew out the overhead light. At the sound of the shot, everyone froze.

Wells took advantage of the silence to say, "Keys, please."

Someone tossed him a set of Ford keys. He leaned down and picked them up off the floor and held them, with the explosive balls in his left hand and the gun in his right, still trained on the stunned Nazis.

"Any questions?" He backed out slowly. He knew that no matter what happened, these guys wouldn't tell the cops anything. The neighbors were used to shots fired over here. Just as he was at the door, however, one of the men charged him. The force of the body block sent the vial flying into the air.

Wells realized he had lost the balls and let the flying man knock him out the door. He could hear the multiple explosions inside just as he and the man came to rest outside in the gravel driveway. Wells didn't wait, just pumped two .22-caliber rounds into the man's thigh, then kicked the screaming man off him. He immediately rose to one knee and faced the open rear screen door. He could see the smoke and a small fire caused by the detonation of the balls. He raised his pistol and waited. As the first man emerged from the confusion, Wells shot him in the knee, causing him to tumble to the ground. He repeated the maneuver on the next man, Dell, the blond guy who had greeted him. No one else tried to follow.

Wells stood up, stuck the pistol in his pants under his loose shirt again and calmly walked to the truck. The Nazis in World War Two must've been tougher, thought Wells, as he drove away in his new truck. Or at least smarter. He enjoyed his special feeling as he took a last look at the confusion he had just caused. And now he had a truck to drive that no one would be able to trace. He knew these morons would come up with a good story when they had the .22s removed from their legs. They'd be too scared ever to come after him.

Tasker took almost an hour going over everything they had developed on the case. Camy Parks took notes while Jimmy Lail sat back on the couch, looking uninterested. They were both still in bathrobes. Jimmy had hardly moved since Tasker stuck him in the stomach with his ASP. He was so quiet that Tasker worried he might have hurt the confused FBI agent. Finally Tasker decided he didn't care.

Tasker told Camy about everything, from the explosives-maker to Sutter's sighting of Alicia Wells.

Camy interrupted, saying, "I knew you guys were interested in her."

"Only because she might give us a clue as to where Wells might really be hiding."

"Yeah, right." Her green eyes rolled at the suggestion. "Is she more or less sexy to you guys now that you know she's a stripper?"

"Camy, I couldn't care less."

"Obviously Sutter does, since he's the one going to topless bars."

Tasker stared at her, wondering if she had some problem with topless bars.

She realized she was going off track and said, "Okay, what's our plan?"

"The first thing I need is for you or Lail to see if there is any real intelligence on Wells. Then I'd like to look at what's been done on your case that might help us. After that, I'm open to suggestions."

Camy said, "We could have an FBI profiler look at the case. They might have some ideas."

"Do they really work? I know we had them look at a murder in Gainesville and the profile was way off. In fact, if we'd have followed it, we never woulda caught the killer."

Camy nodded. "A profile of the bombing might give us some insight into Wells' personality."

"You're right, it couldn't hurt." Tasker looked at Jimmy. "Can you arrange for the profiler to talk to us?"

Camy added, "And keep it quiet so we don't draw any attention."

Making it look like he didn't care, Jimmy said, "Alice Quills? She's not a real profiler. I mean she didn't do the full-year training at Quantico. She just went to some in-service classes and then the thing where she rode with the Metro homicide guys. If you want, I'll call her. And going to her won't raise any eyebrows."

Tasker noticed the loss of accent. Maybe too tired to keep up the façade? "Will you check your intel, too?"

"Technically, we're not supposed to have intelligence files on groups like that."

"Hey, I don't know if he's in any organized group. It was your intelligence files that said he was. I'm just asking you to look."

Jimmy just nodded.

Camy asked, "Is Sutter still involved?"

"We're all equal partners in this thing now."

No one said anything, so Tasker took it as agreement.

Daniel Wells backed his newly acquired Ford pickup next to the small drab building. He'd already found a duplex in Florida City that had a carport in the back to hide the van. He'd settled into his new place with just the clothes on his back and a few things he'd picked up at Wal-Mart. At least now he knew exactly where he stood. These cops were serious and he was obviously wanted. He doubted if even his friend could help him anymore. It definitely meant he had to move on his plan as soon as possible. Since it didn't revolve around a festival or concert, he could do it any time. He had already decided that a weekday was best, but other than that he had no restrictions, other than gathering all the necessary equipment and putting it in place. The only tricky thing was the big rig. First he had to get one, then he had to drive it. A few more lessons and he'd be good to go.

He hadn't bothered to booby-trap this place. Usually, tricks like the Mace bomb only work once before someone is careful approaching a house. He also realized that no one knew he was here. He figured the call by the fire department had given him away at the trailer. That wouldn't happen again.

He tried to watch the little color TV that came with the duplex rental and then tried to read a W. E. B. Griffin novel about marines setting up a weather station in China during World War Two, but he couldn't concentrate. His urge was starting to consume him. He had to pull this off, and fairly soon, or he felt he might fade away, unrecognized and useless. What scared him was not the thought of his plan for downtown Miami, which he hoped might end his need for chaos, but the fact that he was already thinking of a bigger plan. One involving a pedestrian crowd, like at a mall or a music festival.

He got up and milled around the small rented house. Unable to concentrate on anything but his plan, he sat down at the rickety kitchen table and started to sketch out some diagrams for his escape. He was worried. His special feeling had changed, and changed in a big way. He'd always been able to do other things while looking forward to his little stunts, but this was different. Like entering a long tunnel and not knowing which way to walk to get out. He missed his kids, but even that feeling was muted by his need to go through with his plans. A night with Alicia would help. He didn't even know where she was. He looked at his sketch and realized that he had drawn bodies on the sides of the streets. He hadn't meant to, but his hand had a will of its own.

nineteen

derrick sutter had covered most of the obvious topless clubs in the city without finding the lovely Alicia Wells. Not that it was unpleasant duty, but he was getting tired. All he could figure was that the doorman at the Tittie Shack had tipped her off and she was long gone.

He pulled his Buick Century, the one issued to him from the now-closed robbery task force, into a spot near the Club Orion off Biscayne near I-395. He still had use of the car until the lease ran out in two months. He was the only guy from the task force left with one. Not that Dooley needed one in jail. As he thought about his former partner, he realized what a crazy few months this had been.

He straightened his tie in his reflection in the car's window, checked to see if his eyes showed any lingering signs of the Mace attack from yesterday and moved his Glock from his hip to his waist so one of the girls brushing up against him wouldn't notice it. He stopped in front of the simple entrance to the strip bar, looking up and down the street, trying to figure where the employees might park their cars. Every time someone walked in or out of the bar, a blast of loud music pounded in his ears. The dance club across the street had two uniformed cops at the door. He couldn't see who they were, only that they were in uniform. Sutter figured he was far enough away that they wouldn't recognize him.

Just as he was about to walk inside, the door opened and a woman walked out and immediately started up the side street. Sutter wasn't paying attention but realized it was one of the dancers and saw she was blond. As he started after her, he realized the small lot behind the building held the employee vehicles.

"Alicia," he called as he closed the gap on the fast-walking woman.

She gave no response.

When he was a few feet behind her, he said, "Alicia Wells," and reached out for her arm.

She spun toward his touch, and before he could react he had a small canister of OC pepper spray pointed at him.

"No, wait," was all he got out before she hit the button and covered him with orange spray. He immediately felt his eyes burn. He blinked, but it did no good as he went to his knees. "Jesus, what is it with your family and Mace?"

"Just leave us alone. Daniel didn't do nothing wrong." She stared to cry.

He coughed and felt snot pour from his nose. He coughed out, "Just want to talk to him."

"Bull. He says you're gonna arrest him." She started to move away from him. "Please leave us alone."

One of the cops from the dance club had trotted down the street when he heard both Sutter and Alicia yell. The wide, young black officer saw them on the sidewalk.

Just as the cop arrived, Sutter tried to stand. The cop put his hand on Sutter's shoulder and said, "Hold on." Sutter jerked away, not knowing who had grabbed him. Without warning, the cop pulled his own spray. Sutter opened his eyes just in time to realize a cop was with him and he was being sprayed again.

This time the accumulation of different pepper sprays caused him to go to his knees and vomit. He tried to gasp, "I'm a cop," but it didn't come out. He heard the cop yell to Alicia Wells, then spit up again.

Five minutes later, he listened to the cop's apologies after he'd identified himself. Alicia Wells had gotten away without a trace. He was still in distress, but a hose near the parking lot of the dance club had given him some relief.

The young uniformed cop said, "Detective, I didn't recognize you. I am really, really sorry."

Sutter didn't want this incident getting around any more than his earlier Macing. He gathered his breath and said, "If you and your partner can keep your mouths shut, I'll forget the whole thing. But if someone comes up to me and mentions this, I'll whip your ass. Understand?"

The young man nodded his head vigorously.

Sutter decided just to head home and call it a night. It had to be close to dawn anyway. As he stood up, his face burned again and he had to reach for the hose.

He thought, What a shitty couple of days.

It had been four or five months since Bill Tasker had been asked to enter the Miami office of the Federal Bureau of Investigation. During the time he had worked on the robbery task force, Tasker had been housed in the off-site building a few blocks east. The FBI liked the idea of keeping local cops in a site that didn't require as much security. The plain FBI building a few blocks south of Northeast 167th Street held a constantly shifting number of agents that nobody ever seemed able to pin to an exact figure.

As Camy parked in the small, tree-lined lot in front of the building, Tasker's pulse began to rise and he felt a film of sweat forming on his forehead. He just stared at the building, thinking how the occupants had nearly ruined his life just a few weeks before. He'd never been a fan of the FBI, but now he had real anxiety about even going inside.

Camy looked over at him in the passenger seat. "Good Lord, Billy. You look like that kid from *The Omen* when they tried to take him into a church." She smiled, but it had no effect on him. "Don't worry. I want to keep our part in this case as low-key as you do. I think it's important you come with us when we talk to the profiler. Jimmy says she's a friend of his."

Tasker just nodded silently.

"C'mon, relax." She reached over and placed her hand on his shoulder. "What're they going to do, arrest you?"

"They tried that once."

"Believe me. No one is even gonna recognize you."

Tasker sucked in some air for a good sigh. When he first became a cop, he never thought he'd be afraid of the FBI. In the academy, he had even thought about joining the storied outfit. It wasn't until after he worked the streets that he realized how they operated. While most of the agents were generally good guys, the politics of the agency left him wondering how anything ever got done. He looked up at the plain building. "You think Lail is parked in the back yet? I don't want to wait." Tasker had sent the young FBI agent with his own building pass ahead so he could walk them through the front door.

"Billy, you need to move past all this. I bet most people inside don't even know who you are. They're so wrapped up in politics and media they couldn't care less what we do."

He nodded and followed Camy slowly from the car, his anxiety staying steady. He'd purposely left his gun in the car. He didn't know how he might react if he saw the wrong person or someone said something insulting. They entered the small waiting area with the receptionist behind a thick sheet of ballistic glass. No Jimmy Lail.

"May I help you?" asked the middle-aged woman at the desk.

Camy stepped up and showed her ID. "Agent Lail is taking us to see someone in behavioral science."

The woman smiled, looking at Camy's credentials. "And you, sir?"

Tasker looked up, "What?"

"Identification?"

Tasker stepped to the glass and held up his FDLE credentials.

The woman looked up and copied down his name, then cut her eyes to him with more interest. "Oh, Mr. Tasker, I didn't recognize you."

The tone said it all. Tasker felt heat surge through his body. He looked at Camy, who just shrugged, then sat in one of the small plastic chairs facing the receptionist.

After several minutes, Jimmy Lail stuck his head out the door. "Yo, peeps, ready to talk to the shrink?"

They followed him to the elevator, then up to the third floor. Tasker felt several sets of eyes on him during the short trip, and he didn't think he was imagining it, either. Camy gave him a reassuring look once in a while. Jimmy Lail, typically, was oblivious. Tasker noticed that no one really acknowledged the FBI agent, either.

After clearing another security point, Jimmy led them into a small set of offices with one shared window in the common conference room. Stacks of magazines and papers sat on the floor and several of the desks. A poster for the movie *The Silence of the Lambs* hung on the main open wall. A woman in a precise business suit, about thirty-five, with her hair pulled back, walked out to greet the visitors.

"Hi, Jimmy, these must be the people you told me about." She held out her hand limply, reminding Tasker of an old-time school marm. "I'm Alice Quills, FBI agent and Ph.D."

Camy giggled at the self-introduction as she took her hand. "I'm Camy Parks, ATF agent and B.A."

Agent Quills was visibly annoyed, so she turned her attention to Tasker and extended her hand again.

"Bill Tasker, FDLE." He reached for her hand as she suddenly withdrew it.

"Oh my, *the* Bill Tasker."

He shrugged. "I guess."

"I'm sorry, I just meant that I've already been involved in two of your cases."

"Which two?"

"I profiled the Stinger seller at Jim's request." She looked at Jimmy Lail with something approaching lust. "And I actually profiled *your* case. I mean the case where you were charged."

"I was never charged."

"You know what I mean. The case . . ."

"The one where I was framed?" Tasker kept her gaze so she couldn't weasel out of a response.

"The Alpha National Bank robbery case."

Good recovery, thought Tasker. He felt his senses returning to normal. Maybe this was the kind of therapy he needed.

Agent Quills said, "Jim tells me you are interested in my profiling of the cruise-ship bombing from a couple of years ago."

Camy said, "I didn't know that case was ever profiled."

"Oh yes, right after it happened. Then I did an update a year later."

"Why didn't I know about it?"

"It was for the case agent."

Camy narrowed her eyes. "I *am* the case agent."

"The FBI case agent." The woman took a stern tone with Camy. Watching her look at Jimmy Lail, Tasker wondered if she had a thing for the white shadow.

Camy came right back at her. "There was no FBI case agent. I tried, but the Bureau wouldn't work the case with me."

"I can't be sure, but I thought someone in counterterror asked me to look at it. It doesn't really matter, if you've got a suspect." She looked around at the three agents' faces and continued. "Shall we get down to business?"

Agent Quills pulled out some notes as they all sat around a cluttered round conference table. "My profile said that the person responsible for the bombing was a male, twenty-one to fifty-nine, white or possibly foreign-born, with a persecution complex resulting in a need to act out." She looked around the table. "That sound like your suspect?"

Jimmy Lail said, "On the money, honey."

Camy and Tasker exchanged looks. Then Camy said, "It sounds like every suspect I've ever arrested. Is that really all your profile consists of?"

"Profiling is not an exact science, nor is it easy."

Camy said, "I'll agree with the not-exact part."

Tasker stepped in to keep it from going nuclear. "Can you tell us more about the motivation?"

"Not really. People who commit violent acts like this generally are acting on some type of urge or need to feel control. They're simply acting out on immature emotions."

Tasker said, "So our thirty-year-old suspect, who is white, fits your profile?"

Agent Quills replied, "To a T."

"But so do I, and so does Agent Lail here."

"Except for the psychological component."

Tasker nodded, asking, "Would that component be readily apparent?"

"Only to a counselor or therapist working with the subject."

"So how does this profile help a cop looking for the suspect in a case?"

"The profile matched your suspect, didn't it?" She seemed quite satisfied.

"But it didn't help us identify him."

"But he matches it."

"Yes, but it didn't help find him."

"Mr. Tasker, I could play word games here with you all day, but everyone knows you'd never accept anything anyone from the Bureau offered you in the way of assistance, so, if you don't mind, I have work to do."

Now Camy piped up. "Like creating profiles for the gangs in Overtown. Let me help. Black male, twelve to sixty, doesn't like the police."

Agent Quills stood up and turned to Jimmy Lail. "Jim, perhaps you should show your friends the door. I'm sure they have some little crime to solve." With that, she turned and marched into one of the small offices and shut the door.

Jimmy said, "She's smart."

Camy and Tasker just stared at him.

Sutter made Tasker and Camy drive over to South Beach to meet him in a little restaurant he liked off Collins. He couldn't see the beach, but the food was seventy-five percent cheaper. He wanted them to come over the bridge because he'd spent the morning clearing his eyes and face of the pepper spray Alicia Wells and the cop had zapped him with the night before. This was the modern stuff that was easier to rinse away, but it still stung. To make matters worse, as soon as he had arrived home, around dawn, he had tried to relieve the effects by going into the ocean, for the first time in the three years he'd lived on South Beach. The salt water had aggravated the condition until he had finally parked himself in his shower and run cold water over himself until he shivered uncontrollably. Now only his red eyes burned as he sat in the booth, waiting for his partners. He saw them pull up outside in Camy's Ford, appreciating the movement of Camy's lithe little body. Tasker and the others might think she's gay, but Sutter knew better. The little glances she stole at him. The red-faced anger he could cause. She was no dyke, and she had an eye for him.

He stood as they reached the booth.

"You up all night?" asked Tasker. Camy was silent as she slipped in next to Tasker.

"I was up and, no, wasn't drinking."

"You look like shit."

"I ran into Alicia Wells."

"Great, where is she? What'd she have to say?"

Sutter was quiet as he gathered his thoughts.

Camy said, "You did question her? Find out where she lives, didn't you?"

"It's a long story."

Camy kept up the pressure. "Can't be that long. What happened?"

He started slow, avoiding eye contact. "I saw her outside the Orion. She ignored me, and when I caught up, she, she . . ."

Camy said, "I can't wait to hear this. She what?"

Sutter narrowed his eyes at Camy. "Back off, girl. I'm not happy about it, either. She gave me the slip."

Tasker said, "Alicia Wells outran you?"

"After she pepper-sprayed me."

There was ten seconds of dead silence, until both of his partners broke out in a wild fit of laughter. He waited, then said, "Are you done?"

That question was answered with more laughter. Suddenly, Sutter wasn't hungry. He stood to leave, but Camy reached across the table, taking his hand. She squeezed it and said, "C'mon, Derrick, we're just kidding. It's funny. Stay and we'll figure out where we're going on this thing."

Sutter sat back down, with Camy still holding his hand and wondered what thing she meant. This investigation or this thing between them. Either way, he was interested.

twenty

daniel wells was mad at himself as well as at the Big Rig Academy of South Florida. He'd just mangled another row of orange cones, but he'd also learned to accelerate smoothly and was cornering much better. That didn't seem to matter to the teacher. After he'd paid for the second chance, the school had changed instructors on him. This guy, a big tree trunk with a gigantic wad of tobacco in his mouth, oddly named Baby, had bitched about everything from the weather to the cops that had whipped his ass at a bar a few nights before. Wells wasn't sure if the change in the instructors was because they thought he needed a fresh perspective, like they'd told him, or because the other instructor was sick of him.

Wells had listened to the man brag about how it had taken four cops to stop him, then bitch about how they hadn't let up once they had him cowed. He ended by saying, "Fuckin' cops. Always around when you don't need 'em."

Wells had listened to this as he tried to concentrate on the course. He stopped the big truck and turned to his mountain of an instructor.

"That sucked," said the man. "If we'd turned you loose with one of these over in Vietnam, we woulda won the damn war."

"That's why I'm here. Wanna learn."

"Learn? Son, they's some things you can learn and they's some you can't. You can't learn to drive one of these babies."

"But I need to."

"No, son, you don't. Ain't that much money in driving, and there ain't enough money to cover what you might do in one of these things."

Daniel held back a smile, thinking, If you only knew.

The big man continued. "You seem like a smart fella. You could probably do anything. Get a big-ass lawn mower and start a landscaping business. You don't need a big rig, and we don't need people thinkin' you learned to drive at our school."

"But I paid."

"And you done got your money's worth, too. Now, unless you want to try an take it outta my hide, it's time for you to skedaddle."

Wells looked at the man's earnest expression and opened the door to the big training vehicle with BIG RIG ACADEMY painted on the side. He slid out of the cab and walked away silently. He let a small smile escape as he pocketed the truck's extra key he'd taken off the ring. There were three more keys, so no one would notice, and he had one more piece of his plan in place.

Tasker and Sutter walked up the driveway to Wallace Training Academy. The school's main curriculum revolved around teaching people how to handle large trucks. From step vans to eighteen-wheelers.

On the walk up the long concrete driveway, Sutter said, "I think Camy is about to switch back to the coed team."

"What makes you think that?" Tasker could hardly hold back his smile.

"I just know these kinds of things."

"You know all about women, huh?"

"Enough that I know she's got a thing for me."

"What if someone else was already aware of her interest in men?"

Sutter looked at his partner. "You dog. Did you beat me to her?"

Tasker held up his hands. "No, my brother. That fem is out of my division."

"What? Why're you talking like Lail?" He froze and put a hand out on Tasker's arm. "I know you're not saying that the FBI version of Shaft is hitting Camy?"

"You know everything. You'd know if she was never a lesbian and just never corrected the rumors that circulated about her. You'd also know that she and Lail have been together for five months. You'd also know that she thinks you're a conceited ass."

"That's a little harsh. You're my partner."

"I'm just filling you in on what she thinks."

"The only thing that worries me about her is her judgment. Unless that boy Lail is rich or hung like Wilt Chamberlain, she has no business even talking to that idiot."

"No argument from me."

Sutter nodded to himself as they started walking again. "Just a different challenge, that's all."

Camy walked to her car from the office of a construction business in Homestead. When they'd split up jobs, she'd taken the one she thought might produce a valuable lead; she was talking to any regular customers of Naranja Engineering. Tasker and Sutter were going around to truck-driving schools, and Jimmy Lail was searching all possible intelligence databases to see if Wells was listed anywhere. He kept saying that the FBI wasn't allowed to keep that kind of information, but everyone knew they had some indices. Otherwise they wouldn't have been able to claim that Wells was associated with a terror group in the first place. Jimmy could also check the county, and they had some big reports on the various crazies. Since they only had to concentrate on Dade County, they put some real effort into creating a broad database on members of extremist groups, and they didn't have to worry about the Department of Justice looking over their shoulders. This was Dade County; there wasn't time to worry about outsiders.

This construction company was straight up. They had hired Wells to repair some of the small Bobcat tractors and specially configured trucks. The manager liked Wells because he did good work at half the price of the companies that were certified to repair the Bobcats. Camy just moved down her list to a pressure-cleaning company in Florida City. On the short drive down US 1, she found herself thinking about Billy Tasker. He was a sweet, good-looking guy, but she'd checked around and found out he had two kids. That was a lot of baggage. He did have a good body and those blue eyes. But he had kids.

After a few minutes, her mind wandered to the arrogant, but definitely attractive Derrick Sutter. He was a legend among some of the Miami PD female employees. A gentleman who never had any complaints. And unlike Jimmy Lail, he really was black. Camy smiled, thinking about him as she headed south.

FDLE criminal-intelligence analyst Jerry Ristin had eliminated almost all of the phone numbers Daniel Wells had written in his address books. He had found several relatives in Florida and had agents from Gainesville to Fort Pierce on their way to check the addresses. He had a whole bunch of commercial numbers probably associated with the engineering business, and then there were half a dozen numbers he couldn't identify. These were probably nonpublished. No one had used them on credit applications or mailing lists. A subpoena to Bell South hadn't come back yet on all of them.

Ristin ran them through the computer again, using general public Web-search sites like Google and Yahoo! Still nothing. Ristin hated being beaten by information. That was his job. While the agents liked to reminisce about shootouts or chases, he always relished a good challenge to find information on the computer.

He looked at one number for a few moments and thought it sounded familiar. He went to one of the undercover phones and dialed the number, knowing the phone he was using would come back as an insurance agency. An answering machine with an electronic voice merely told him to leave a message. He looked at the number again. It appeared to be in a sequence. The last four were 8005. He dialed 8000, and after two rings a female answered: "FBI, may I help you?"

Ristin hung up, thinking, What the hell was that?

Tasker and Sutter pulled up to the last of the five schools listed for teaching the skills needed to drive an eighteen-wheeler. The other four had had no idea who Daniel Wells was and didn't recognize his photo. They parked Tasker's replacement car, a gold Jeep Cherokee, next to a sign that read BIG RIG ACADEMY. Tasker didn't think they would ever get all the CS residue out of his car since Wells had booby-trapped it. Now he had a state car and personal car that were Cherokees. He had been able to slip the Monte Carlo to the dealer and have a buddy there keep his mouth shut. They were washing the interior and if necessary replacing the carpet. Tasker told him he'd pay for it out of his own pocket. It was worth it to keep the events of that day secret from his coworkers.

They walked up to the front desk, which was manned by a tired-looking woman with graying, greasy hair held back with bobbie pins.

"Help you?" she asked as the two cops walked into the small building surrounded by acres of asphalt. Through the glass, Tasker could see two trucks without trailers parked in the corner of the lot.

"Yes, ma'am," said Tasker, flipping open his identification. "We're looking for a man who may have come here for lessons."

She took his credentials in one hand as she read them, then looked at his face to ensure he was the right man in the photo. She cut her eyes to Sutter, who didn't bother to show her any identification. "What's his name?"

Tasker said, "Wells, Daniel Wells."

"Name don't ring a bell. Hold on while I look it up." She turned to an ancient Tandy SL1000 computer. The old monochrome screen flickered and then displayed a list of names. She scrolled down to the end and studied it for a few seconds. "Nope, no Wells."

"Can I show you his picture in case he used a different name?"

The woman just looked at him, apparently waiting for the photo. When Tasker handed it to her, she looked at it carefully, then looked at her computer again and said, "Westerly was the name he gave us."

"When was the last time he was here?"

"You'd have to ask Baby about that." She looked at Tasker as he waited for her to tell him where he'd find this Baby. "Out back near the trucks. Think he's eatin'."

Tasker nodded and followed Sutter out the door, across the lot to the parked big rigs. A monster of a man in a tight T-shirt that said "I Am Not a Fucking People Person" stood next to one of the trucks, eating a bologna sandwich.

"Help you?" he said, eyeing them carefully.

Tasker smiled, saying, "The woman inside said this guy took lessons from you." He held up the photo of Wells. "If you're Baby, she said to talk to you."

"I'm Baby. Why you want to know about him?"

"Just need to ask him some questions."

"Who're you?"

Tasker flipped out his identification.

Baby leaned over to look at the official credentials. He nodded and said, "You know I had a little trouble with the cops the other night over at the Last Chance saloon."

"That's rough," said Tasker, then held up the photograph again. "Did this man, Wells or Westerly, ever talk to you?"

"I coulda stayed if ya'll didn't have them batons and pepper spray."

"I'm sure. Now about this man."

"You two wouldn't even get my attention other than to make sure one of you didn't get stuck under my shoe."

Tasker smiled and said, "You're probably right. When is his next lesson?"

Baby seemed frustrated in his failure to provoke a fight. As Tasker looked at his partner, so did Sutter. His hand had subtly reached around to the ASP he kept in his back pocket. Tasker shook his head slightly. He already had his hand on his own ASP.

Baby pointed at Wells' photo and said, "What'd he do, anyway?"

Tasker didn't miss a beat. "He *may* have molested a child. That's why we need to talk to him."

Baby's eyes widened. "A girl or boy?"

"Does it matter? It was a child."

"You're right, you're right, it don't matter. He just left a couple of hours ago, and I don't think he'll be coming back. He had no aptitude for this at all."

"He say why he wanted to learn?"

"Naw, just that it was his dream. If ya'll wait a minute, I'll get his file. See what we can find out." Baby started to hustle toward the office. He looked over his shoulder down toward Tasker and Sutter trying to keep pace. "A child molester, that's low. I hope you catch that nasty sumbitch. That just makes me sick."

Tasker felt a little guilty leading the man on like this, but he'd never said Wells *did* molest a child, only that he *may have*. Tasker didn't want to have to fight this guy either, so he figured it all came out in the wash. Now Baby would answer any question they asked.

twenty-one

nothing was adding up on this case. No matter what Tasker did, Daniel Wells seemed to stay one step ahead of him. This wasn't some kind of master criminal, either. He had no record. Or maybe that was the mark of a master criminal: no tracks. Either way, with the effort and manpower Tasker was putting into looking for this guy, he'd have thought someone might at least run into him at the grocery store. The southern section of Dade County just wasn't that big. He had people covering every angle but had yet to put his hands on Wells. The Big Rig Academy proved he was still in the area. Tasker and company couldn't even find his stripper-wife.

Along with the case problems, Tasker felt guilty about leaving the girls alone during the morning. It was so unusual to have them on a weekday. Thanks to a Jewish holiday that the Palm Beach County school system called a "fall break," he had been able to have them on a rare Thursday and Friday.

Now Bill Tasker sat at his kitchen table while his girls played a PlayStation game. He'd worn them out before dinner shuttling from a Home Depot to hobby shops, letting them think he was looking for a certain type of glue, when he was really looking for signs of Daniel Wells. He figured that Wells might be looking in places like that for supplies of some kind. If Donna knew he was dragging the girls around on that kind of mission, he'd have been in for a fight. And that woman could fight. He still missed her, but she could lay a big hurt on you if you crossed her.

He looked up at Kelly and Emily as they concentrated on the TV screen. The two sisters shared no qualities other than being sweet. Kelly, the artistic, cerebral, quiet ten-year-old. And Emily, the athletic firebrand. He didn't deserve such beautiful, well-mannered girls. That was one of his biggest problems in a nutshell. He didn't deserve much of anything. He'd always been focused on work and tended to exclude everything else. Even after the West Palm shooting, while he was under investigation he could only focus on that. After he'd eventually been cleared, he'd still sulked about it to the point that Donna had thrown his ass right out of his own house. Now that he did deserve.

Every time he made a promise to himself that he'd spend time with his family, something happened to sidetrack him. He loved them and loved doing things with them. He just couldn't let things at work drop. Tomorrow he had one meeting in the morning at the office with everyone—then he was coming straight back to these two. He didn't care what happened.

He looked down at his and the other agent's notes and knew there was a pattern somewhere, he just couldn't see it. Unlike the FBI profiler, he didn't think his own analysis was beyond question. He needed something confirmed. The one thing that the profiler had said that he continued to contemplate was the bomber's motivation. To be in control. Tasker ran that through his maze of a mind to see if he could relate to it at all. From some of the shit he'd pulled, it seemed like Wells liked to *lose* control, not gain it. But maybe he was misreading what the profiler had meant. That psychobabble tended to cloud issues. Tasker thought in practical terms, and he couldn't see a practical reason for Wells to risk his family and bomb that ship. On the other hand, he was running awful hard if he was not involved. What scared Tasker the most was that he felt Wells was working on something else. That had to be the reason he hadn't left town. That's why he had a gas tank welded in his step van. Tasker knew he was up to something, and that's why when he looked up at his daughters and saw they were occupied, he went back to his notes.

Derrick Sutter followed Tasker through the front doors of the Miami Regional Operations Center of the Florida Department of Law Enforcement. It was a severe culture shock after the constant bustle of activity at the Miami PD. In the city, local citizens stood in line to get accident reports, report minor crimes and complain about some unknown cop who either didn't enforce some city ordinance or enforced it too rigorously. Here, west of the airport, in a brand-new, sparkling clean, three-story building, no one waited in the lobby. One well-dressed, nice-looking woman sat comfortably behind thick, bulletproof glass. Sutter was shocked to see her smile and wave to Tasker as he walked inside. That shit wouldn't happen at the PD. Sutter realized that the mission of FDLE was entirely different from that of a local PD. FDLE worked on big cases which generally weren't reported directly to them by the public. Sutter decided police work was more efficient if you didn't include the public.

On the third floor, they turned into an immaculate squad bay with big, clean windows and working computers on every desk. In a spacious conference room at the end of the bay, Sutter could see the delicious Camy Parks sitting with her perfect legs crossed. As he came closer, he saw she was talking to that FBI moron, Jimmy Lail. Tasker's analyst, Jerry something, stood at the end of the conference table, not even concealing his feelings about Camy's legs, or the rest of her.

Tasker said, "Sorry we're late. Thanks for seeing them in, Jerry."

The older, portly man nodded, not taking his eyes off Camy.

Sutter grabbed the seat next to Camy. "Hey, baby," he said quietly. It still got a harsh glance from Jimmy Lail. Sutter wondered when he'd realize that a real black man was trying to move in on his territory.

Tasker addressed the whole room. "Let's see where we are. Who's first?"

Camy started right up. "No clues from any of the companies he worked for. They all said he was a great guy who worked hard."

Tasker asked, "None of 'em had any idea where he might be hiding out?"

"Nope. One place, South Florida Metal Works, said he worked on some welding and even hauled away bags of metal scraps that had been lying around for a year. Just little corners and shavings from making shelves and things like that. They loved the guy. Kept turning them down for a permanent job."

Sutter gazed at her while she delivered her professional report. He nonchalantly let his hand drop off his lap and brush her leg. He got no response.

Sutter said, "Bill and I covered all the truck-driving schools in Dade and found out Wells used the name Westerly at the Big Rig Academy, but didn't graduate. In fact, they booted his ass 'cause he couldn't get the hang of it."

Camy asked, "When was his last lesson?"

"An hour before we got there."

"So he's still in the area."

Tasker said, "That's what bothers me. If he didn't have some kind of plan, wouldn't it be smart to leave Florida?"

Jimmy Lail chimed in, "That's whack, my man. You guys love jumping to wild conclusions. We don't even got any four-one-one this cracker even bombed the cruise ship. So far, all we got him for is running from you." He gave a hard look at Tasker.

Sutter said, "Then why's he running? As a cop, that always raises my suspicions." Sutter doubted the FBI man would catch the inference that he wasn't a real cop.

"That's off the hook, my brother. I think we might be running on a wild-goose chase." Jimmy moved his hands like an L.A. gang member making a point with different fingers pointing down.

Sutter said, "You get anything from your intelligence index, J. Edgar?"

Jimmy opened his notepad. "We got this dawg all over the script. He hangs with the original ragheads all the time."

Tasker, swallowing his annoyance, asked, "Who are the 'original rag-heads'?"

"The nightriders, homeboy. You're from Florida, you don't know them?"

Sutter said, "Who the fuck are you talkin' about?"

"The Ku Klux Klan, my brother. The KKK. Our dawg Wells is one of their butt-boys. He's been seen at the KKK crib off Krome, west of Tamiami Airport."

Tasker said, "You sure? He'd didn't strike me as that kind of nut. I mean, it was bad FBI intel that helped get him locked up for the wrong crime."

"You tell me to check the intel base, and when I find something, you don't want to hear it. Don't be dissin' my work product." He slid the chair out like he was prepared to fight anyone who challenged his credibility.

Sutter said, "Sit your white ass down. He was just asking a question."

Camy jumped in: "We could keep a little watch on the house. We don't have too much else to check."

Tasker turned toward his analyst. "What about it, Jerry? You got anything else for us to work on?"

Sutter knew that Tasker revered the heavy older man with the funny dark-tinted, Coke-bottle-thick glasses. He could see the deference the FDLE agent showed the analyst with his every move.

Ristin started slowly. "I have a couple of odd numbers in the personal phone books taken in the search warrant at Wells' house." He cut his eyes hard to Jimmy Lail. "I want to get the subpoena information back before I make any comment on the numbers. Right now I only have a hunch I don't want to throw on the table yet."

Jimmy spoke up, virtually ignoring Ristin. "Camy's right. We need to drop a five-O cover on the Klan house. That's better than wasting our time on all these useless leads."

Tasker asked, "What's a 'five-O cover'? Surveillance? You need to cut that shit out."

Sutter stepped in to ask Jimmy directly, "Who says the leads are useless? I've found that in police work you don't know what's important until all the pieces are in place." Sutter couldn't believe he'd gotten two shots in on the witless FBI man in one conversation.

Jimmy fired back. "Okay, what do we do, then?"

At once everyone looked to Tasker. He shrugged and said, "If that's what we have, that's what we have. All we need is one eye on the house, and it doesn't have to be round-the-clock. That way we save a little manpower."

Camy agreed. "Three six-hour shifts shouldn't tax us too much."

Tasker nodded. "Seven to one, one to seven, and the last guy goes till midnight or so unless the place is dark before that. But no one try and grab him alone. He gave us the slip too many times and proved he's smart enough to be dangerous."

Everyone nodded. That was all there was to do. Sutter liked the way Tasker could articulate a decision and jump right in.

Camy said, "I'll take this afternoon."

Sutter said, "I'll take tonight. It's all OT for me."

Tasker turned to Jimmy and added, "If you take tomorrow morning, I'll take both shifts in the afternoon. My daughters are here today, but I'm free tomorrow."

Jimmy Lail nodded, obviously not happy to be giving up a Saturday. None of the federal agents got extra pay to work weekends.

Camy looked at Tasker. "I'll get ahold of you when I'm done today. Let you know what it looks like."

Sutter wasn't sure, but he thought he saw something in Camy's eyes that had nothing to do with being a lesbian or being hooked up with Jimmy Lail.

Daniel Wells slowly cruised past Emerson-Picolo Transportation in Miami, near the Miami International Airport. He'd welded some of their perimeter fence a few years back and knew the layout of the big yard. Most nights they stored three or four big tanker-trailers. Some even held aviation gas. That was some of the most flammable material an artist like him could work with. He picked up speed so he wouldn't be obvious as he passed the main office that faced Thirty-sixth Street. He still had a key to the gate. He doubted they had changed it in the past year or so, and they liked that he worked at night and didn't interfere with business. They trusted him with the key, and they were right. He had never stolen anything from an employer and never overcharged on a job. His dad had always insisted that he give a fair day's work for a fair day's wage. Even as a kid, when he was a bag boy at Winn-Dixie in Ocala, he'd never taken long breaks or left early. He'd bag groceries and be polite to the customers because that was his job. He would flirt with the cashiers occasionally. That was something he couldn't help. A pretty girl was a pretty girl. But he didn't mind working.

Today he could see three long trailers and three shorter ones. He couldn't risk going in to say hello because he had already heard that the cops had been talking to his former employers. The woman from the ATF, the cute one with big boobies, had gone by several of his old jobs. He had friends everywhere. That was one of the reasons he could stay ahead of the cops. Friends in key places.

twenty-two

tasker had raced home from the office to do something with the girls. He didn't want to know what Donna did with a free Thursday night. She had seemed in a good mood and had even said she'd pick the girls up right from his town house. If Emily hadn't had gymnastics and practice for some play, they could've stayed another night. He'd made use of the afternoon. He had learned the intricacies of the board game Cranium and learned about the interesting lives of a pair of young black twins separated at birth and now living on Nickelodeon.

By late afternoon, he stood in his small front yard, throwing a junior-size football to Kelly, who would toss it a few feet to her little sister, who could wing it back to Tasker like an NFL quarterback. At least like a Baltimore Ravens quarterback.

He stopped one pass in front of his face, just before it took his head off, as Emily said, "Let's run some patterns."

Tasker smiled as she hustled over to him to line up. Kelly, avoiding the discomfort of sweat, casually strolled up to Tasker. "I'll hike the ball. She can run any pattern she wants."

Tasker smiled at his ten-year-old's attitude, obviously borrowed from his ex-wife. She had her mother's looks and mannerisms. Tasker wasn't sure if some young man would be lucky to meet her in twelve years, or doomed. To him it didn't matter, because she was perfect.

Emily said, "Hit me past your car by the tree." She took off like a small blond rocket.

Tasker let a high floater sail and watched as his youngest daughter plucked it right out of the air, never breaking stride. She tucked the ball under her arm and darted across the yard, dodging imaginary tacklers all the way back to him.

"What do ya think, Daddy? Can I play in the league at home?" Her high, doll-like voice made her seem younger than eight years old.

"Sweetheart, you can do anything you put your mind to." He leaned down to kiss her, when he saw a Ford Crown Vic rolling down the residential street. As it crept along slower, he realized it was Camy Parks. The fading sunlight reflected off her light-orange hair. He said to his daughters, "You guys go in and play on the PlayStation for a few minutes. I'll be right in."

The girls didn't need coaxing. They raced into the house from the front door. Tasker stood near the patio courtyard as Camy parked in his driveway. She smiled, strolling up to the surprised Tasker.

"Didn't mean to chase off your girls."

"No problem. What's wrong?"

"Nothin'. Just thought I'd give you a rundown on the surveillance. Sutter relieved me a little early and I wasn't up to his efforts to get in my pants, so I decided to drop by and fill you in." She smiled, obviously pausing to see what he'd say about getting in her pants.

He avoided the whole issue. "I appreciate it, but a call would've been fine."

"You're on my way home, and I was curious what your house looked like. I knew it wouldn't be a bachelor pad." She looked the house over. "This is very nice. Cozy."

Tasker smiled. "You should see my other house. It's beautiful."

"The one your ex-wife has?"

"Exactly."

"Your girls are cute as can be. Their mother must be a knockout."

"She is," he said as a casual statement of fact. Tasker couldn't take his eyes off her. In simple jeans and a T-shirt after a full day of work, she looked like a miniature model from Victoria's Secret.

After a few seconds of awkward silence, Camy said, "You wanna talk out here or can we go inside?"

"It's nice out. Let's sit on the patio." He led her through the wooden gate that stood in front of the open patio. "Wanna beer?"

"Sounds good," she said, sprawling into a lounge chair.

Tasker hustled inside, checking on the girls, who were playing one of the Super Mario Brothers games, and then grabbed a couple of Icehouse beers from the fridge. He had already decided that he didn't want to introduce Camy to them. She was just a coworker and he didn't want to confuse them. Besides, if they saw Camy, they might slip up and tell their mother about the sleek, beautiful red-haired woman Daddy was talking to. He didn't need that.

He checked his watch and noticed that his ex-wife Donna would be by to pick up the girls soon. He might need to hurry this up a little bit.

"Here you go," he said, setting the beer on the small table next to her.

She sprang up and spun to face him as he sat on the lounge chair next to her. "I'm not sure this surveillance is a good idea."

"Why not?"

"I watched that place for a little over five hours, and in all that time only one car came and went. A black F-250 owned by an E. Conners. He's the listed owner of the crappy little house, and it just looked like he was doing errands."

"Is he in the KKK?"

"Yeah, all that checks out. The house belongs to Conners. ATF knows that much. Something's not right. It's not the kind of place that they just hang out at. Conners is probably the only one of those morons who owns a house, so he's the leader. The house has an orange grove around it, and Conners owns the twelve-acre pepper farm on the same street. Daniel Wells doesn't even show in our intel base."

Tasker thought about it. He also thought about the hand that Camy had placed on his knee and left there. This lead might be thin, but it was all they had to go on for now. "Let's do this: we sit on it over the weekend. If there's no movement, next week we'll get together and talk about it again."

"That's fine." She leaned into him a little. "Now that you've got me in this thing, I want to go all the way." She cut her green eyes up to his.

He could feel her breath across his face. His body tightened. "I'm glad you're here. I mean on the case." No, he meant he was glad she was here.

"I'm glad of both." She smiled.

As he was thinking of something intelligent and profound to say, he heard a voice from the fence.

"I'm not interrupting anything, am I?"

Tasker jumped at the woman's voice and jerked his head toward the open gate. His ex-wife, Donna, stood at the opening, looking right at him. He couldn't get a sense of her feelings. Was she pissed? Surprised? She was smiling, but she didn't exactly look happy.

Tasker stood up, causing Camy's hand to flop back in her lap. "Hey, Donna." He glanced at his watch. "Didn't realize it was so late."

"Apparently not," Donna said, looking over at Camy.

Tasker cut in. "Donna, this is Camy Parks. Camy, this is my ex-wife, Donna."

They smiled and nodded at each other.

Donna asked, "Do you work with Billy?"

"I'm an ATF agent. We're involved"—she waited a second—"in a joint investigation right now."

Donna looked at Tasker. "I'll get out of your way. Are the girls ready?"

Tasker gulped a little air and nodded.

Then Camy said, "I was just leaving." She was moving toward the gate before Tasker could say anything. After she was past Donna, she said, "Call if anything happens tomorrow."

"Sure thing," was all Tasker could say.

Camy said, "Nice meeting you," to Donna and turned toward her car.

"She's cute," said Donna, as she watched her hips sway away.

"That she is." Tasker felt like he was having the same conversation twice in twenty minutes. He added, "She's an ATF agent working on a case with me."

"So I gathered," Donna said. "I saw what she was working on."

"It's not like that. She has a boyfriend."

"She may have a boyfriend, but she was interested in you. A woman can tell these things." She walked over and sat on a lounger. "Billy, is it smart to have the girls around women?"

"Aren't they around men?"

"No."

"What about Nicky? He is considered a man, isn't he?"

She let it go and said, "I mean, women the girls don't know."

"How would they meet them?"

She shrugged.

"What's the story on Nicky Goldman? Is he divorced?"

She nodded.

"How does his ex-wife feel about you seeing him?"

"They didn't have kids, but she's fine with it. You know her."

"I do? Who is it?"

"Laura, the woman who builds the websites and helps at the girls' school."

Tasker stared at her. "Nicky was married to Laura Parker?"

"That's her maiden name. She changed it back after the divorce. Why's it so surprising they were married?"

"She's a little out of his league, isn't she?"

"Oh, and I'm not? Thanks a lot."

This chat wasn't going to get any better. "Sweetheart, you're outta *my* league."

She smiled and said, "Don't you forget it."

"*You* know you're outta Nicky's league. What do ya see in him?"

She gathered her thoughts. "He's sweet, and very neat."

Tasker laughed. "That's the new criteria? Sweet and neat? According to that, Richard Simmons would be a great catch."

"He's very nice."

"Is he a boyfriend or a girlfriend?"

She frowned at that, as she let out a short snicker but didn't scold him.

"What happened to the girl who loved excitement and thrills?"

She looked into his eyes. "Excitement shut me out and thrills moved to Miami."

That hurt enough for Tasker just to keep his mouth shut.

Daniel Wells pulled out his phone card and settled into the phone booth at the Denny's in Cutler Ridge. He only had two people to call, but these might be long conversations. It seemed like he only ever called two people. He sat on the stool between the two phones and thought about who to call first and what to talk about. As he sat there, an elderly lady walked up to use the other phone. Wells immediately sprang from the stool and pushed it closer to the other phone.

"Thank you, young man," said the woman.

"My pleasure, ma'am." He waited until she was finished with her short call and settled onto the stool again. He dialed Alicia's cell phone. No answer. He dialed the other number and immediately heard a male voice.

"Hello."

"It's me, Daniel."

"Where the fuck you been?"

"Everywhere."

"So I heard."

Daniel leaned back to hear what was new in the world.

twenty-three

bill tasker pulled onto Krome Avenue and headed north. The road was most famous for the huge INS holding facility through which it seemed like half the population of Dade County had come at some point. He picked up speed in the Gold Cherokee he was still using for work. His friend at the dealership said his Monte Carlo was being rehabbed. It no longer made the technicians at the Chevy dealer cry or vomit. The residue of the CS with which Daniel Wells had booby-trapped the car was slowly being eliminated.

In the distance, Tasker could see the parking lot of the empty convenience store that served as the surveillance post. It was two blocks from the small farming road where the house they were watching sat. From the store they could see the side yard and driveway. On the bright side, no one coming or going from the house would be likely to see them. As he came closer to the vacant store, he saw Jimmy Lail's tricked-out Honda parked next to the shabby white building. Tasker had to admit that, although the car was an embarrassment to look at, no one would ever make it as a police vehicle.

He pulled in behind the Honda, expecting Jimmy either to call him on his Nextel or come out and greet him. After a minute of no response, Tasker climbed out of the Cherokee and eased up to the Honda's driver's window. Through the tint, Tasker could see Jimmy's head resting against the glass. He was asleep. Not just dozing, but all-out dead asleep.

This was not an uncommon event on long surveillances. The hard hours and boredom contributed to cops just drifting off. That was why, when there was enough manpower, you traded off the eye every hour or so. Tasker wasn't angry, but he didn't think he could let this slide without some sort of practical joke. He knew Jimmy Lail didn't like him and that you shouldn't play jokes on people you don't like or who don't like you, but Tasker couldn't help himself.

He took a minute to look around the lot to see what he could do. There was no one around, so he didn't have to worry about startling an innocent bystander. The area had a few gang members who harassed local businesses or picked on the poor migrant workers occasionally if the dope trade was slow, but generally people didn't frequent this part of Krome Avenue.

Tasker wasn't sure how soundly asleep Jimmy was, but he'd work in stages and find out.

Daniel Wells had the old Ford Ranger loaded with stuff he might need later. He had just picked up all the scrap metal he had stored from the company he'd done work for a few months back. When he had seen the pile of sharp-edged cuttings, he'd known he could put them to good use. They'd loved him for hauling away the dangerous jagged metal pieces, none larger than his hand; the whole box of them hadn't weighed more than fifty pounds. They had just kept sweeping them into the corner day after day, never giving any thought as to how to get rid of them.

Wells headed south on Krome Avenue from an old farm shed on one of his former employers' land. They didn't mind him leaving things inside the unused shed and liked the idea of a reliable person checking on the outlying acres of the tomato farm once in a while. The old Ford pickup backfired for no reason about every ten miles. Wells knew mechanical machinery pretty well and knew the fundamentals of car repair, but it seemed like this old truck was haunted. As long as it got him where he was headed and didn't draw any attention, he didn't care.

He knew he'd never hear anything more about the tussle he had had with the Nazis. At least three of them would have had to go to the hospital with gunshot wounds, unless they had some low-life ex-doctor that took care of things like that. It seemed like there was every type of professional available on the black market to handle services that people outside the law might need. Wells decided no matter what, they wouldn't want people to know one man had come into their clubhouse and taken a truck without getting a scratch.

He was headed to his secret box over by the power plant to hide a map, a .38 revolver and a thousand dollars in twenties he'd saved up in case he needed it to leave the area after his show. He didn't think he was being optimistic. He felt that his simple but spectacular plan, executed only by him with no other help, would cause enough terror and confusion that he would walk away cleanly and be able to enjoy it for a long time. He had been fighting to keep his mind on the task, even though he had started to get a better idea involving Turkey Point nuclear power plant. Finish what those damn Arabs had started. Shit, it had taken those two idiots months to bring him into their plans and then to try to recruit three others even to attempt to pull it off, and they hadn't come close. It was true that the reason they hadn't come close was because of Wells himself, but that was their failure. Too many people involved. At the time, Wells hadn't realized the wild disorder the plan might cause. It would also have cost a lot of lives. He hadn't wanted that to happen two years ago. Now it was a tradeoff. A few lives for a lot of chaos. He obviously was past that concern.

Just after he passed the road where that Klan idiot, Ed Conners, lived, his truck let loose with a booming backfire. It scared even him. He hoped the old racist had jumped at the sound, too. He never took his foot off the gas. A block later, he saw a couple of cars in the old closed Manny's Market. A god-awful gold-colored Cherokee next to a little low-rider Honda. He saw a guy walking around the Honda with some kind of tarp and thought he looked familiar. Wells shrugged and kept driving.

Tasker was about halfway done setting up his prank when he heard what sounded like a gunshot. He ducked behind the Honda, still holding the plastic sheet he'd found near the empty building, behind an old sign that read MANNY'S MARKET. As soon as he discovered that the loud boom was a backfire from an old blue Ford Ranger pickup coming down Krome Avenue, Tasker turned his attention back to the Honda to make sure the noise hadn't awakened Jimmy. To Tasker's surprise, Jimmy Lail's head still lay motionless against the driver's-side window. The car was idling to give the worn-out FBI agent air conditioning. Tasker could hear the soft thump of the bass from a CD or the radio. He continued to wrap the opaque plastic, probably used for farming, all around the small car. It was thicker than a garbage bag and about three feet wide. Tasker wrapped the whole car twice, blocking out all light. He had looped over the passenger door so he could slip inside when he was finished.

He'd paused just after the blue Ranger had driven past. He didn't know why, but the lone vehicle gave him a funny feeling. He had seen that it hadn't come from the house they were watching but didn't understand why it made him uneasy. He shrugged it off, like so many other odd feelings cops get, and went back to the task at hand. The little Honda was now covered with black plastic. Tasker could walk away now, but he wanted to see Jimmy Lail's reaction. He carefully parted the strips of plastic so he could open the passenger door. Pulling the handle in steps took over a full minute. Once it was opened a crack, Tasker realized that the music Jimmy had been listening to was much louder than the car had let on and had masked all of Tasker's activity. He slid into the seat and pulled the door shut, allowing the plastic from outside to fall into place on his window, too. The interior was surprisingly dark. Little cracks of light slipped in here and there, giving him just enough light to make out the snoring form of Jimmy Lail. Drool ran down the corner of his open mouth as air rushed past his apparently swollen adenoids.

Tasker was going to enjoy this.

Daniel Wells was a couple blocks down the road before the eerie feeling that he had just avoided danger passed. He took Krome all the way into Homestead, then turned east toward the racetrack. He kept his speed down, remembering the officious Homestead cop who'd written him for speeding in the Toyota a few weeks earlier.

Arriving at the little dirt turnoff, he turned south, toward one of the canals that cooled the giant nuclear reactor over at the power plant. No one would notice the disturbed dirt and lime where the box was buried, but if you knew where it was, it was obvious. He pulled right next to it and took out a small army-surplus folding shovel from behind the seat of his Ranger pickup. A minute of scraping the dirt from the box gave him good access. He opened it and was relieved to see it was still watertight and in good order. He threw in the gun, cash and map and pulled out some of the TATP he had stashed. In a matter of three minutes, he was on the road again without anyone knowing where the box was hidden.

He headed back to his duplex to finish up his van.

Tasker smiled to himself as he knocked lightly on the dashboard. Jimmy Lail stirred but didn't wake. What was it with this guy? Tasker pounded a little harder. No response. This was impressive dereliction of duty. Finally, Tasker smacked the dash and yelped, "Jimmy!"

Jimmy didn't spring awake, at least not at first. He stirred, then opened his eyes, then hissed, "Shit!" and looked at his watch, hitting the illuminate button. He studied it, not even noticing Tasker until he looked up at the dark windows again and turned toward the FDLE agent laughing in the seat next to him.

"What the fuck!" It came out in a Texas twang. "You think that's funny?"

Tasker could only nod as he laughed and gasped for air. Tears started to run down the corners of his eyes.

"Shithead, you coulda got shot."

"When? After you had your coffee?"

"What is this shit, anyway?" He started to calm down and tried to roll down his window.

"Relax there, Mr. Surveillance. It's just plastic."

Jimmy pulled the handle, then shoved open his door, ripping the plastic. Tasker followed his lead. In thirty seconds, they had all the plastic off the Honda, then Tasker followed Jimmy to the shade of the old market's overhang.

Jimmy sighed and said, "That was pretty funny. I always heard you didn't have much of a sense of humor."

"I didn't have time with your guys on my back. But I couldn't pass this up."

Jimmy nodded, taking a deep breath. "I musta just dozed off. You're pretty stealthy."

"You just dozed off like Adams was just president. You were out for a while."

Jimmy just glared at him. "Long night. You seen my squeeze."

Tasker nodded. He'd seen her up close. He looked down the road toward the house. "Anything happen? At least while you were awake?"

"Not much, but I bet we give this a few days and our man will show."

"Why do you think that?"

"Dunno, just do."

Just when Tasker was getting used to his almost pleasant Texas drawl, Jimmy added, "I'll leave it with you, aiiight? I got other peeps to check out."

Tasker just nodded, then asked, "You ever check with Sal Bolini on any info on Wells?"

Jimmy shook his head. "Why?"

"He's always yappin' about his great sources. I thought he might come up with something. Probably just all talk."

"No, man, he's for real. He made a couple of solid terror cases. The man grabbed the two Jordanians who were going to blow up Turkey Point."

"That was Bolini's?"

"For true. He also stopped some homegrown terror boys when some local Nazi tried to destroy a Metro bus."

Tasker nodded. "No shit, I remember that, too. Guess I just thought Bolini was another empty FBI suit." He looked up at Jimmy, forgetting for a second who he was talking to. "Sorry, I didn't mean it like that." Tasker watched as Jimmy Lail slowly started for his car in silence. "Hey," Tasker called out. "That's a good surveillance car."

That stopped him. "Seizure. No one else wanted it. Can you believe it?"

"You're a lucky man." Tasker watched him squeal out of the lot and head north up Krome. He looked up at the sun and stretched. It was going to be a long Saturday.

twenty-four

jimmy lail kicked his little supercharged Honda in the ass and shot north on the turnpike extension toward Pembroke Pines. A quick, surprise booty call on Camy might be just the trick to straighten out her attitude. He decided not to mention Tasker's prank. He got the feeling that Tasker didn't do shit like that to brag, just for his own entertainment. He'd find out on Monday.

He cranked up the bass on his DMX CD and eased back into the seat. He hit the fifth speed dial on his cell phone, barely able to hear the numbers beep over the thump of the bass.

"Hello." The male voice was short and to the point.

"Hey, it's working like you said."

"What?"

He raised his voice. "I said, it's working."

"Jimmy, cut that rap bullshit off if you want to talk to me."

Jimmy hit the mute button on his stereo, shocked by the sudden silence. He spoke back into the phone. "I said, it's working."

"Told you. Sorry you have to do it but we need the time."

"No sizzle off my shinizzle."

The phone went dead as the man hung up.

Jimmy shrugged and hit the number-one speed dial.

"Hello," a female voice said.

"Hey, my lady. Just finished my five-O duty and thought we might share some lunch." He laughed, then said, "And then eat."

"Who's this?"

Jimmy sat up straighter. "Whatchu mean? Camy, it's me, Jimmy."

Her giggle carried over the phone. "Really. How was I supposed to know that?"

Jimmy relaxed. "Everyone's in a funny mood today."

"Anything happen on surveillance?" she asked.

"Wells didn't show yet, but it's only a matter of time. Tasker is on it the rest of the day and night."

"That was nice of him to take two weekend shifts."

"Why not? Whole thing's his fault."

"That's not true and you know it."

"Check it out, awright. I arrested Wells and he sprang him."

"You didn't arrest him for the bombing. *We* arrested him for something he didn't do."

Jimmy sighed. "That's just work, baby. What about it? I'll be to your crib in thirty minutes."

"Sorry, Jimmy. I can't see you today. Got too much going on."

"More important than me?"

"'Fraid so. Sorry." The line went dead.

Something was up with that girl, and he didn't like to think what it could be.

Tasker settled into his surveillance like most any cop looking at a sixteen-hour stint: slowly. He pulled his Cherokee back a few feet to catch the shade of the empty building's overhang as the sun slid west across the sky. Even though he knew he could leave the area for food or a bathroom break, he was prepared and had packed two sandwiches, though more out of economic need than dedication to duty. His little cooler held four canned Cokes, and his empty Gatorade bottle was on the seat next to him. The big bottle, or as the drug guys call them, the "portable John," eliminated the need for repeated runs to the nearest gas station, which in this case was ten minutes away. Tasker asked his neighbor to save the bottle since he wouldn't buy Gatorade. Being a Florida State alumnus, he had an aversion to anything developed at the University of Florida. He had bought Powerade for years before the commercial showing the origins of Gatorade began airing. Keith Jackson aside, he had no reason to be reminded of anything worthwhile coming out of Gainesville.

The day was uneventful, with several more cars than usual visiting the house. From his current position, with the help of binoculars, Tasker could clearly make out faces coming and going at the old, run-down house. None of the drivers coming up or down Krome even seemed to notice him. No pedestrians walked past. That was the only way to tell his Cherokee was running. He had his fanny pack with a Beretta model 92—the .40 caliber—and two extra magazines in his belly bag. To be on the safe side, he had pulled his Heckler & Koch MP5 nine-millimeter machine gun and put the short black weapon on the front seat with an extra thirty-round magazine next to it. It seemed like overkill. He wasn't what some cops called a "gun queer." He just thought that if something happened way out here in the middle of nowhere he should be prepared. He had just been issued the .40-caliber Beretta to replace his old nine-millimeter. Between the two guns he had almost a hundred rounds in case of trouble.

The hours passed, until the sun finally set over the Everglades and he stepped out of the car to stretch. He turned off the engine and leaned against the warm hood, twisting one way, then the other. In a matter of seconds, he felt first tiny gnats, sometimes called "no-see-ums," then the bigger, louder mosquitoes started to land and attack his ears, neck and exposed arms. He tried to brush them off a few times, but they landed in greater force each time. Finally he retreated back into the Cherokee and slammed the door, cursing the tiny bloodsuckers. He cranked the engine and then spent ten minutes killing all the mosquitoes that had followed him into the vehicle. The small incident turned his mood sour and focused the frustration of the case. In fact, he felt frustration at this surveillance. There had to be a better use of his time. How had he gotten talked into it? As he tried to recall the chain of events that had him sitting next to a swamp watching an old man's house with seventy-five mosquitoes at eight o'clock on a Saturday night, an old Chevy Caprice rumbled into the lot and parked near the rear edge, about a hundred feet from Tasker. His lights were off, but the engine was running. He kept an eye on the vehicle as five young men poured out of the lime-green, beat-up car. They huddled around the hood talking for a few minutes, then, almost in a single-file line, started slowly strolling toward Tasker's car.

Four of the men stopped next to the building as the one in the lead came to within a few feet of the Cherokee. Tasker looked at his passenger seat, where the *Miami Herald* sports page was covering his MP5. He looked through his tinted window, knowing the twenty-year-old white kid couldn't tell who was inside. He heard the guy in jeans and a plain white T-shirt say, "Yo," then, after no response, get louder and say "Yo" again. Two of his friends came up to join him. One moved to the passenger side of the car. Tasker smiled thinking of a Discovery Channel show he'd watched with his girls about the pack behavior of wild dogs hunting antelope in Africa. The big difference was that the antelope didn't have automatic weapons.

The leader took a step forward and tapped on the window. "Yo, mister."

Tasker knew that they had a problem with gangs out here. Some preyed on migrant workers, some sold crack. Tasker hoped these might be the bullies who bothered the poor migrants. Rolling down the window, he could've made these losers a mile away for redneck dropouts from some high school south of Kendall.

The leader said, "Man, why didn't you answer me?"

Tasker kept his voice low and calm, "Didn't know I had to."

The kid looked at him sideways and said, "Yo, whatchu doing out here? You lost?"

"I'm fine, thanks." He started to roll up the window.

"Wait, wait, wait."

Tasker stopped the window. "What?"

"This here is private property."

"Is it yours?"

"Naw."

"Then don't worry about it," said Tasker, rolling the window the rest of the way up.

The kid stepped closer and rapped on the window with his knuckles.

Tasker appreciated these young men breaking his boredom, but he had to put an end to it. As the window came down again, he said, "What'd ya want, son?"

"Naw, man, what do *you* want?"

"I don't want a thing from you."

"Then you must got something. 'Cause out here you either keep driving, you need something or you got something. So what do you got?"

Tasker shrugged, sliding his hand under the unfolded *Miami Herald*. "I don't know. All I got is this submachine gun." He pulled the MP5 up from under the newspaper. "You want some of it?"

The young man stumbled back, saying, "No sir, I'm sorry to bother you." By the time he was on his feet, his friends were in the car, throwing it into drive.

Tasker chuckled as they burned rubber out of the lot. His temporary good mood faded quickly as he felt the frustration rising in his mind again.

Derrick Sutter had never been obsessed with anything or anybody, except maybe himself. He acknowledged this character trait and attributed it to his mother, who used to tell him, "No one will ever love you like your mom or yourself." He'd found it to be true. Both his mom and he tended to focus on one subject: his happiness.

Now he had to admit that he was very nearly obsessed with this crazy case, or at least with Alicia Wells. Not 'cause she was a knockout, which she definitely was, but because she was the only person who had ever successfully escaped from him in the city. It was bad enough he had trouble finding her, but to have his hands on her then have to cry like a little girl for the second time in two days. He had to find her. Luckily, hanging out at topless bars wasn't the worst form of police work.

He didn't mind working on a Saturday night late when he thought about poor, obsessed Bill Tasker. That boy was gonna work himself into an early grave. When Sutter had called him, about an hour ago, the FDLE agent was still on post, watching the damn KKK house. He was a better man than most. Even Sutter admitted to himself that if he was out there alone on a Saturday night, he'd risk missing Wells and head out to have some fun. Tasker took things too seriously to have much fun.

Sutter leaned back in his tall chair at the Harem Club and surveyed the line of stages as he took a swig of his Bombay and tonic. A blond on the last stage might be Alicia. He couldn't tell, and he damn sure wasn't going to get too close this time.

It was near dawn, and Alicia Wells had broken her rule of not drinking while working, but the young lawyer who had helped Daniel had showed up and was so nice. A public defender for the federal court. Whatever that was. He was nice, cute and had some cash. The next thing Alicia knew she was a little drunk, giving him a lap dance in the back room. One lap dance turned into another and another, until they were just making out in the small room with two couches. No one even checked on her. She lost interest when he ran out of money, and nice and cute just didn't cut it. Besides, she was a married woman, though that seemed less and less real every day. In fact, the longer she was away from Daniel's hellion boys, the better she liked it. She did miss little

Lettye. She was just a sweet little Barbie doll. But the boys never stopped, and Daniel encouraged them all the time. He talked about how he liked to "disturb the natural flow of the universe." Whatever that meant, she just wished the boys weren't one of the ways to do it. Daniel would watch the news about the riots or some explosion like it was one of her soaps. Like *General Hospital* without a plot. She knew he had some weird ties to different people and believed he might have helped them do some crazy things from time to time but never let on. He thought she was a little stupid because he had three years of college, but she wasn't. She had her GED, and a month and a half of beauty school besides. She may not have known the capital of Florida for sure, she figured it had to be Orlando 'cause of where it was built, but she was smart in other ways. Like he didn't have ten dollars to his name. He'd work and work and charge people for only the hours he put in. She made four hundred, sometimes six hundred, a night after expenses, and untaxed. Unlike the other girls, she didn't use drugs or drive fancy cars. She had almost nine thousand dollars stashed away. That made her smart as far as she was concerned.

All this ran through her head as she stumbled down the long path that led to the small apartment she rented from the nice Cuban family in North Miami. The bungalow-type building sat way off the road and no one ever bothered her.

As she stuck the key in the lock and started to turn it, she heard a man's voice say, "Found you finally."

Tasker was a little drowsy at the wheel of the Cherokee on the way home and then fell into a deep sleep on his couch ten minutes after turning on the TV to unwind. He caught a little of *Saturday Night Live*—the "Weekend Update" bit with the really hot babe in glasses—before he was off dreaming of water skiing with the girls in the Keys while Donna drove the boat. The phone snapped him awake at eight in the morning.

He reached for the portable handset, unable to focus on where it could be. Finally he grabbed it and mashed the talk button. "Hello."

"Billy, it's Jerry. Did I wake you?"

"Yeah, I was on the damn Klan house until almost midnight."

"Sorry, Billy, I thought you had it this morning and the only number I had handy was home. I was trying to get you before you left."

"No problem, Jerry. Camy has some ATF guys covering the surveillance for us today. What's up?"

"Hey, I didn't want to say anything in front of the Feds, but there is something weird about one number in Wells' phone book. I was in the office yesterday, cleaning up some stuff, and noticed a subpoena to Bell South had come back."

"Yeah, go ahead."

"There's a North Miami number that according to Bell South is an unassigned number. The problem with it is that it rings. Unassigned numbers have a phone-company recording. This unassigned number rings, but no one answers when I call."

"You think it's a police UC line?"

"Not even a UC line. When I call another number close to it with the same exchange, guess who answers?"

"No idea."

"The FBI."

Tasker was silent while he thought about what that might mean.

It took Alicia Wells five minutes to calm down after being surprised at her front door. She sat on her couch, looking at the source of her surprise next to her.

"How'd you find me?"

Daniel Wells smiled. "Your mama told me where you were. Why would you hide from me?"

"I knew you didn't like me dancing, and I needed a break from the boys."

"They doin' okay?"

"If starting fires all over your uncle's neighborhood and blowing up a little bridge across the canal is okay, then they're fine."

"I miss those boys. But I had to see you to let you know what was gonna happen."

"What?"

"You need to go collect the kids and wait at Uncle Tom's for me to call. End of the week I'll ride over to Tampa and we're all heading for Louisiana."

"New Orleans?" she asked hopefully.

"No, way further west. West of Baton Rouge. Little compound there run by some mighty serious boys. Boys that hate the government and need my help."

"I don't want to live in Louisiana."

"That's fine. We'll be moving on to Montana after a couple of weeks."

She put her hand on Daniel's arm. "No, Daniel, you don't understand. I want to stay."

"Can't stay."

"Why not?"

"You'll see. You won't wanna stay after Thursday."

"What happens Thursday?" She was getting frustrated. She hated it when he treated her like she was an idiot.

"Gonna stir some things up. Nothing you should worry your beautiful little mind about. Just gonna cause a little pandemonium."

She looked at his handsome face with a sideways glance. "You ain't gonna hurt anyone, are you?"

"That's not the point. It may happen, but it's not intentional." He put his arm around her. "You're the only person in the world I've said anything to about this. I just need you to pack up and go get the kids. Then we'll go back to bein' a family."

Alicia pulled away and stood up. "You know the cops are looking for you."

"Yeah, I know. How do you know that?"

"That black cop, the one that came with Bill Tasker, tried to question me."

Now Wells stood. "What'd you tell him?"

"Nothing. I used the pepper spray you gave me. And ran."

He hugged her, laughing. "That's my girl." He held her at arm's length and said, "Don't look so worried, baby. I got an ace up my sleeve with the cops. They won't touch me."

She smiled at him but felt a wave of uneasiness. He'd changed since she'd last seen him. He had a wild look in his eyes. She didn't know what he had planned, but she didn't want to see anyone hurt, and definitely didn't want to ever see Montana, let alone live there.

twenty-five

"it's as hot as Pamela Anderson's ass out here," said Derrick Sutter to Bill Tasker.

Tasker looked at the empty lot and tall sawgrass along the unkempt edges of Manny's abandoned market and had to agree. He'd brought his partner lunch at the surveillance post and thought he'd break up Sutter's day with a visit.

Sutter looked at the FDLE agent and said, "What's bothering you now? You got everyone to agree with you, Wells is a bad guy. You got the FBI to work on a Saturday. You've performed miracles, and you still don't look happy."

Tasker smiled at that. "Something's not right with this."

"The case?"

"This surveillance. *You* think Wells would be here?"

"No, not really. He does seem too smart to be mixed up with them. He's got a job, or at least did have a job, which most of the Klan jerk-offs don't, and he seemed too normal. But that doesn't mean shit, because apparently he's not if he likes blowing things up."

"This seems like a huge waste of time."

"Almost everything you investigative agencies do seems like a waste of time. I'm a street cop. Hit fast and hit hard—that's what *I* like."

"But this specific surveillance used all our manpower and brought the rest of the case to a dead halt."

"Yeah, that's true. But I'm a black man watching the Klan. I can't complain. Told my dad and even he was impressed."

Tasker smiled at Sutter's positive outlook, then caught sight of a pickup truck coming out of the street. It was the third time in twenty minutes it had come up Krome Avenue and driven past them. He let his eyes follow it. The big F-250 had three men in the bed and two up in the quad cab.

Sutter said, "What is it?"

"Just nervous."

"About the truck that's filling up with rednecks?"

Tasker nodded. "Exactly."

"Now you were about to tell me why you were worried about the case."

"Jerry Ristin called me yesterday."

"On a Sunday? *Our* analysts aren't quite that dedicated."

"It was a sensitive matter. He didn't want to talk in front of the whole group."

"That include me?"

"I'm tellin' you, aren't I?" Tasker looked outside to see the F-250 slowly pass again, headed toward the house, this time with another man in the back. "Jerry said one of the numbers in Wells' personal phone book comes back to the FBI."

"No shit! What'd you suppose he was doing with that?"

"We're gonna find out." Before he could add to his comment, Tasker saw several men at the corner of the yard looking back toward Manny's Market. "I got an idea."

Sutter cut his eyes to Tasker. "This doesn't sound like a *smart* idea, but go ahead. What's your plan?"

"I pull away, maybe down the road, and see if they hassle one guy sitting alone."

"So I'm bait?"

"Yeah. You could be better bait if you rolled down the window."

"So they could see I'm a black man?"

"They *are* supposed to be the KKK."

"All you want is a pretext to question them and maybe get in the house."

"And end this fucking surveillance."

"Go hide like a baby." Sutter smiled.

Tasker said, "Let me call for reinforcements."

Camy Parks was uneasy herself. She had just searched all the ATF intelligence files available and found pages and pages on Ed Conners, but not one sentence about the house off Krome being a meeting place. It was true the FBI had different sources, but usually not that different, and with the limited flow of information there was often something that overlapped. She couldn't figure out why there was no overlap, unless Jimmy Lail was lying about the connection. Then she couldn't figure out why he would lie. She looked over at Jimmy, who was sitting at her desk, bobbing his head to some beat only he could hear. Because he had such a good body and acted so goofy, she always thought of him as kind of stupid. Was he smart enough to mislead a group of veteran cops? Why?

Before she could ask him, her Nextel chirped and she heard Bill Tasker's voice. "Camy, you out there?"

She keyed the radio button. "Go ahead."

"We're at Manny's and need some help right now."

"On the way." She jumped up and hustled past Lail, tapping him on the shoulder. "We gotta go."

"Whazz up?" asked Jimmy.

"Billy and Sutter need help at the house."

"The Klan house?"

"Where else?"

"What the hell could be going . . ."

She looked at him as she grabbed some gear by the desk and headed out the door.

Jimmy followed at a trot.

Daniel Wells had it all mapped out. Alicia would get the kids. Wednesday night he'd grab the truck. He'd park it and get everything ready. Thursday afternoon, maybe two-thirty, or a little later, at the start of rush hour, he'd make his move. A move that would make him part of history as well as create a scene of anarchy never seen before in Miami. By five, he's a legend and his itch would be scratched. At least for now. There'd be plenty of opportunity in Montana to plan for travel, if necessary. He settled down for his noontime nap with a smile on his face.

Tasker had pulled his Cherokee straight back into the tall grass when the pickup was parked at the house. Sutter had told him over the Nextel that there was no way he could be seen from the road. Sutter knew where he'd pulled in, and he could see the grill of the Cherokee, but someone off the road wouldn't pick him up. Tasker had pulled his MP5 from the back of the Cherokee and checked his Beretta. If they could get these rednecks to do something stupid they might catch a break.

Over the Nextel, Sutter said, "The F-250 just rolled by real slow with five guys in the back, and none of them hid that they were staring at me."

"Just give me the word and I'll roll out." He quickly raised Camy on the Nextel. "What's your twenty?"

"Five minutes." There was a strain in Camy's voice.

Tasker waited. The wind would blow the sawgrass to one side or the other occasionally, giving him a glimpse of the parking lot and Sutter still safe in his car.

During a period when his vision was blocked, Sutter came over the Nextel. "Bill, they're in the lot. I'll beep when I need you."

Tasker acknowledged him and then raised Camy. "How far?"

She came right back. "We're on Krome, thirty seconds."

Tasker said, "Just come in the lot. The truck is here and we need to—" Tasker heard Sutter beep the horn. He let the phone drop and hit the gas. The gold Cherokee roared out of the field like a charging rhino and rolled into the lot over potholes and garbage and obviously surprised the rednecks, who were now in a ring around Sutter's door. One of them had a shotgun and two had ax handles.

Tasker brought the Cherokee to a screeching halt right next to the surprised men. He popped out of the Cherokee with his MP5 already up. At almost the same time, Camy rolled into the lot and secured the two guys standing near the F-250. Jimmy Lail had his gun up sideways and started yapping, "Five-O, five-O, nobody move." He looked at the young man closest to him and added, "That mean you, be-autch."

Tasker focused on the man with the shotgun and said, "Police. Drop the gun."

The man looked at him with scared eyes.

Tasker yelled, "Now!"

The shotgun clattered to the ground.

Tasker turned his machine gun on the others. "Now the ax handles."

The two men in their thirties let them fall to the ground with hollow clunks. Their hands wavered and shook in the air. Tasker felt the anger flash through him when he thought about what they had intended to do to his friend with those handles. He checked his emotion before he did something stupid like whack one of them in the face with the butt of his machine gun.

Sutter moved from his car to collect the shotgun and kick the ax handles out of reach. "Damn, this is the new millennium. Who uses ax handles anymore?"

No one answered.

Jimmy Lail moved closer, shoving one of the men. "On the ground, crackers."

Tasker looked over to Camy, not surprised she had both her subjects already sitting next to the truck with their hands on their heads.

After a minute of surveying the situation, Tasker had all the men together near the truck and his MP5 slung over his shoulder.

"Now, what's this all about?"

One of the younger men, about twenty-five, said, "We was worried when we saw y'all hanging out down here. We didn't know what was goin' on."

An older man, near fifty, barked, "Dale, shut up. We ain't done nothin' wrong."

Tasker smiled. "Mr. Conners?"

The man nodded reluctantly.

"You're wrong. Looks like you assaulted Officer Sutter here."

The man didn't acknowledge him.

Tasker said, "Get up and come over here." He waited until the man had stood and walked to him, then led him away from the group, now under the watchful eye of Sutter, Jimmy and Camy.

At Sutter's car, Tasker stopped, turned and said, "This can all go away with a little information."

The man had a sour look, then said, "What kind of information?"

"I need to find someone."

"Who?"

"Daniel Wells."

Conners looked at him, then asked, "Who?"

"Daniel Wells, from Naranja."

"The handyman?"

"Yeah, I guess you could call him that."

"Why would I know where he is? I only took my lawn mower to him once to get fixed."

"He hasn't been staying at your house?"

"Not unless he's screwing my wife behind my back."

"You're Ed Conners. You're with the Ku Klux Klan, right?"

"That ain't against the law. I'm proud to be Ed Conners and to be the head of our klavern."

"Your what?"

"Local Klan group."

"These fellas other members?"

"These boys work the different farms up and down my street. They was worried you fellas was crack dealers. We been having a problem. All they wanted to do was scare you off. They ain't no Klan members. Hell, two of 'em is Mexican. They couldn't join if they wanted to."

Tasker could have kept questioning the man, but there was no point. He wasn't holding back, and Tasker had someone he wanted to question more. He felt his frustration level rise and took a deep breath to control it.

He started back to the F-250 with Conners. "Okay, you guys can go. Why not just call the cops next time you think someone is dealing dope?"

Conners said, "Yeah, they come right out. Why don't you go find some real criminals?"

Tasker said, "That's a good idea." He stood and watched the men hop into the back of the truck, then waited as the truck rumbled out of the lot back toward the house.

Jimmy Lail said, "What was that all about? I should've busted a cap into the air to get those be-autches talkin'." He pulled out his automatic and, holding it sideways again, pointed into the sawgrass, showing his partners the motion he'd use to fire it. "That woulda made 'em shit." He looked at Sutter. "Ain't that right, my brother?"

Tasker couldn't take it anymore. He sprang toward Jimmy, knocking his pistol out of his hand, then kneeing him in the leg, and finished by throwing the stunned FBI man to the ground and landing on top of him. He had Jimmy by the shirt, his face two inches from Jimmy's.

"The word is bitch. B-I-T-C-H. One fucking syllable. Never hold your gun any way except perpendicular to the ground. That's how they're intended to be held. I don't care how many movies you've seen, your pistol is not supposed to be held at an angle. Never sideways. You got it?" Spittle flew from his mouth into Jimmy's face.

Sutter stood up and calmly tried to move Tasker. "C'mon, Bill."

He stood and looked down at Jimmy Lail, who said, "Bolini is right. You're an asshole."

"Bolini? You been talkin' to him?"

He hesitated, then said, "Yeah, sort of. I mean, I work with him, dipshit."

Now Sutter stepped in. "Now that sounds like you. Why you trying to talk like a street kid all the time?"

Jimmy didn't answer.

"Now I'm not on as short a fuse as my man Tasker here, but if you ever use that fake urban bullshit accent around me again, I'm gonna whip your ass."

Tasker added, "Me too." He took a step back and looked at Camy, who didn't seem to mind having her boyfriend set straight. Tasker added, "And I don't know what this idiotic surveillance was all about, but if you lied, you'll be in for another ass-whippin'."

They watched Jimmy silently slink back to Camy's car.

Camy said, "If the counseling session is over, I better get him cleaned up."

Tasker took a deep breath as he realized they were all the way back at square one.

twenty-six

alicia wells blew her nose like her mama had taught her, mouth open and with full force. The honking sound was not very ladylike, but it cleared her clogged nose.

Ever since Daniel had told her of his plans, she had been sinking lower and lower into a funk. She wasn't sure if it was the idea of moving to Montana that upset her so much as the idea of moving to Montana with Daniel's two boys.

The other thing that was bothering her was Daniel's comment that he was going to do something in Miami. She didn't want Daniel doing something he'd get in a lot of trouble for, and she didn't want anyone getting hurt.

She sat on her couch and started to sob again as the rush of ideas flooded her mind again. She had some money and could just take off. Daniel wouldn't find her if she didn't want him to, and he wasn't the kind of man who'd bother her mother to find her, or even look that hard. But it didn't seem right somehow. She couldn't just walk away. She wouldn't ever see him again, or little Lettye. She could live without seeing the boys, but even the thought of losing them forever had a sobering effect.

She looked out her window at the backyard of the main house. Mrs. Garcia's granddaughter was kicking a ball in her pretty white dress. The squat Cuban lady held her two-year-old granddaughter's hand to steady her from time to time. That was all Alicia wanted: a normal life, and to watch her kids grow up. Was that too much to ask? She started to cry again.

Tasker concentrated so hard on the computer screen that Sutter's voice made him jump in the chair.

"What's with you?" asked Sutter, as he sat in an empty chair. In fact, the whole FDLE squad bay was deserted. He had followed Tasker over after their run-in with the Krome Avenue farmers.

Tasker returned to the computer screen, saying, "Something about this case stinks."

"Everything about this case stinks. Be more specific."

"You ever wonder why the FBI has been no help at all?"

"Actually, that's the only thing that *isn't* a surprise. I can't remember them being much help on anything."

"But think about it. Sal Bolini won't even acknowledge the case, but he talks to Lail about it. Jimmy Lail's only suggestion wastes our time for four days. Something doesn't add up, and I'm gonna find out what."

Sutter spun in the chair once. "Why?"

"Why what?"

"Why find out? You could always walk away. You could pretend that none of this fiasco ever occurred and no one would blame you or say another word."

"You serious?"

"Would FDLE discipline you if you dropped this and moved on to something else?"

"No, of course not."

"Would your supervisor think you're less of an investigator if you worked on something else?"

"I don't think so."

"Then why not drop the whole thing? You've had enough trouble with the FBI to last a lifetime. Move on."

Tasker considered this. Logically, it was a sound argument. Tasker prided himself on his logical reasoning and rational thought, whatever the subject, and this was both logical and rational. He looked over to his partner, now learning the intricacies of the adjustable office chair by spinning it up, then lowering it.

Tasker said, "That's a good idea."

"Glad you agree."

"I can't do it, but I recognize the good sense of it."

"Why can't you walk away?"

"Because it's not right. This guy killed someone with a bomb and may do it again. The FBI is involved with him, and someone has got to stop him."

"And you're the only one in the world who can stop him?"

"Yes. Me and you."

"Good answer. I just wanted to make sure this was as important to you as I thought it was. What's our next move?"

Tasker leaned to one side so Sutter could see the computer screen. It showed a *Miami Herald* news-archive article on two Jordanian nationals the FBI had arrested for attempting to attack the Turkey Point nuclear power plant.

Tasker said, "First stop, MCC."

Sutter just stared at him.

"To interview either Samir Al-Soud or Kaz Jourdi. The article doesn't specify which agent arrested them, but Lail said it was Bolini. Maybe they can tell us something."

"You think the Bureau would be pissed if they found out we were talkin' to their prisoners?"

"Do you care?"

"Nope."

Without another word, they were off.

Jimmy Lail would never admit that he'd hurt his back when Tasker threw him on the ground. He sat at the lat machine at the Bally's in western Dade, just staring at the bar. He realized he was zoning out and looked around to make sure no one thought he was acting strange. He rubbed his head where the nylon sock cap irritated his skin, then reached for the bar and pulled it down with no real enthusiasm. This sucked. He couldn't even concentrate, because that state cop had disrespected him so bad in front of his woman. And that Miami cop didn't hide what he thought of Camy. It was a lot easier when everyone had thought she was a lesbian. It'd explained why she never wanted to go out of the house with him. It kept other men away. And the thought of it kept Jimmy in a general state of arousal.

After finishing up with some lackluster squats, Jimmy headed over to the ATF office. Camy might be able to keep him from coming by her house, but she couldn't keep him from a federal law enforcement office.

Forty minutes later, he strutted through the main door and waved to the older receptionist, who was so used to his face she buzzed him in without calling Camy. He bounded up the stairs to her squad and was able to sneak within five feet of her desk before she even noticed him.

She looked up from her report, but didn't smile. "How'd you get in here?"

"Walked, baby. How you think?"

"I think you're supposed to call first."

"I never used to have to call."

Camy leveled her stare at him. "Jimmy, this is work. You're supposed to be professional at work. Act like a professional."

Jimmy didn't reply. He decided he needed his space, anyway, and sulked back out of the building. This case had ruined his life. His woman wasn't giving him his props, the other cops disrespected him and he was starting to think people didn't like him.

The thing that bothered him most was that an FDLE agent, a damn state cop, thought he was better than him. That wasn't right and it wasn't true.

Jimmy always excelled at anything he did. He'd been teacher of the month at Prairie Middle School in Laredo two different times before he joined the FBI. The multicultural class he'd taught had been talked about all over the county. It was the first time the other culture considered hadn't been Mexican. If they wanted that, they could cross the Rio Grande on the west side of town. He had brought Kwanzaa to South Texas. He didn't need any of this shit.

They could complain about the Klan surveillance all they wanted. They still did it. And Jimmy felt satisfied on a number of different levels. The cops had done what he'd told them to do. He'd impressed some people who mattered at the Bureau. And most important, he had harassed the Klan a little, and that would burn up his racist father back on LBJ Lane in Laredo more than anything Jimmy could do. The Klan had never changed its out-of-date views, but Jimmy could still strike a blow for the peeps wherever he worked.

The Miami Metropolitan Correctional Center was quiet this time of the evening. The administration didn't like visits after six, but for law enforcement they would make exceptions. Tasker found that Kaz Jourdi had already been moved to Atlanta, where he was being evaluated for a future destination. Samir Al-Soud was still at MCC waiting for transportation. Neither had caused any trouble while guests of the Federal Bureau of Prisons.

After a thirty-minute wait in an interview room the size of a small closet with a rickety table and three folding chairs, two burly Bureau of Prisons officers escorted a small dark man about thirty-three with a wicked comb-over hiding a large, shiny head. He had intense dark eyes which he immediately trained on Tasker, trying to assess who he had to talk with now. He was thin but had some muscle. Tasker wouldn't want to tangle with him if he was pissed or had a cause.

The prison officers let him step inside the small room alone and said to Sutter, "We'll be in the control room. If you need us, stick your head out the door. We have to see you."

Sutter smiled, looking at the prisoner. "No problem. I think we could handle this one."

The second officer laughed and said to the first, "How many times have we heard *that*?"

Tasker asked, "Is there something we should know about Mr. Al-Soud?"

"No, nothing specific. We just seen more than one FBI agent get his ass kicked down here."

Al-Soud seemed to follow the conversation with interest.

Sutter said, "Don't worry, I'm a Miami cop."

The first officer said, "Seen *that*, too." He turned and shut the door.

Tasker pulled out the chair next to the table and offered it to the small man.

Al-Soud slowly sat, exchanging looks with both cops.

Tasker said, "Mr. Al-Soud, you speak English, don't you?"

He nodded.

"My name is Bill Tasker and this is Derrick Sutter."

The man made no reaction.

"We wanted to talk to you about your arrest. It has no bearing on your case, which, from what I understand, is already concluded."

The man looked at Tasker and said, "Why would you want to talk to me? Why not talk to another FBI agent?"

"I'm not with the FBI."

He looked at Sutter. "And you're a Miami cop?" He had no trace of an accent. He could have been from Los Angeles.

Sutter said, "That's right."

Tasker said, "I'm an agent with the Florida Department of Law Enforcement."

"So an FDLE agent and a Miami cop are interested in an FBI case. This must be some turf war."

"Not really. The opposite, actually. We're on another case that the FBI is not interested in." Tasker looked at the calm little man. "Who arrested you?"

He looked surprised. "Why, the FBI, of course."

"I mean, which agent? Do you remember?"

He nodded vigorously. "Oh yes. Of course. A most disagreeable man. Agent Bolini."

Tasker cut his eyes to Sutter. Then said, "I read the news article, but what exactly did you do?"

"I am afraid, due to legal considerations, I shall not answer that." He looked at Sutter. "And nothing could make me talk."

Sutter shrugged, stood up and said, "Okay, that just means I'm outta here quicker." Sutter took a step toward the door. The small Arab man looked to Tasker.

"Okay, okay, wait. I'll talk to you."

Sutter let a small smile cross his face.

Tasker winked at him, turned to Al-Soud and said, "We're listening."

The man gazed ahead as he recalled details. He began, "I've got to tell you—it was brilliant."

Tasker smiled. "Hold on, ah, what should we call you? Samir? Mr. Al-Soud?"

"Call me Sami. Everyone does."

"Okay, Sami, tell us your idea."

"It was mostly mine, but Kaz added some logistics."

Sutter cut in. "Summarize this shit, Sami. We're not investigating you. We're just interested in your case."

Sami nodded, anxious to get on with his story. "Well, you know that Turkey Point used to be relatively unguarded. I am an electrical engineer and had done some contract work out there a few years ago."

"At the nuclear plant?" asked Tasker.

"No, the fossil fuel plant, but they're right next to each other and the engineers showed me around plenty of times. They have that typical American pride in their accomplishments. They love to brag and show off how smart they are." He took a second and asked, "Now, where was I?"

"You were saying how brilliant you are," said Sutter.

He nodded, "Yes, of course. So, as I was saying, I talked it over with Kaz, my friend, and we thought that if someone attacked the plant from the ocean side, they could make quite an inroad to this facility. There used to be a dock there and everything."

Sutter said, "Why'd you want to attack it?"

"It was a popular idea among some of us. Make a statement about America's vulnerability."

Sutter took a harsh tone. "A vulnerability based on freedom that you enjoyed."

"Correct," said Sami, like he couldn't understand Sutter's reasoning.

"And you liked living here?"

"Yes, of course."

"But you wanted to attack us?"

"Yes, the power plant."

"Why?"

"I told you, to make a statement about America's vulnerability."

Tasker looked over to Sutter and shook his head so they could move on.

Sami was silent for a few seconds, then said, "So, I had the idea that a big enough bomb planted on the ocean side of the plant might not destroy it but would scare a lot of people and disrupt life."

Tasker asked, "How were you going to get the bomb in? Suicide attack?"

"No, of course not. Not unless Kaz wanted to ride in a boat loaded with explosives. And he wanted to live as much as me."

"So what did you plan?"

"A sealed explosive that when it was dumped in the water and reached a certain depth, it armed itself. Then, after we were gone, it exploded."

"You could build something like that? Where'd you learn how to do that?"

"Not us. We met a man. An engineer who told us he wanted to see the same thing—the plant to go up in a big show. He had the whole device made up. He had the explosive, too. But before we even had a boat, the FBI grabbed us and we abandoned the plan. They had us, they knew everything, so Kaz and I pleaded guilty. I start a twelve-year sentence next month."

"What happened to the other guy, the engineer?"

"I don't think they ever caught him. I gave his name to Agent Bolini, but I don't know what happened."

"What was his name?"

"Daniel Westerly. He lived in Naranja."

Tasker just stared at Sutter.

Wells had almost everything ready to go. He was about to get some rest for the night, when his pager went off. Within a minute, he'd hustled down to a gas station and called the number back, and when a man answered, Wells said, "Hello?"

The man just said, "They talked to Al-Soud."

"So?" asked Daniel.

"So be careful."

"I always am."

Wells heard the line go dead and shook his head. If that little Arab fella couldn't tell the device he'd made for him and his buddy Kaz was as bogus as a three-dollar bill, then Wells wasn't worried about what he might tell the cops.

Wells chuckled at the memory of him showing the two would-be terrorists the heavy marine fuel tank with the few fake gauges and switches welded on the outside, and then saying it was a pressure-triggered bomb that could bring down Turkey Point. The confusion on their faces when the FBI had swooped in was worth its weight in gold. That was the sort of thing that everyone liked. It satisfied his urge to a degree and had bought him some goodwill, too. If Sami Al-whatever wanted to blab, he could, but that dumb son of a bitch didn't know anything useful.

twenty-seven

tasker knew it was a dream, but he went with it anyway. In his mind he was with an old girlfriend and she wanted him, not the satchel of cash he was accused of taking. Her dark, shapely legs were about to encircle him when, just like in real life, somebody pounded on his front door and ruined the moment. It took a couple of seconds for him to realize the rapping was real and he was still in his own bed, alone. He rolled to his right and looked at the alarm clock. Who would be pounding on his door at seven-fucking-thirty in the morning? Normally he'd be up and around, but his interview with Sami Al-Soud at MCC had kept him up late, as he and Sutter had contemplated, over a beer until nearly two in the morning, what the hell was going on with the case.

He sat up in bed and ran his hands through his sandy, short hair. He slipped on a pair of gym shorts that were lying on the ground and pulled an FSU T-shirt off the chair near his bedroom door. He padded through the town house, clearing his head as he went. Just as he reached the door, the pounding started again. He turned the knob, leaving the chain on, and peeked out the crack.

He let his eyes adjust to the sharp Florida daylight and said, "What the hell are you doing here? Is everything all right?"

His ex-wife, Donna, in jeans and a casual shirt, smiled back. "I just needed to see you." She hesitated, then added, "You alone?"

"Yeah, sure. Come in." He closed the door and unlatched it, then re-opened it to let her walk in.

As she crossed the threshold, she said, "I'm sorry, bothering you like this, but I need to talk to someone. That's not correct, I needed to talk to *you.*"

They sat on the couch. "You want something? Juice? I could try and make coffee."

She smiled and shook her head.

"The girls are okay, otherwise you would have said something. Why aren't you at work?"

"Called in sick. I left the house for here as soon as the girls were ready for early-morning activities at school."

Now he just looked at her. It was a treat to be able to look at such a pretty girl up close, and without being self-conscious. That was one of Donna's great charms; she was an unpretentious, natural beauty. No need for makeup; looked as good at seven-thirty in the morning as at seven-thirty in the evening. He waited for her to gather her thoughts.

"I was feeling lonely and missed you. Then last night I just couldn't get you out of my mind."

He waited for the "But."

"So I took a chance and raced down here first thing."

He smiled and felt a rush of emotion sweep over him. Then he checked back to reality. "What about Nicky Goldman?"

"We broke up."

"I'm sorry." He didn't like lying but had managed to keep a straight face.

"So am I. He was sweet. But you were right—being sweet and nice doesn't make you Mr. Right."

"What does?"

She let loose with that brilliant smile. "A lot of things." She reached over and pulled him to her for a long kiss. When she was done, she said, "So what do you want to do today?"

He stared at her for a moment. "What do you mean?"

"We have the day to hang out. What would you like to do with it?"

He paused, brushing a strand of blond hair from her face. "I didn't know you were coming."

"That's why it's called a surprise."

"What I mean is, I didn't take the day off."

"You have such a flexible schedule I didn't think it'd be a problem."

"Usually that's true, but we're right in the middle of something that's going morning to night until we're done."

"With no days off?"

"Not for a few days, anyway."

She looked into his eyes. "It's still work first, family second, isn't it?"

"No. Absolutely not. It's just that this is really important. I mean life-and-death important, and it's basically my fault that we're in it."

A tear built up in her eye, then ran down her cheek.

He went to brush it away, but she caught his hand. "Is the redhead working with you?"

"Camy Parks? Yeah, her and half a dozen other cops."

Donna stood quickly and turned to the front door. "I understand."

"Donna, wait."

She paused at the door.

"Please stay."

"So we can spend the day together?"

"An hour, anyway."

She opened the door and stepped out without a word.

Sutter sat at an FDLE conference table with Bill Tasker and his squad analyst, Jerry Ristin. Sutter had never been so impressed with a non-sworn member of a police agency as he was with this heavyset, raspy-voiced man. The guy treated them almost like they were students in a class, as he laid out his theories on what had happened on the case and what he'd found through his computer searches.

Clearly, the FBI had a tie to Daniel Wells and had not been completely truthful with the other law enforcement agencies involved in this case. Jerry couldn't be specific, his job was to discover trends. Now he told the cops, whose job it was to get very specific.

The older man summed it up, saying, "Well, boys, it looks like you were hosed by the Bureau again. This is getting to be a habit. I woulda figured you'd catch on to their shenanigans by now."

Sutter and Tasker just looked at each other.

Ristin shrugged. "Maybe next time."

Tasker asked, "You got anything else?"

"Nope, not really." He smiled and chuckled like a senior Christmas elf. "Don't look so down, boys. The FBI has been fucking cops since before you were born. Don't be embarrassed that you fell for it." He paused. "Twice." He paused again. "In two months."

Sutter felt his blood pressure rise. "Wait a second. I wouldn't call that shit with the money typical FBI bullshit. They don't usually frame cops."

Ristin smiled again. "Ah, the innocence of youth."

Tasker said, "At least with Dooley and the money, I knew what was going on and why. This one has me more confused."

Ristin said, "You mean the KKK surveillance?"

They both nodded.

"I don't know why you were on that. But the fact that Wells had an FBI number in his phone book and was probably a snitch in the case against Al-Soud tells me that the Bureau has used him."

Tasker said, "So he's no threat now?"

"I didn't say that. If he really wasn't a threat, he'd go to the Bureau and lay low. If he had no reason to stay here, he'd be gone quicker than a doughnut at a Weight Watchers meeting."

Tasker said, "We need one or two more pieces of the puzzle."

Sutter said, "I know where we can find those pieces."

"Where?"

"Jimmy Lail. He's not as stupid as he acts."

"How?"

Before he could answer, an intercom buzzed and a female voice said: "Bill, you have a visitor in the lobby."

Tasker reached over and hit the button on the intercom. "Who is it?"

"She wouldn't say."

"Thanks, be right there." Tasker looked at Sutter and said, "Had an issue with my ex-wife this morning. She may have come to her senses."

"I gotta head over to the PD for a few minutes. I'll follow you down and take care of my shit, then meet you at one at ATF." He turned to Ristin. "Sir, you have done a great job. I appreciate it."

Ristin smiled. "It's a team effort to keep Billy out of trouble."

"Ain't that the truth."

Heading down the stairs, Tasker said, "I like how you two bonded over my misfortune."

"I say always find the bright side of a situation."

Tasker smiled. "Let me introduce you to Donna real quick, then I'm gonna take an hour with her to make sure she's okay."

Sutter nodded as they reached the ground floor and headed through the double security doors. He looked into the lobby, curious as to what this ex-wife Tasker was always talking about looked like.

They stopped at the door and both cops froze. Alicia Wells stood up when she saw them. Her eyes were red and she held a tissue.

Sutter said, "Now, *this* is gonna be interesting."

Camy Parks sat at her desk, gazing out a window that looked over a fenced parking lot where they held seized vehicles. The file from the cruise-ship bombing sat on her cluttered desk. She had to admit that after two years without any progress at all, the case had lost a lot of its original interest for her. At first, when there'd been media activity and people were asking her about it, she had attacked the case like a pit bull, but over time, as leads washed out—and with them the inquiries—she felt like she had been placed on some kind of inactive squad. That was what she had liked about the Bureau of Alcohol, Tobacco and Firearms—they were never inactive. She loved the feeling of having too much work and being the underdog agency. Now, with her duties restricted to the one case, she had lost some enthusiasm. That is, until recently. Now people were interested in the case again. She had the two good-looking cops working with her, Tasker the quiet and introspective one, and Sutter the too-sharp-for-his-own-good one. She even had been able to bring Jimmy Lail along on the case. That had been a thrill at first, but now he was wearing on her nerves.

Something about the case had never seemed right and she couldn't put her finger on it, but lately it had just gone plain spooky. This guy Wells moved like a ghost. He was in the area, but no one could put their hands on him. Then there was that business with the Klan house. Where had the FBI gotten that info?

Her cell phone rang. She looked at the face of it and saw: "Incoming Call." That meant that it was a number that was blocked. Had to be Jimmy calling from his office.

"Hello," she said into the tiny phone.

"Hey, baby."

She let out a small sigh. "Hello, Jimmy."

"What's my girl up to?"

"Work. It's ten-thirty. You should be working, too."

"What's with my lady this morning?"

"Jimmy, did you call for a reason other than to annoy me?"

"Whoa, girl, I was gonna ask you if you wanted to have dinner and some lovin' tonight."

"Can't tonight."

"Even for Joe's Stone Crab?"

"That'd be nice, but it's September. Joe's is closed."

"I'll take you anywhere you wanna go."

"Not tonight."

"Why not, baby?"

"I've got to wash my hair." She cracked a smile at that old one.

"C'mon, baby, that's a bunch of—"

She didn't hear the rest as she mashed the "end" button on her phone. She smiled, thinking that between Sutter and Tasker, one of them had to be free tonight.

twenty-eight

tasker focused on east Palm Drive as it turned into Southwest 344th Street, the empty Homestead speedway a few miles behind them. Sutter sat in the backseat of the Cherokee, talking—more like reasoning—with Alicia Wells. She had come in from the cold, like a spy from the sixties. And she had problems. Alicia told the investigators some of her story, but obviously held back quite a bit. What she did say was that Wells might have a secret box near the Turkey Point power plant and she thought she could find it. Knowing that the discovery of physical evidence might help them find the elusive repairman from Naranja, Tasker decided Alicia could talk in the car and headed out to this quietly modern part of the county.

Alicia sat, half-turned toward Sutter in a sundress and, clearly, no bra. She had garnered a few stares back at the office, which was another reason Tasker thought it best to hustle her out of the FDLE building. She had cried on and off during the brief interview, and now Sutter was waiting for her to regain her composure. He handed her a tissue. She held it to her nose and cut loose with a deafening honk as she blew her nose. Tasker thought a semi had rolled up behind him.

Alicia said, "That's better, thank you." She wiped her eyes again.

Tasker asked, "Still up this road, right?"

"I'm guessing it's on the dirt road to where we used to fish. The boys told me that Daniel could see them from where he liked to park on the bank of the canal."

"And you can find it?"

"I'm not stupid. Just choose not to deal with everything. Wish I didn't have to talk to you fellas, but I do." She looked at Sutter. "And I'm sorry I pepper-sprayed you."

Sutter smiled. "It was a good move. A smart move. I never expected it." He handed her another tissue. "And believe me, I cried and blew my nose a whole lot more than you are now."

She smiled and let out a short giggle.

Tasker said, "You said Daniel worried you. Did he give any specifics?"

"Naw, only that it was gonna be spectacular and on Thursday." She blew her nose again, earning an amazed stare from Sutter. "And that it was gonna be in Miami."

"Anything else?"

"Just that he didn't seem to care if people got hurt. He might be a little confused. He gets that way sometimes. Focused on something and then forgets other stuff. If he was working in his workshop, he'd sometimes forget to eat." She put her hand on Sutter's knee. "I couldn't live with myself if someone got hurt and I didn't do anything."

Sutter said, "There's a lot of that going around." He threw his intense stare over to Tasker in the driver's seat.

Alicia went on. "Daniel is a good man. He's a great father and treated me better than I ever been treated. I don't want him in trouble, neither. I reckon if you catch him before he hurts someone, he might just get probation."

Tasker remained silent. He didn't want to mislead her. He left his eyes on the straight road and kept driving.

"Daniel is a little different in some ways."

"How do you mean?" asked Sutter.

"He likes order in his workshop, but everywhere else he likes things just . . . goin' nuts. I mean, he lets those boys of his run wild. They're holy terrors."

"If everyone who let their kids run wild was crazy, we'd all be in asylums," said Tasker.

She leaned forward and rested her hand on his shoulder. He looked up in the rearview to see her piercing blue eyes. It felt like electricity was shooting through his body where her hand touched.

Alicia said, "No, it wasn't like they were bad. He punished them if they sassed or didn't eat good. He *liked* them to start fires and break stuff. He watched them and sometimes gave pointers on how to make it *worse.*"

Sutter said, "They ever hurt anyone?"

"Not that I know of."

Tasker thought back to the FBI profiler. Maybe she wasn't so full of horseshit. "Did he ever say he liked to be in control of things like that? Like fires or breaking things?"

"Naw, but he told me once that he liked when things were out of order. When they were in . . . I can't think of the word he used."

Tasker and Sutter said in unison: "Chaos?"

"Yeah, that's it. He liked to see how people reacted to chaos. He had an idea, a what-do-you-call-it?"

This time nothing popped into Tasker's mind.

Alicia said it herself. "He had a *theory* that the bigger the flash, the crazier people acted. Didn't matter if there was any real danger—it was all show."

Tasker asked, "He ever say how he tested this chaos theory?"

She shook her head. "Nope."

"You don't have any idea where he might be staying?"

"Nope. He just calls me or my mama from a pay phone. I don't even got an idea where he uses the pay phones. One time it was in a Publix, 'cause I heard the people talkin' on the store speaker."

"He have any close friends he might go to?"

"Naw. He did call one fella a lot, and the guy called him, too. He came by the house a coupla times."

"What's his name?"

"Never heard it. He was from up north. New York or Boston. Talked real fast, and funny, but always dressed nice, like he was a banker or a lawyer."

Tasker thought of one more thing as she said, "Turn here."

He slowed and pulled off the paved road onto a soft, muddy road that cut between two long strips of Brazilian peppers. Some people called them Florida Holly, but they definitely weren't native plants. The thin long branches of the low trees crept out toward the two-lane asphalt road. Tasker turned off 344th onto the uneven, winding trail. Several times the Cherokee almost bogged down, feeling like it might get stuck in the soft sand.

Once he had a grip on the vehicle's handling, he asked Alicia, "Why was Daniel learning to drive a big rig?"

"He just wanted to learn. I asked him if that meant he'd be gone truckin', 'cause I didn't want to stay alone with them kids. He said he wouldn't be leavin'. But he kept going to that school."

Tasker nodded. He slowed the car when he saw the narrow canal with the lime-green water. The patchwork of canals here were used to cool the power plant. The fresh water was pumped in and out of the plant, keeping this marsh area off-limits to developers. As a result, it was also one of the largest habitats for crocodiles in the Northern Hemisphere. Over the years, Tasker would occasionally see one on a bank or in the water, but never up close. Their reputation for being more aggressive than alligators made him keep his distance. This little dirt road was about as close as you could get without trespassing on Florida Power and Light land.

Alicia said, "This was his place. He came out here all the time."

"Any idea where the box is buried?"

She shook her head.

Sutter said, "Can't be that hard to find. Look for disturbed dirt."

The problem was that with the dirt-bike tire tracks and the soft dirt, it was a giant upturned sandbox.

Tasker said, "Let's look at it like a crime scene. Figure where he would stand to fish and how far he could see." He had Alicia point out the tree Wells usually sat under. Tasker took his place and turned to survey the field. Almost immediately, he saw the square patch of upturned dirt near the edge of the brush line where they had entered.

Tasker said, "Jackpot."

Jimmy Lail was frustrated by the way Camy had been acting. The girl's attitude was downright disrespectful. He could handle a lot but not being disrespected by his bitch.

He dialed her cell phone again. When her message came on instead of her, he pushed the "off" button so hard the phone casing cracked.

Between the way Tasker had treated him and now Camy, he was losing his cool.

He'd show them. When he got the good spot at the Bureau, they could all kiss his ass.

It was time for Daniel Wells to gather the last pieces of his plan together. He probably had enough TATP left to do the job, but wanted to get the rest from his box in case he needed it later. A run out there to clean out the box, and then off to borrow one of the Big Rig Academy's teaching units. He even had a place to stash it for a day until he needed it. He was still a little worried about backing up to a tanker unassisted, but decided that for a one-time shot he could do it.

He barreled down East Palm until he saw the Homestead speedway, when he remembered the vigilant cop who had stopped him a while back. He backed off the gas and slowed to fifty-five. It was a nice afternoon and he wished he'd had a fishing pole, since he was headed to his favorite spot, but he knew he'd never be able to concentrate on fishing with his plan so close. His body had tingled all over for the last three days as the time drew closer.

This would be big, but nothing compared to what he intended next. He already knew his target. He had grabbed a book from the library about how to do it. He would make this feeling last and last.

He slowed as he approached his turnoff.

It didn't take much to uncover the lid to the box, buried about eight inches under the soft sand. Tasker and Sutter focused hard on the box, to give Alicia a few minutes to handle private business. Even though they offered to drive her to a restroom, she said she had used the bushes plenty of times and headed into the thick brush.

Sutter reached down into the box. "Looky here." He held up a glass container. "Don't need no lab tests to tell me what this is."

Tasker nodded. "What else is in there?"

Sutter leaned back down, setting the bottle gently on the soft dirt next to the box. "Let's see. A box of fuses, some cash." He sat up again and ran his fingers against the tightly bound twenties. "Bet it's close to a thousand."

Tasker nodded his head.

Sutter said, "No, really. I bet you. If it's within fifty bucks off a thousand, I get to keep it. If not, then it's yours." He flashed his smile.

Tasker said, "Funny." He snatched the money from Sutter's hand before he could count it and crammed it in his front pocket. He looked at his friend. "Evidence."

"Man, you are paranoid." He leaned back into the box. "Whoa, now here's some evidence." He pulled up a small Smith & Wesson .38-caliber revolver, his two fingers holding it by the trigger guard. "What would an engineer need with this?"

Tasker took the gun, also by the trigger guard, and added, "Why would he hide it out here?"

Sutter grabbed the last item, examined it briefly and said, "A map of the county." Then he looked in the box and added, "And a roll of duct tape."

Tasker stood up and said, "He's done if we ever find him."

Sutter said, "We'll find him in time."

"But do we have any time?"

Wells whistled a Rush tune, "Free Will," as his Ford Ranger bumped over the entrance to his fishing hole. He was hardly paying attention until he saw the gold Jeep Cherokee. It took him a second to notice the two men near his box, then another second to recognize the state cop, Bill Tasker, and that Miami cop named Sutter.

"How on earth did they find this?" he said out loud as he spun the wheel. The Ranger turned slowly in the soft sand. He saw the men spring up from the box and turn his way. For a second, he thought they might not recognize him. Then he heard Tasker yell, "Daniel, wait!"

Wells hit the gas, spraying dirt back onto the men. The only problem was that the sudden spinning of his wheels sunk them into the soft sand. He heard some pops as his side mirror shattered. Someone was shooting at him. He ducked instinctively and steered for the break in the tree line.

Tasker was running in his direction just as the wheels finally caught on harder ground. The truck lurched up out of the soft spot, and Wells yelped with relief—until he saw that Tasker had jumped onto the rear of the truck, then tumbled into the bed of the pickup.

"Oh shit," said Daniel, as he saw the paved road. He hammered the gas pedal and turned the wheel hard when he hit the pavement, both to get some speed and in hopes of tossing the persistent cop out of the truck.

As he headed west on 344th, he looked in his rearview and was relieved to see an empty bed.

Tasker heard the vehicle coming down the dirt path and didn't give it a second thought. "Fishermen," he said to Sutter. Neither man recognized the old blue pickup, but it only took a second to recognize the driver. Without thinking, Tasker shouted, "Daniel, wait." Like he was trying to catch up to an old friend at a ball game.

Sutter didn't hesitate. He dropped to his right knee and pulled his backup Beretta .25 from an ankle holster. He brought the tiny, nonregulation semiautomatic pistol up in both hands like it was his full-sized Glock and started to pop away at the truck as it spun wildly and sprayed them with dirt. The small-caliber bullets had little effect, and in a few moments the truck's tires caught on firmer ground.

Tasker raced ahead without hesitation. When the truck bogged down again, he made a wild leap and landed on the tailgate, then tumbled into the bed. He felt his face rub against the rough, rusty floor of the bed, then his head slammed into the cab. He lay there for a second to regain his composure, checked to make sure his belly bag was still secure and then, finally, got up on his knees in the wildly rocking truck. He was about to set himself to kick the rear access window out when the truck hit the paved road with a thump and sent him first into the air, then back against the tailgate, then to one side. By the time the truck was on smooth pavement, Tasker was on his back, looking up at the sky, trying to determine if anything was broken. He was wedged near the cab and didn't think Wells could see him, so he stayed put for a minute to grab a few breaths of air and devise a plan.

Sutter grabbed the bottled explosive and the pistol as he sprang to his feet. He didn't give Alicia a second thought when he ran to Tasker's Cherokee. It wasn't until she darted out of the bushes, her dress still hiked up, that he remembered he couldn't leave her.

"In the Jeep. Get in the damn Jeep," he shouted.

She was inside before him. "What's goin' on?"

"Hold these." He shoved the gun and bottle in her lap as he jerked the seat up where he could reach the gas. "Your husband just showed." He reached down the steering column, relieved the keys were in place. He cranked the engine and hit the gas, getting much the same effect as Wells, spinning in circles and kicking up dirt. He pushed the Cherokee almost into the bushes, rubbing the thick Brazilian pepper branches hard against the gold paint to stay on firmer ground. It worked, and he darted onto the road at thirty miles an hour, immediately catching sight of the truck up ahead. "Hang on," he said as he punched the gas.

Alicia, close to tears, said, "Where is Mr. Tasker?"

Sutter looked ahead. "I *thought* he was in the truck." His stomach shifted toward his throat as he quickly scanned the sides of the road to see if his partner had been thrown from the truck.

"There he is," said Alicia, pointing at the truck ahead of them.

Sutter felt a breath of relief come to him as he saw Tasker pop up in the bed of the truck. He had his Beretta in his hand and leaned back, holding on to the side panel as he kicked the small window in the center of the rear glass. Tasker's foot went into the cab as the window came right off its tracks.

"Oh shit, girl, this could get ugly."

Tasker felt the blood come back into his brain and reached down for his pistol. The truck's motion was fairly steady now as they headed west toward Homestead. He thought about waiting until Wells stopped for something, but was afraid there might be innocent bystanders. He took a deep breath. He counted to three, then jumped up on his knees. He wanted Wells to see the gun and know what could happen. Tasker braced himself and brought up his right foot with the hiking boots he'd slipped on instead of tennis shoes. Thank God the heavy, reinforced shoes had been close to the door of his closet. He pulled back his leg, aimed for the rear access window and let fly. The force of his kick sent his foot into the cab and made him lose his balance.

Wells, apparently unnerved by the action, swerved hard one way, then the other, causing Tasker to fall again.

"That's enough," he said out loud, sticking his right hand—his gun hand—into the cab and up to Wells' head. "Stop the truck, Daniel," he yelled into the cab over the sound of the rushing wind. He then followed his arm through the wrecked rear window. He squeezed his head and shoulders through, just as Wells hit the brakes. His momentum carried him mostly into the cab, but gave Wells the chance to bat away his hand and send the Beretta rattling to the floor. The truck instantly picked up speed as Tasker balled his fist to bash Wells' brains out. He raised his fist.

Wells said, "Hang on there, slick."

Tasker froze at the sight of a Ruger .22 auto pointed in his face.

"Now slide on in all the way before you get killed."

Tasker complied.

"I could just shoot you and be done with it."

Tasker stayed silent. He'd been on the wrong end of a gun before and never liked the feeling.

"When you sprang me on the Stinger charge, I said I owed you. Remember?"

Tasker nodded.

"Now we're even." He tilted his head back to look at the rearview. "You're buddy is in the Jeep, so I can't stop." He looked hard at the mirror. "Son of a bitch, that's Alicia, isn't it?"

Tasker didn't respond. His eyes worked their way down to his gun on the floorboard between the gas pedal and the console.

Wells said, "That's how you found the hole." He turned to look at Tasker. "What'd you do to her to make her talk?"

Tasker shrugged.

"I know you cops. You probably told her she'd lose the kids if she went to jail. Didn't you?" He shoved the pistol closer to Tasker's head.

"Yeah, Daniel. She just talked to save the kids."

"You bastards." He took a couple of breaths. "A deal's a deal. I'm gonna let you out, but I can't stop 'cause of your pal."

Tasker looked at the Beretta again.

Daniel saw the glance and fired his .22 without warning.

Tasker jumped and raised his hand to his face, feeling for the wound. It only took a second to see that Wells had only added a hole to the truck, shooting high, into the roof.

"Don't even think about going for that gun." He slowed the truck. "Up here where the swale is grassy by the track, I'm gonna slow to about ten miles an hour. If your buddy tries to bump us, the deal's off, so signal him if you have to."

Tasker felt the truck slow.

Wells stepped on the Beretta with his left foot, then slowed the truck some more.

Tasker looked over his left shoulder and saw his Cherokee closing on them. Tasker held up his hand to Sutter, who immediately backed off a few car lengths.

Wells said, "Now, open the door and get out."

Tasker pulled the handle slowly, opening the door a crack.

"We're even," said Wells.

"Daniel—" started Tasker, but Wells poked him with the gun.

Tasker went with the motion and flopped out of the truck, hitting the grass, then rolling head over heels into a slow side tumble as he came to the edge of a gravel lot. He shook his head. "Ow" was all he could say. He watched the truck gain speed, then saw Wells toss out Tasker's Beretta a few hundred feet ahead as the truck sped away. Wells beeped a little rhythm and took off.

Sutter skidded to a stop a few feet from Tasker.

Jumping out of the Cherokee, he gasped, "Jesus, you all right?"

Tasker didn't honestly know. "Catch him." He shoved at his partner. "Go."

Sutter looked him over and said, "No way. You need some attention. Look at this shit." He pointed to a puddle of blood gathering around Tasker.

Tasker tried to respond, then just blacked out.

twenty-nine

"where's alicia?" asked Bill Tasker.

"I got a room at a hotel in case Wells tries to look for her."

Tasker nodded, avoiding words that rattled in his head. He blinked hard at the bright overhead light as the small Latin doctor inspected the last of his stitches.

"Not bad," said the forty-year-old doctor, with a light accent. "You won't have much of a scar on your arm, and the two deeper cuts on your left leg will look like a Christmas wreath. Good work if I do say so myself." He smiled, filling out crow's-feet that showed he was sincere. "Judging from some of your other scars, these won't bother you a bit."

Tasker timed the throbbing in his head and let out a quick "Thanks."

"You'll be sore for a week. That was some tumble you took. Next time you two are fishing, you should ride in the truck's cab."

"Will do," managed Tasker.

"Nothing's broken, but I want you in bed for at least five days. Understood?"

Tasker nodded.

"Why don't I believe you?" The doctor looked at Sutter, standing silently in the corner of the small walk-in clinic's main exam room. "Like I don't believe the fishing story. But my job is to patch up, not lecture."

Sutter said, "Good plan." He handed the man a stack of twenties. "We gotta boogie."

"Let me get his prescriptions and give this to the cashier," the doctor said, as he ambled out of the room.

Sutter quickly turned to his partner. "Tell me again why we didn't go to Jackson and you claim worker's comp?"

"No time. They'd have me on my back for a week."

"Like this guy wants."

"And I will. After we find out what the fuck is going on and grab Daniel Wells." Tasker looked at him. "And these twenties came from where?"

"Your front pocket."

"Derrick, that was evidence."

Sutter nodded his head. "So, when you bend the rules and don't use worker's comp and lie to a doctor, it's to save time. When I do something like that, it's 'destroying evidence.' "

Tasker's eyes bulged of their own will. "It *is* destroying evidence." They sat in silence a few seconds. Tasker realized these were extraordinary times. "Okay, what do you think we should do next?"

"Let's go talk to Bolini and figure out what the damn FBI is up to."

"Not if we're just fishing. We need some proof."

"This feels too damn close to the business with Dooley. Fuckin' Bureau causing shit, and we got our thumbs up our ass."

Tasker winced as he pulled his shirt up to look at his bruised ribs. Along with the twenty-seven stitches he'd just received in three different places, his legs had a few good patches of road rash, his left arm was turning blue with bruises and he thought one of his teeth felt funny. "We've gotta tie up the loose ends." He slid off the examining table.

Sutter put his hand on Tasker's tender shoulder. "I know exactly how to tie up the FBI loose ends."

Jimmy Lail snatched his phone off the front seat on the first ring. "Yo," he almost shouted. He'd been in a foul mood since Camy had stopped answering her phone. That's why he was shocked to hear her voice.

"Hey, baby. Sorry I was such a bitch earlier."

Jimmy smiled. "You da bomb, baby."

"You wanna come over?"

"When?"

"I'll be home in an hour. Don't work out, you'll need your strength."

The smile spread across his face. "You got it, baby. I gotta swing by my crib and shower."

"You may want to wait on that, too." Her voice had none of the defiance she'd shown the past few weeks.

Now his erection swelled as fast as his smile. "Whatever you say." He vaguely heard her say goodbye, then tossed the phone back on the front seat. He'd show her what goin' all night really meant. Some good lovin' would go a long way to straightening out that attitude she'd had for a few weeks. She'd beg him not to leave. He reached down and cranked NWA until his windows shook.

Just after nightfall, he rolled down Camy's street in the way-too-white-bread development she lived in. The upstairs was dark and a few lights were on in the rear of the downstairs. Jimmy parked in the driveway, something she normally didn't approve of. In fact, she usually liked him to park a house or two down. She said it was her old-fashioned streak. She didn't want the neighbors to think she allowed men to spend the night.

He knocked on the front door and it flew open almost instantly.

All he could do was stare and say, "Wow."

"Like it?" She laid on her Dixie drawl and smiled.

He nodded, taking her in his arms. The sheer material of the tiny pink teddy smelled like lilac. She bit him on the neck playfully and took his hand, leading him through the living room to what was normally the guest bedroom downstairs. They had done it in there before, rattling the huge brass bed frame and tilting the mirror on the vanity to watch themselves.

Once in the room, she turned and whispered in his ear, "Let's get dirty tonight."

"Anything you want, baby."

She winked and pulled a matching pink teddy from the dresser near the small bathroom.

"Really?" This *was* new.

She held it up to him and nodded vigorously. Then she pulled out some handcuffs.

That wasn't too unusual. He shrugged and started to yank off his shirt.

Camy turned him toward the bathroom and said, "Come out ready. I wanna be surprised." Then she gently shoved him toward the open door.

Inside he flipped the light switch, turning on the bright, clear lights around the mirror. He held the teddy up to the mirror and shook his head. If it made her wild, why not. Even though he'd rather just do it, sleep an hour and do it again. He slipped out of his street clothes and had to survey himself naked for a few moments, then dropped the teddy over his head. It looked miniscule but had amazing stretch capabilities. He pulled it down but was unable to button the crotch over his genitals. What did it matter? He checked himself in the mirror again, then, satisfied, he shut off the lights and made his entrance.

"Look at you," said Camy from a sprawled position on the queen-sized bed. She patted the mattress. "C'mon, stud."

He bounded into the bed and grabbed her, trying to unsnap the teddy immediately.

"Hang on there, big fella." She stroked his rising erection. "Let's do it right." She pulled the handcuffs off the small table next to the bed.

"If that's what you want." He obligingly stretched out his arms and allowed Camy to run the cuffs through the brass frame and secure his hands.

"That's a little tight, baby."

She smiled. "That's not all that's tight."

He felt his breath get short as she slipped off the bed and made a show of walking around the bed. She went back to the dresser and retrieved two sets of leg chains.

"Where'd you get those?"

"Amazing what being nice to the Marshals will get you." She casually strung one set on each side of the foot of the bed frame, then walked to the bathroom. A couple of seconds later, she walked out with two washcloths. She folded one and placed it inside the metal cuff on the leg chain, then secured his right ankle. The cloth made the tight cuff comfortable. He sighed as she did the same to his left leg.

"Try it," she said as she gazed at his toned body, spread-eagled on the bed. The pink teddy stretched to its seams around his chest, the white, puffy frills on the shoulders brushing his nose.

He pulled his hands, then each leg, and said, "Baby, that's tight. Now let's get dirty."

She ran a hand down his chest. "You bet, baby," she purred. Then she walked to the door to the family room and opened it a crack. She walked back toward the bathroom, flicking on the overhead light in the ceiling fan. The room was suddenly lit up like a classroom.

Jimmy squeezed his eyes shut. "Baby, I know you like to see me, but that's a little bright." Behind his closed eyelids, he saw a brighter flash and opened his eyes. Two men in bedsheets with pillowcases over their heads like old-time Klansmen stood at the foot of the bed. One had a camera in his hand. He shot another picture, and the flash blinked.

Each man had holes cut out of the pillowcases. One man fumbled with the case to get a better view. Camy remained motionless by the bathroom door, still in the see-through teddy. The broader of the two men, the one without the camera, pulled a slender three-foot baseball bat from behind his back. He slapped it in his hand. Jimmy could read the Fish Billy logo on the handle and knew it was used to club hooked game fish. A chill ran down his back and he felt his bowels loosen.

One man said, "You are so fucked."

At which moment Jimmy's bladder just emptied.

"Jesus," said the man.

Daniel Wells looked down from the cab of the Freightliner with great pride. He had walked onto the Big Rig Academy grounds unseen, used the key he had stolen to start and then drive a tractor right off the lot and through traffic with hardly an incident. He had clipped a parked Chevy, then bumped another car near Seventy-second Avenue, just hard enough to knock it onto the median. The man looked dazed and no one else was around this time of night, so Wells wasn't worried. First he was headed over to Emerson-Picolo Transportation, and then his problems would begin. He had to hook up to a trailer, alone, then get off the lot. He knew no one was there, he'd already driven past. He had used a series of stolen cars during the evening to get from one spot to the next. They had all been Hondas, that being the only car he knew how to hot-wire. Getting into the cars wasn't pretty, either. He just shattered the side window and opened the doors. He turned on Thirty-sixth Street and slowed almost immediately as he came up on the lot. He stopped the rig with its blinkers on and hustled to the gate. He tried the key he'd kept from the year before and it worked perfectly. Sliding open the double gate, he trotted back to the truck. After a minute of maneuvering, he was in the lot and close to the small tanker opposite the open gate. That solved a couple of problems. First and most important, it was pointed in the right direction. Second, it was fairly small, about two-thirds the size of a full tanker. He'd checked it to make sure it was full. The cargo was avgas. The small warning placard on the side had the numbers 100/130 written on it, confirming that the cargo was, in fact, aviation fuel. It would blow. He had already tested that theory.

He backed the truck, slowly watching the rearview the whole way. This was something they usually used two men to do. He heard a thump, then a click. He threw the tractor out of gear and set the brake. Jumping out, he raced to the rear, only to discover he had missed the "fifth wheel," the connector for the trailer, by three feet to the left. Now the trailer was hooked on the truck's supporting beam.

Back in the cab, he gunned the engine to pull free, but ended up dragging the tanker a few feet. The noise and sparks were horrendous, especially considering the tanker's load. He hopped out and inspected the connection again. Still hooked to the side.

Then he used his problem-solving mind. He let some air out of the rear tires. When they were half empty, he jumped back in the cab, and the tractor pulled out smoothly.

He lined up the tractor again and then inched it back. As soon as he heard metal on metal, he hopped out and inspected the alignment.

"Incredible," he said out loud to himself. The connection lined up perfectly, the ball of the trailer-tanker directly in the center of the fifth wheel. Just like a pro. He backed the tractor some more until it locked in place, then secured the trailer, brake lines and electrical connections. His first solo. His heart raced with the engine as he headed toward the open gate. He couldn't resist blasting the horn like a real trucker. No one was around, and if they were, who would expect a thief to announce himself like that? He was on top of the world.

He reached the gate and turned east on Thirty-sixth Street. He turned a little sharply and took out the fence with the tanker-trailer. He shrugged as he dragged a seventy-foot length of chain-link fence a block before it broke free. He looked in the mirrors. The right one was missing. No problem—still no one around.

An hour later, having to drive much more conservatively and even taking the tanker through part of his planned route, Wells parked it on the side of a residential street that had a patch of pine trees and grass on one side. Two other big rigs sat there. If someone cared to check, they'd think he was just another trucker visiting someone on a long trip.

He hopped out and found a Honda a block away. A swat with the blunt edge of his Buck knife and the window cracked. He used his elbow to finish. It made almost no noise. He was inside the small blue Civic, about to rip the steering column to pieces, when he noticed someone already had. He didn't know why; if the car was locked, someone had a key. He went with it, touched the two already stripped wires, which caused the small engine to hum to life. He pulled out, appreciating the ease of handling compared to a big rig. A block later, he turned onto a small side street and could see the Orange Bowl right in front of him. That was the best landmark for miles around. He'd thought about leaving the tractor-trailer in the Orange Bowl's parking lot, but this was less conspicuous. After the Big Rig Academy reported the theft, someone might notice it in the parking lot.

Wells headed south to his duplex to finish the step van, because that was all he'd drive from now on.

thirty

"now, *this* is embarrassing," said Derrick Sutter, pulling off his makeshift Klan hood. Tasker followed his lead, waving it in front of his face to dissipate the odor.

Camy, still standing in the room, quietly slipped into the bathroom, but not before both Tasker and Sutter got a good eyeful. Tasker believed that was a calculated move. He wasn't sure to what purpose, but he appreciated it nonetheless.

Sutter said, "See, I told you I knew a way to tie up the FBI loose ends." He smiled, showing his gold tooth on the side of his mouth. "I just wish his end was a little more tied up. I think he shit the bed."

Tasker shook his head. "Nope, just had his bladder let go. Happens to the best of us." He winced at the pain his own voice brought to his banged-up head.

Sutter snapped two more digital photos while Jimmy Lail thrashed in the bed.

"You guys are in such deep shit! This is kidnapping."

The bathroom door opened and Camy, now covered by a thick terrycloth robe, said to Jimmy, "I think they call this kinky sex. I don't recall you objecting."

Jimmy's face flared red as he yanked his legs again. "Now, tell me, what the fuck is going on?"

Tasker kept his voice calm and even. "Blackmail. Simple and direct." He looked over to Sutter, who snapped another photo. "You talk and we erase the photos. Tell us everything and you can have the camera. Hold out and you're an Internet star before you get to work in the morning."

Jimmy stared at him. "I never thought you'd stoop this low."

"You should be more optimistic." Tasker waited for Jimmy to calm down and said, "Now tell me about Sal Bolini's connection to Wells."

"Kiss my ass."

Sutter smiled, handed the camera to Tasker, and said, "Maybe if I snuggle up close and bury my face in the covers. That'd make a good photo. At least it'd look like he has some taste."

"Fuck you both!"

Sutter started to unbutton his shirt.

Jimmy immediately said, "Okay, okay, okay. What do you want to know?"

Tasker asked, "Is Bolini protecting Wells?"

"Sort of."

"Did he tip him about the search warrant at his house?"

Jimmy hesitated.

Sutter unfastened another button on his shirt, and Tasker raised the camera.

Jimmy nodded with some passion. They had definitely found his weak spot.

Tasker continued in a good interrogation voice. "Has he told him to lay low?"

Another nod.

"Why?"

Jimmy shrugged. Sutter started to open his shirt.

"Okay, okay, stop doing that." He cleared his throat. "Wells has been giving us info for years. He's saved a lot of lives."

"According to who?"

"Bolini."

Sutter stepped in. "What about the Klan surveillance? That was all bullshit, wasn't it?"

Jimmy nodded. "It was designed to buy time for Wells to clear up some personal business so he could leave the area."

"What personal business?" asked Tasker.

"Dunno."

Sutter slid one shoulder out of his shirt.

Jimmy kept an even voice. "You can come down here and give me a blow-job, but I really don't know. Now, have I earned that camera?"

"Did Bolini know he bombed the cruise ship?"

"Yeah. After. Wells said he wouldn't do it again."

Tasker was speechless. Too bad this moron wasn't the responsible party.

Jimmy said again, "Do I get the camera?"

"One more thing."

"What's that?"

"We need you to call Bolini and set up a breakfast meeting."

"Where?"

Tasker said, "Denny's over off Thirty-sixth."

Jimmy thought about it, then nodded.

Tasker looked at him. "And after I meet with him, you'll get the camera to see the photos erased. I don't want him warned."

Jimmy said, "That's bullshit. I want that camera or there's no deal."

Tasker looked at Camy. "All right, leave his ass locked up till morning."

Jimmy said, "Shit, get me a phone."

Camy added, "I'll keep an eye on him tonight." She winked at Jimmy, who brightened slightly.

Tasker saw the look Sutter gave the chained FBI man and thought it was best to get him out of there fast. Besides, if Tasker didn't get off his feet and give his aching head, back, shoulder and hip a rest, he might faint.

Tasker watched Sal Bolini park his Bureau-issued Ford and walk into the Denny's without a glance around the lot. A minute later, Tasker strolled in the front door and then right to Bolini's table just as the waitress brought his coffee.

Bolini said, "What're *you* doing here?"

"Filling in for Lail."

Bolini took a second and then said, "Vanilla Ice spill his guts?"

Tasker just smiled. "He had reason to."

"You didn't hurt the little shit, did you?"

"I didn't think you'd care about things like that."

Bolini shrugged. "You got me all wrong. In fact, all I care about is the public good. Did you hurt Lail?"

"Not physically." Tasker remembered the look on Camy's face as they left her house and added, "He was all right when I last saw him."

Bolini took a sip of his coffee and waved away the waitress when she wandered over. He looked at Tasker silently.

Finally, Tasker asked, "Why?"

"You wouldn't understand. Cops never do."

"Try me."

"He was a good source. He knew how to keep his mouth shut."

"But he bombed a ship. He killed a guy."

"What? The baggage handler? He wasn't even an American."

Tasker stared at him with his mouth open.

"That's what I'm saying. If it was up to cops, you guys would just arrest him without thinking of all the good he could do. He saved a lot of lives. He kept Turkey Point from getting blown up by Al-Soud and Jourdi."

Tasker shook his head in frustration. "But they couldn't have done it without Wells. He tricked them. The device Al-Soud described to me wouldn't have worked."

"Then they would've picked another target. The point is we stopped them."

"I thought the point was to enforce the law."

"I have enforced a lot more than you." Bolini's voice became sharper.

"Why'd he do the cruise ship?"

"I have no idea. We had a gentleman's agreement not to discuss it."

Tasker felt like drawing his Beretta and sticking it in the FBI agent's face to bring him back to reality.

Bolini said, "If I had been there the day you morons arrested him, I could've put a stop to it right then. Thank God you're persistent."

"What's that mean?"

"I saw you were trying to help him after you realized your mistake. Who do you think sent you that little intel photo?"

"You were in it from the beginning." Tasker felt like a little kid.

"I'm tellin' you, Tasker, he's a great source. Look at me. He put me on top. You back off and we can work something out. Make you a star over there at FDLE."

Tasker balled his fist but took a deep breath instead of throwing the punch.

"What about his next little act?"

"What next act?"

"Whatever he has planned for this afternoon. He told his wife to steer clear of downtown."

"That whore. She's not smart enough to know a warning if it bit her on that luscious ass of hers."

"Can you contact him?"

"Not unless he calls me. I'm not worried."

"Why not?"

"He's on your dime now."

Sal Bolini was a little shaken by his breakfast meeting with the serious state cop. He'd known about the cruise ship and let it slide. He had no idea why Wells had done it but knew the guy had a screw loose. He loved to see the shit stirred. It was obvious, the way he wanted to be at arrests as the undercover when he didn't have to be. He once told Bolini how the only excitement he felt was in watching people run scared. And it seemed to have gotten worse in the past two years. Every time they had an arrest or search warrant, Wells had to be there. Still, Bolini had no idea he had anything else planned. He'd told the FBI agent he had to clear up some family matters. Bolini figured it was with that kooky wife of his, or some money issues. Not some kind of stunt to scare people.

Bolini dug in his inside suit pocket to find his secret address book. He had Wells' pager, which only he was allowed to call. After all, the FBI had paid for it. He dialed the Miami number.

Five minutes later, Bolini's cell phone rang. He said, "Talk to me, Daniel."

"Hello, Sal." Wells' voice was clear, but there was wind noise and traffic in the background.

Bolini said, "What's goin' on?"

"Nothing, Sal."

"When you leavin' town?"

"Tonight."

Bolini's stomach turned a little. "Can we meet?"

"No time today, Sal."

"Later, before you leave?"

A semi blasted its horn on the interstate. Bolini realized he heard the same horn over the phone. Wells was close.

"Naw, Sal. We're done meeting. You always treated me right, so I'll give you one last piece of info for free."

"What's that?"

"Stay out of downtown Miami today." The phone went dead.

Bolini absently put it back in his coat pocket. He thought, Oh shit, what have I done? How was this going to make him look? He could always blame Tasker.

He reached for his phone book.

He dialed quickly, tapping his foot as it rang for a third, then a fourth time. Finally, he heard a male's voice say, "Hello."

Bolini said, "No bullshit. We gotta meet right now."

thirty-one

daniel wells watched the dial of the old fuel pump roll up slowly. He put five gallons in the van itself. Why not, it wasn't going anywhere after today. Then he started filling the tank he'd welded inside the van. He was careful not to let the clerk see he had the nozzle actually inside the beat-up step van. It probably didn't matter because the guy never looked up from his perch inside the tiny building. There were sixty-five gallons in it already, and he intended to use at least eighty gallons. He looked at the tank. No leaks, and the bags of scrap metal fit on top and around the sides like moldable sandbags.

He looked at his watch. No, no, he wanted to wait at least two more hours. He looked up at the interstate a few blocks east. He'd put the van in place in an hour and a half. First he'd find some place to eat. His stomach had been growling, but he was so excited he hadn't eaten since yesterday afternoon. He needed to clear his mind and think. After this he'd have to clear out, get the kids and be ready for anything.

He shut the pump off at ninety-six gallons, including what he'd put in the van's tank. He checked his wallet. A hundred and sixty-three bucks pretty much wiped him out. He walked toward the cashier, looking over his shoulder at the van. Still no leaks. He had stripped off the sign for his business, but you could still see the outline of the letters. In a couple of hours, that old van would be in a million pieces and no one would care what was written on it.

"We've got to make this work even though it's a desperation Hail Mary," said Tasker, looking at Derrick Sutter, Camy Parks and the dozen or so agents recruited from FDLE and ATF. Tasker hadn't briefed them on anything specific, only that Daniel Wells was a fugitive, was armed and had last been seen driving a blue Ford Ranger pickup. They were at the last rest stop on Florida's turnpike extension near Homestead. Tasker went on: "You've each got a grid on the map. We've got no specific leads, but with some luck we might spot him. He's supposed to be moving today, probably in the truck, but you've all got photos, too." Tasker looked at the other cops. "Use the Nextel if you see anything and we'll all come running. Don't make a move on your own." Tasker closed his eyes as his headache from his ride in Wells' truck came back. Tasker had told the others that he'd fallen off a neighbor's motorcycle and that it just looked bad. He said he felt fine, which was one of the biggest lies of his life.

"You okay?" asked Sutter quietly.

Tasker nodded. "We go until there's no chance left. Any questions?"

All of them started for their cars.

Camy walked over to Sutter and Tasker. "He should be in bed," she said.

"Tell him."

"Look, I'm fine, I'll ride with Derrick."

Sutter said, "I could see the others believed you when you said you fell off a motorcycle."

"Really?" He brightened a little.

"No."

Tasker's head hurt too bad to worry about what rumors might spread about him.

Tasker's phone rang. He answered it, "Bill Tasker."

"No bullshit. We gotta meet right now."

"Who's this?"

"Bolini."

"So?"

"What if I said I believe you?"

Twenty-five minutes later, after a harrowing ride up the turnpike, Tasker, Sutter, Camy and Bolini stood near Interstate 95 and downtown Miami.

"You sure?" asked Sutter.

"Look, I heard the horn here and it came over the phone, too. I'm tellin' you he's right around here."

Tasker looked at him. "Either you've come to your senses or you think we're the most gullible cops in the world."

"No bullshit. He's here." Bolini paused. "He gave me some information."

"What?"

"He told me to stay out of Miami today."

Sutter said, "Oh shit, we need to get some help out here."

Tasker said, "We still have no specific leads. If he heads back south, our guys will see him. What if you get your guys at the substation to cover Thirty-sixth Street north and we'll go from there to downtown?"

Sutter immediately jumped on his phone.

Bolini said, "I'll keep trying to get him to answer his pager."

Tasker nodded, but didn't want to stray too far from the older FBI man. He still didn't trust him completely. As he stood there with Camy, a small, tricked-out Honda pulled up.

Camy smiled. "What are you doing here?"

Jimmy Lail said, "Bolini called me." He had no accent but his Texas drawl. He wouldn't look Tasker in the face.

Camy gave him a hug. "I thought you were okay."

He glared at her. "With you, not with him."

Tasker nodded. "That's fair. I'll get the camera."

As Camy followed him to his Cherokee, Tasker had to ask, "Why's he pissed off at me but not you?"

"I'm the one who unlocked him last night. We had a nice talk and he's feeling a little better about himself and his roots." She smiled slyly. "I'll send you the bill from the company that's going to clean my bed downstairs."

"He still your boyfriend?"

"He never really *was* my boyfriend. But now he understands that."

"Can we trust him?"

She looked over at Jimmy by the Honda. "Sure. He can help. He knows what Wells looks like. What could he screw up now?"

thirty-two

miami police detective derrick sutter was now completely in his element and intended to show the FBI what that meant. Whereas the Feds were just driving around aimlessly hoping to see Wells, Sutter knew who to ask. He'd already called four of his snitches and had them out and about. Now he was checking with the convenience stores and gas stations along Seventh Avenue. They might not talk to most cops but they'd talk to him. And he didn't have to spend half an hour introducing himself. They all knew him. This was what local cops were paid for: knowing the community and its residents.

The first three places were able to say quickly they hadn't seen a blue pickup or even a white man anytime during the day. Sutter gave them each his cell number, increasing the number of eyes working for him every time he stopped. If Wells was still in the area, Sutter would hear about it.

Farther south, moving toward a more industrial area, Sutter stopped at a place with a sign that simply said GAS. The clerk was encased in a cement building the size of a port-a-let with one pane of thick bulletproof glass and an old window air conditioner cemented into the side of the building. It hummed and labored in the humid Florida heat.

Sutter tapped on the glass with his open badge case.

The clerk looked at him without moving.

"I need to talk to you," said Sutter in a loud voice.

"So talk," said the young black clerk calmly, as he set down some kind of textbook and leaned into a microphone. His hair was braided neatly against his scalp.

"Come on out."

"Can't."

"What d'you mean?"

"No key. Boss locks me in for four hours, then lets me out for a break. That's how he keeps three stations running."

Sutter snapped his head back. "Where do you shit?"

"I don't."

"What if there's an emergency?"

"I call his cell."

"What if you got robbed?"

"Can't be. No way in and the glass is solid." He rapped the tinted slab of ballistic glass with the edge of his book.

Sutter scratched his head. This was a new one. "Tell you what, I'm busy right now, but I'm gonna rap with your boss later. That cool?"

"Cool," said the young man, obviously not a fan of the system.

"Let me ask you about your customers. You been here since eleven or so?"

"Yep, since ten."

"You see a white guy in a blue pickup?"

"Nope. Only white man I seen was in a big ol' step van. He bought a lot of gas, too."

Sutter nodded and started to walk away. He paused and opened the folder he'd carried all day long. He pulled out an eight-by-ten photo of Daniel Wells. "Was it this man?" he asked the clerk, holding the photo to the window.

"That was the man," said the clerk with no hesitation at all.

Daniel Wells finished his second Cuban sandwich. This was a great little place. He sat at a small patio table under an umbrella somewhere south of where he needed to be. He ate a leisurely lunch, waiting for the afternoon traffic to start to kick in. This quiet lunch place catered to truckers, and he was a trucker—right?

He sat in the cool shade and drank a Coke, satisfied with himself. He'd planned and prepared this huge event all by himself. No sponsors, no extra cash, no cops on his ass, no one to even drive him around. He'd just used his American know-how and ingenuity. This would take some damn Arabs fifteen men to do, and half of them would blab. He didn't need his own terrorist cell. He could be a damn example to the young people of America. If you use your head, plan and follow through, there is nothing you can't achieve.

He finished his drink, laid a healthy three-dollar tip on the table and crossed the street to his van. In ten minutes, he was driving past the Orange Bowl. He could see the Interstate 95 traffic building. A smile crossed his face as he headed north to get on the interstate headed south. He'd already decided that the perfect place to leave the van was the overpass where 95 tangled with the Dolphin Expressway on the way to Northwest Eighth Street, creating a spiderweb of ramps, one on top of the other. He waved to a couple of kids who looked at him like he was the ice cream man.

Tasker had spread the word as soon as Sutter called. Wells was now in a step van. Some of the agents from down south were headed up to the city. He had a lot of people working on extremely vague information. But they were all ready to do their duty. Bolini had been very hesitant to call in FBI agents. Tasker didn't know if the Fed thought he'd look like a fool for letting Wells operate for so long or if it was something else. He didn't have time to talk to Bolini about it now and wasn't sure the FBI would be able to help if they did show up.

Tasker knew the van with NARANJA ENGINEERING written on the side. A clerk from a gas station said the lettering was peeled off but you could still see it. Tasker was so worried about what Wells had planned that he hardly noticed the constant throbbing of his head or the ache in his ribs or the increasingly bloodstained bandages over his various cuts. He knew that if they had enough time they'd find him. He kept his eyes open for anything that moved. Bolini was on the next street, trying to coordinate the search with Tasker. They moved their cars like sharks through the unsuspecting drivers and pedestrians crowding the streets.

On Eighth Avenue, Tasker, cruising slowly in his Cherokee, spotted a van taking the ramp up to Interstate 95.

He clicked his Nextel radio to reach Bolini. "I may have him."

"Where?" came back after the beep.

"Getting on a southbound ramp to 95." Tasker punched the gas and closed the distance until he saw the side of the van. Clearly the removed letters said NARANJA. He grabbed his Nextel. "That's him, that's him. Ninety-five southbound." He scanned the phone for Sutter and clicked it again. "Derrick, we see him. Southbound from Fifty-fourth Street on 95."

A beep, then Sutter's response: "We're on our way."

Tasker was up the ramp and in southbound traffic in thirty seconds. The van was in sight ahead in the right lane. Bolini pulled up behind Tasker. They followed him a mile. He made no funny moves and gave no hint of where he was headed. Tasker closed the gap to three cars. He didn't care if Wells burned him now. There was no way he was getting out of Tasker's sight again. One way or the other, this would be over soon.

Then Wells slowed to a crawl and started to pull off at the Eighth Street ramp near the Orange Bowl and the Miami PD. The four-story rise of ramps where the north-south highways met the east-west stood in front of him.

"What the hell?" said Tasker quietly to himself.

The van came to a complete stop right under the overpass, on the shoulder of the road.

Tasker didn't like the looks of this one bit. He started to hit the gas, but was cut off by a big refrigerated truck which abruptly slowed to a near stop. Tasker couldn't see anything but the truck's rear doors.

Wells patted the van's dash like it was a dying pet. "You been good to me." He looked out the window, then up to the layers of roads running overhead. He smiled and twisted around in his seat. A four-inch square with a simple battery-operated clock fastened to it was strapped onto the interior gas tank. Wells never used the same type of timer twice. Sometimes digital, sometimes analog, sometimes motion sensors. He loved the variety. This timer had about five minutes on it. Long enough to clear the area and move on to the next phase of his plan.

As he was leaning out of the van, ready to move, he noticed two other cars on the shoulder, then realized one was Bolini. It only took another second to recognize Tasker in that ugly gold Cherokee. "Oh shit!" he breathed out and leaned back into the van, pushing the minute hand ahead four minutes with his finger. He didn't know how long he had left, but it wasn't much time. He jumped through the van and out the passenger door, then let his momentum take him down the little embankment until he ran across the loop coming off the interstate, headed toward the Dolphin Expressway, and then for the fence in a dead run.

thirty-three

tasker jumped from his cherokee and fell into an all-out dash after the fleeing Wells. The loose gravel on the shoulder of the highway made him slip one way, then the other, jarring his battered body, but he regained his footing and kept moving. Sensing Sal Bolini trying to stay close behind him, he focused on Wells.

Tasker skidded to a stop in front of the van, torn between chasing Wells and checking the van. He glanced inside, then leaned in the open doorway into the van and froze, seeing the clock on the metal box welded into the rear. He knew how much gas had gone into the box a few hours ago. It didn't take a genius to figure out what would happen when the big hand of the clock caught the little hand. His bladder almost let go when Bolini skidded into him, saying, "What is it?"

Tasker leaned out of the way. "Look."

Bolini stuck his head in, then popped out. "You know anything about detonators?"

"Enough to see we only got a minute left."

"What do we do?" Bolini started to pant like a dog.

"It looks like we could just rip the clock off the tank and it'll be inactivated."

Bolini shook his head. "No, no, no good. Wells is too fuckin' smart for that. He'd have it booby-trapped."

Tasker thought about the CS Mace trap and had to agree. He looked up at the traffic. "We gotta do something. This thing could take out the whole overpass."

Bolini floated a suggestion. "What about running?"

Tasker just stared at him. He then jumped into the back and started pulling the bags of scrap metal away from the tank. He handed them to Bolini, who tossed them away from the van.

Bolini said, "I got an idea. The keys in it? We could drive it outta here."

Tasker looked and shook his head. "I got a plan B," he said, jumping out and racing back to his Cherokee. He jumped in, cranked the engine and threw it into drive two.

Bolini jumped back as Tasker eased the Cherokee onto the bumper of the van, then gunned the engine. The big van wobbled but moved forward, following the contour of the ground. It slid off the shoulder onto the slope that led to a pond in the center of the loop coming off the interstate.

The van picked up momentum as the decline of the slope grew. Tasker started to back off with the Cherokee, but gravity had grabbed it too and he started sliding in the loose dirt right behind the van. He hit the brakes, but in the pebbles and debris on the slope the Cherokee didn't slow down at all.

The van hit the water with a splash, then rolled and floated into the shallow water. Tasker couldn't stop the Cherokee, and followed. The Jeep felt like it was sucked in by the van as Tasker reached over to open the door and get the hell out. The quickly rising water slammed the door back on him. He hit the window button, but the electrical system had already shorted.

Tasker prayed that the water would disarm the bomb as well. He knew the Cherokee wouldn't be any protection against a gas bomb that big. Even with the bags of shrapnel removed from the van.

He banged on the window with his fist, then, without hesitation, pulled his Beretta from the belly bag, pointed out the side window, pulled the trigger and blew it out. He tried aiming low so the round would travel harmlessly into the muddy water.

He slid out of the shattered window, feeling the glass slice his left knee and bumping his back hard as he reacted to the cut. He flopped completely into the water and struggled to his feet in the four-foot-deep pond. He slogged to the edge, knowing the bomb was about to explode. Gasping for breath, he flopped onto the bank, exhausted.

Wells was in a pretty good trot with his Ruger .22 tight in his right hand. He was passing some apartments near the interstate but hadn't heard a blast yet. It didn't really matter. It was just to divert traffic anyway. He was a little surprised Tasker or Bolini weren't chasing him. They may have been crazy enough to defuse his bomb. Wouldn't be hard. Just yank off the timer. He looked over his shoulder again. Nothing. Then, as he reached the next block, he heard it. Like a beautiful symphony. The boom reverberated through the neighborhood and houses, almost sounding like several explosions. He looked back to see the fireball just above the trees. That didn't make sense, because the overpass should have absorbed the blast and fireball. It was pretty all the same.

He turned at the last block and saw his semi still secure and waiting for him. He fumbled for the keys and climbed up the small ladder to the cab. He cranked over the engine and gave the motor a little time to warm up. Looking up, he noticed the traffic already backing up from the van blast. Black smoke was rising from the area of the massive overpass. The way these people stopped to stare at a car with a flat tire, traffic would be backed up to Broward County soon, and people would be fighting to get off the highway and crowd onto the city streets.

Tasker started to get up when he felt hands on him. He looked up as Bolini dragged him out of the mud and onto his feet.

"Move it," Bolini grunted as he pulled Tasker along on a trot.

From the shoulder of Interstate 95, Tasker saw Sutter, Camy and Jimmy Lail running toward them. Bolini pointed to the fence and shouted, "Cross the fence here and cut him off. He's right there." Bolini pointed into the neighborhood just west of the interstate.

Without a word, Sutter and Jimmy turned and bolted for the fence, Sutter taking it in one graceful leap. Camy raced back to Jimmy's little Honda on the side of the interstate. Tasker watched as she backed the car and turned it facing the fence separating the road from the neighborhood. She gunned the engine and ripped through the old battered chain-link barrier.

Tasker was running on his own power now, headed for Bolini's car, when he heard the boom and then felt the shock wave of the blast. They both turned to see the fireball climb from the exit loop and rise straight into the air where no overpass of concrete could block it and cause damage. They both headed back toward the blast and were relieved when they saw no cars charred on the loop. The bushes around the pond smoldered, and it looked like the water had absorbed a lot of the blast.

Tasker's gold Jeep Cherokee was an unrecognizable heap in the shallows of the ponds. The van looked like Godzilla had kicked it. Tasker still smiled.

Bolini patted him hard on the back. "Let's get that son of a bitch."

Sutter gulped air after the first two blocks. He was good at sprints and even the occasional long jump, but distance events were not his strong suit. Jimmy Lail had surprised him by having some wind and good legs. He was half a block ahead, weaving through yards and checking parked cars with his Sig nine-millimeter already drawn and ready.

They'd come straight from the interstate and headed toward the Orange Bowl, then cut into this neighborhood. A kid on a bike said he'd just seen a man jogging and pointed them in his direction. They knew he had to be here somewhere, but this street was about to end at some pine trees. Then Sutter intended to go left toward the Orange Bowl and send the FBI man right back toward the interstate.

Sutter started to notice a second uncomfortable sensation other than being winded. He was starting to sweat. In good slacks and a nice shirt. That didn't happen to a cop that was thinking properly.

Then came the blast. Just the concussion and sound made Sutter and Jimmy duck. He looked over his shoulder and saw the fireball rising from a few blocks behind, the orange and yellow dissipating into the sky.

"Oh shit!" Sutter said. "We need to check on Tasker and Bolini."

Jimmy Lail was too far ahead of him to hear.

When Sutter was about to yell to him, Jimmy saw something at the corner and aimed his gun. He waved excitedly.

Sutter used his sprinter's speed and was up to Jimmy in a few seconds and immediately saw the idling semi tractor-trailer with Wells in the front seat. A smaller tanker was hitched behind the cab. Sutter didn't want to think what was in it.

Jimmy said, "I'll stop this asshole." He marched forward with his pistol out for Wells to see.

Wells opened the truck's cab door, leaned out and popped two rounds off with a small-caliber pistol.

Jimmy Lail immediately dodged behind a parked car and crouched.

Sutter moved toward the truck, his Glock drawn. He fired once at the truck cab to keep Wells' head down, then advanced quickly. He could hear Jimmy, behind him now, start to shoot, too. The sound of the nine-millimeter rounds smacking into the semi cab made Wells duck.

The truck started to move, but when Sutter raised his pistol he felt a stabbing pain in his left foot and ankle. He went down, watching as Wells carefully drove around him to get the big rig moving. Sutter turned and saw Jimmy dive out of the truck's path as Wells blasted the giant air horn.

Now Camy in the Honda turned down the street. She squealed to a stop next to Sutter and burst out of the car to him. She looked at him, then pulled a white gym towel from inside the car and immediately held it to his ankle, saying, "You'll be okay."

"What happened? I thought I twisted my ankle."

Jimmy was with him now. "Man, are you okay? I'm so sorry."

Sutter just looked at him. "Don't tell me."

"I didn't mean to shoot you."

Sutter wanted to smack him, but turned to Camy. "Catch the truck, catch the truck. Wells is in it."

She looked up quickly, but no one was sure where the semi had gone after it took the first turn.

thirty-four

tasker felt like a train-wreck survivor. He was wobbling his way through the neighborhood after his partners and Wells, blood running down his face, hair burnt in patches, legs bloody and soaking wet. This was no dignified day at the office.

Bolini was checking the area of the blast for injuries and to explain to responding cops what happened. Tasker couldn't risk losing Wells. He was about to sit down and rest for a second when he heard the gunfire. It was coming from the end of the street. He picked up his pitiful pace.

He reached the last street just in time to see a semi tractor-trailer driven by Daniel Wells roll down the street, blaring his horn. In its wake he saw Jimmy Lail standing with Camy over Sutter, who was down, a block away. He turned and moved as fast as he could to the injured Miami cop.

"What happened? You all right?" he gasped as he came upon his partner.

Sutter seemed more pissed than injured. "That jerk-weed shot me."

"Why?"

Jimmy, walking up behind, mumbled, "It was an accident."

Tasker stood up and spun to meet the FBI man face to face, but instantly realized how embarrassed Lail was and that it really had been an accident.

Camy started to jump in the Honda. Jimmy followed her. She said, "We need to find the truck."

Tasker nodded his head. "Go, go. Bolini will be here in a second."

A minute later, Bolini pulled up in his Ford Taurus and Tasker grabbed Sutter, then piled in, Sutter careful with his leg but fully mobile.

As the car started to roll, Bolini said, "Wells shot you?"

Sutter shook his head but didn't elaborate, and Bolini let it ride.

"Which way?" asked Bolini.

Tasker said, "He's gotta be headed to the area where the undercover Miami cop saw him. Head toward Biscayne, we'll pick him up."

Bolini stepped on the gas.

From the front passenger seat, Tasker turned around to Sutter. "That's it!"

"What?"

"The van was a diversion. The real attack is the tanker. He wanted to drive the tanker into the small side streets. That's why he learned to drive the big rigs."

Sutter's eyes widened. "You mean he's gonna detonate the tanker?"

"Exactly. And that'll make the van look like a firecracker."

Bolini pushed the Taurus up to fifty in the tightening traffic, swerving in and out and up over curbs. He fumbled with his Nextel. "Hey," he yelled into the handset. "It's Sal. I need every swinging dick in that office out here. I'm going down to Biscayne by Bayfront Park. We got a semi that may be used as a bomb." He listened to someone, then said, "Now!" And shut the phone. He turned to Tasker and said, "We gotta get to him before he arms the bomb. I'm no bomb tech. None of that red-wire, blue-wire bullshit."

"I'm with you," said Tasker. He still didn't trust the FBI man, but he'd been a help and now seemed to realize the truth of the situation. Sutter sat, quietly simmering in the back. Tasker was impressed with Sutter's restraint, unless it was due to loss of blood.

Tasker turned to face his quiet partner in the backseat. "You okay?"

Sutter, holding the red-stained towel Camy had given him to his ankle, nodded curtly.

Tasker's Nextel chirped, followed by Camy's voice. "We're off the interstate, headed for Biscayne. I'm gonna call Miami PD and fill them in."

Tasker responded, "Ten-four. We're near the interstate, coming up on Fifth Street."

When Bolini made a turn onto Fifth, heading for the Port of Miami, he said, "Up there, straight ahead."

The tanker was slowing in the growing traffic. There were still a lot of cars between them and Wells.

"Shit," said Bolini, slowing to a stop behind traffic and pounding the steering wheel in frustration.

Tasker yanked the door handle and was gone.

Wells was glowing. He had slowed in exactly the kind of traffic he had expected. No cops questioned the tanker's movement because all the cops had hightailed it to Interstate 95 a minute after his van went up. Now, with the radio playing Toby Keith and the air conditioner humming, Wells felt like he was in control and about to send the whole world out of control.

He shifted his eyes to look out the side rearview, but remembered he'd banged it off on the gate to Emerson-Picolo Transportation. Since leaving the little neighborhood by the Orange Bowl, he had knocked off the left side mirror, too, and taken out a mailbox, a parked moped, two parked cars and clipped a lunch truck. The truck was the only one anyone noticed. The owner jumped out, screaming something in Spanish while shaking his fist. Wells just waved and got back into the groove of the music.

He looked at the buildings on both sides of the street. It would be better to go three or four blocks south, closer to downtown. This road was still a little open for traffic to the port and Bayfront Park.

He changed radio stations until he caught a news bulletin about the interstate. A woman solemnly reported, "A car fire on I-95 near the exit to Northwest Eighth Street is starting to cause major tie-ups. No word yet on the cause or injuries. The Florida Highway Patrol is on the scene and we will give you updates as they come available. Avoid this area if at all possible."

Wells smiled, knowing his plan had succeeded without a hitch. He could feel his tingling sensation grow, then, without any warning, his door opened and a strong hand had a hold of him.

Tasker jogged toward the stopped semi, moving from car to car, not only for cover but support. There was no part of his body that didn't throb, and some body parts were positively screaming. His stiff legs bled from several places and he was still wet. He had his Beretta out of its belly-bag holster and a badge dangling from a chain around his neck. The few drivers that noticed him recoiled in disgust and fear. As he passed one car, a woman grabbed her baby from the car seat and held her. He glanced over his shoulder to see if Bolini had caught up. He didn't expect Sutter would be running anywhere.

This was it. The culmination of his fuck-up. Like most of his errors, this one looked to haunt him for a long time if he wasn't lucky and fast. He had to stop at a white Lincoln Town car with a tiny elderly man in a worn-out cap behind the wheel. He rested his head on the cloth roof for a few seconds as he caught his breath. The passenger window whirred down and he heard the old man bark, "Off the car, you wino. Get a job."

Tasker pushed off the car, noticing the blood drops on the roof and smeared on the door. He put a hand to his forehead and felt the warm flow. What was that from? he wondered.

Finally he was directly behind the semi; then it lurched forward a few feet. He popped his head around the tanker and didn't see a mirror. He stepped from behind the tanker and started a quick march forward. There really wasn't a mirror on the cab. He paused just behind the door. What if it was locked? Should he wait for help? He looked and didn't see anyone coming. It was time. He made his move.

Jumping onto the running board, he held his gun tight in his right hand and tried the handle with his left hand. The door opened wide and there was Wells, startled by the activity. Tasker reached in and grabbed him hard with his hand.

Wells leaned away from him but didn't strike at him. Then Tasker saw why: he had flipped a switch. Tasker swung the butt of his Beretta in, landing a blow sharply across Wells' head. Then he pushed the dazed man hard into the cab so they were both inside. Tasker looked out the rear window and saw a digital timer with blinking red numbers: 01:58 . . . 01:57. This wasn't good.

"Shut it off," screamed Tasker.

Wells didn't respond.

Tasker shoved the barrel of his gun to Wells' temple and growled, "Shut down the timer, now."

Wells blinked and said, "Can't."

"Daniel, I'm not kidding, I'll keep you right here until you shut it down."

"I'm not kidding, either. There is no way to stop it."

"What'll happen?"

"The explosive on the tank will detonate, rupturing the tank and causing the aviation fuel to ignite. It'll be big. Big and flashy." He grinned, showing slightly crooked lower teeth.

Tasker didn't have time to get into the reasons. He looked at the timer: 01:42.

Suddenly the passenger door flew open and Sal Bolini stood on the running board. He grabbed Wells. "Got him!"

Tasker pointed back to the timer. "We gotta disarm it."

Bolini stood on his tiptoes, straining to see the timer. "No way. Let's get outta here and clear out these people."

Tasker said, "No time. Get out. I got an idea."

Wells turned and pushed Bolini, causing them both to tumble from the cab. Tasker couldn't be concerned with that right now. He pushed the pedal on the far left and shoved the gear shift closest to him. He heard gears grinding. He looked at the dash and saw a big white button. He mashed it, and the big air horn sounded. He laid on the gas and eased the truck forward. The cars right in front of him got the message and started moving up onto the curb or forward as far as they could go. He risked a look over his shoulder at the timer: 00:52 in red numbers.

Bolini was surprised by Wells' aggressive movement. He fell hard onto the sidewalk, with Wells landing right on top of him. Bolini was stunned but not out. Wells reached for his gun, but Bolini was a veteran, not some new recruit. He head-butted Wells hard in the face, the younger man's nose exploding in a haze of red. He quickly slipped from under the stunned man and threw an elbow into his head.

For his part, Wells was game. He took the blows and returned a knee that just missed Bolini's crotch. He had the upper hand for a second and appeared about to capitalize on his advantage when the tractor-trailer started to move forward. Both men froze in their belligerent embrace and stared at the big rig as it jerked forward, bumping a car harmlessly out of the way, then bumping another. It started to pick up speed, and rolled over the rear of a pickup, squashing it under its massive tires. Now people were abandoning cars in the tanker's path as it crushed and grinded several more, then knocked a light pole down. Finally, it hit some open space near the intersection and its blasting horn stopped.

Wells completely let go of Bolini and stood up to watch. He was mesmerized. "Now that is some good chaos," he said, still staring at the truck.

Bolini stood next to him, also watching the progress of the tanker. Tasker was doing a good job of getting it away from the buildings and other cars. He snapped back to reality and smacked Wells in the head with his pistol. He looked down at the man on the ground holding the back of his head and said, "That effectively ends our association, shithead."

thirty-five

tasker had never been in a big truck like this before. Still, the clutch was on the left, gas on the right and brake in the middle. The gear shift had a diagram with what looked like ten gears. He stomped on the clutch and jammed the shift stick into first, grinding the gears in the process. He eased off the clutch and on the gas, feeling the huge truck start to inch forward. He thought he hit a curb, then realized it was the hood of a Ford Mustang as the Freightliner rolled right over it. He spun the wheel to the left to try and center the semi tractor-tanker in the road and squished an abandoned Toyota, then a Corvette. The rig straightened out and he hit the gas as he found he had more room. Driving this big rig didn't seem that hard, except for the cars that kept getting stuck under his wheels. He had to blink hard to clear the blood and sweat out of his eyes. He could see that people were getting the message and abandoning their cars. In front of him, a whole family fled from all four doors of a brand-new Buick. He prayed that no one was stuck inside any of the cars he had already flattened. He had no choice. He knew the buildings would intensify the blast's shock wave. He headed for the causeway leading to the port. At least it was open. He hit the intersection at Biscayne, and traffic cleared. He stomped on the gas and heard the engine rev higher. He wasn't sure how to shift gears, so he just pointed the tanker toward the open road. When he spotted the bridge, he looked behind him. The timer read 00:42 in red numbers.

Camy had left Jimmy's Honda a block off the interstate, away from the growing traffic problem on Fifth. Jimmy had already sprinted toward the semi tractor-trailer they could just see in the distance. She had tried to raise Tasker and Sutter for an update, but had gotten no response. She had already gotten the Miami cops off their asses and heading this way, but they would have been moving already once they saw cars were starting to jam the roads of the city.

Camy searched the streets for any sign of the other agents working with her, then started to jog in the same direction as Jimmy had run. She left his Honda locked and hoped it wouldn't get towed from the no-parking zone where it sat.

Tasker mashed down on the brakes, bringing the lumbering machine to a stop past the base of the bridge headed toward the port. The American Airlines Arena was to the left and back toward the city a few hundred feet. He didn't hesitate to leap off the truck onto aching legs and start to run back downhill toward the snarled traffic. There was not another vehicle on the bridge. What kind of moron would follow a tractor-trailer that had just smashed fifteen cars? He ran about ten steps and realized that in his present condition he'd never clear the tanker before it detonated. He took a sharp turn, cut across the two empty lanes and headed for the side of the bridge. As he climbed the small guardrail and prepared to jump the forty feet into the Intracoastal Waterway, he heard another engine and saw a large truck cresting the hill coming from the port. He stood high on the rail, waving his hands to stop the truck, then heard a faint beep from the tanker. He turned and saw only a flash.

Sal Bolini, with Jimmy Lail's help, had dragged Wells to the intersection to watch the tanker's labored climb up the incline of the bridge. Why didn't Tasker shift gears, Bolini wondered. He stared at the tanker, willing it to move faster. Then he did something he hadn't done since high school: he prayed. "Please, God, let him get out." He closed his eyes and repeated the prayer. When he opened them, Tasker was hobbling along the side of the stopped tanker. He mumbled, "Thank you," out loud.

Bolini's grip tightened on Wells' arm as Tasker turned toward the north side of the bridge. Tasker climbed onto the rail, then hesitated.

"Jump," Bolini said. "Fucking jump!"

Tasker turned and stood and started waving his arms.

Bolini looked up the bridge and saw a tractor-trailer headed over the span of the bridge. The driver saw there was a problem and stood on the brakes, causing the box trailer to slide sideways across the four lanes of the bridge, nearly jackknifing, but stopping well away from the tanker.

Then the tanker exploded.

The sight and sound of the blast took him by surprise. It looked like a mini atomic bomb as it flashed, then traveled vertically, instantly melting the electric and communication cables over the bridge. The signal on the stop gates on the bridge crackled and popped, the lenses shattering. The grass along the arena property withered instantly as the flame licked all the way down the bridge and to the sides. The paint on the side of the building bubbled and changed colors as the sign over Bongos Restaurant popped and sizzled.

Everyone ducked instinctively, and the sound of the blast echoed through the streets and into the spaces between buildings.

Part of the fireball shot straight down the bridge, guided by the rails and ocean breeze until the intersection flashed with flames. No people were still in the vicinity. The smashed Chevy closest to the bridge instantly ignited, as did the two cars next to it. One, a Chrysler, burned out immediately. The other started to burn from the tires up. Black smoke started pouring from both vehicles and drifted across the area, adding to the mounting confusion.

Bolini squinted to see through the smoke but couldn't see Tasker.

Sutter, limping up to where Jimmy stood with Wells in cuffs, casually kicked the prone man just on general principle. Unable to see what they were all staring at until he reached the line of spectators in front of Wells and Jimmy, he pushed through the crowd just as the tanker blew up. The sound rattled his intestines, and the flash hurt his eyes.

"Jesus, where's Bill?" he shouted to Bolini as they both ducked.

Bolini just shook his head.

Sutter felt sick to his stomach.

He stared at the flame as it just sort of evaporated into the sky. If it had blown down here, the blast would've killed fifty people. He himself never would have thought fast enough to move the tanker to an open place.

He went to one knee and felt tears build in his eyes.

Wells stared at the unfolding scene. This was getting pretty good, with the black, sooty smoke filling the streets and the people screaming. The tanker wasn't where he would've put it and hadn't done nearly its potential, but people were scared and it was because of him. This was cool.

Bolini and Jimmy bolted into an all-out run to the bridge. Sutter put his hand on Wells and forced him to prone out on the ground again. Then he sat across his legs. The crowd was starting to grow as more people left their cars to see what the hell was going on.

Bolini reached the bridge and started the long slog up the incline. Finally he had to move all the way to the right because of the heat of the burning hulk of the tanker. The cement guardrail was flashed with a brown, burnt color. They looked down at the water for any sign of their partner.

Jimmy hopped onto the rail at the spot they'd last seen Tasker, then leaped down into the water before Bolini could protest. It looked like a long way to Bolini, but Jimmy hit the water with a splash and was immediately up and thrashing around.

Bolini leaned over the side, anxiously looking over. "See anything?" he shouted.

Jimmy was too intent on the search and too far away to respond.

Bolini started to pray again. "Help us out—*please,* God."

At that moment, Jimmy broke the surface with Tasker, unconscious in his arms. Jimmy flipped his head so he was face up, cupped an arm across his chest and started for the seawall nearest him.

Bolini raced down the bridge faster than he realized he could run, and jumped to the embankment under the base. He half-ran, half-tumbled to the edge of the water, then scurried around the small bay on the seawall to meet Jimmy Lail.

"Here," gasped Jimmy, holding Tasker's motionless body up from the water. Bolini grabbed his shoulders and tugged. With effort they had him up onto the grass, and Jimmy pulled himself up.

Tasker had the cuts and bruises from earlier, and now his hair was singed. His left eye had swollen shut.

Bolini said, "You know CPR?"

Jimmy laid Tasker out completely flat, and as he was tilting his head back, Tasker coughed and water sprang up out of his mouth like an oil well.

Tasker coughed again and gasped, "Anyone hurt?"

Bolini let out a laugh. "No, I don't think so."

"What about the truck on the bridge?"

Bolini paused, then stood, looking up past the burning tanker. "He's stopped right at the crest." He kneeled back down to Tasker. "You did good. With both bombs. Maybe you should be a bomb tech."

Tasker coughed and let out a slight smile, "No, thanks." He sat up. "Where's Wells?"

"We got him. Sutter is sitting on him."

Jimmy Lail chuckled. "Literally."

"Get me to them," said Tasker, slowly standing to his feet.

Tasker didn't intend to argue when the first paramedics arrived and told him he had to go to the hospital. He walked slowly, with Jimmy and Bolini on either side of him. They cut through the crowd and saw Sutter still sitting across Wells' legs.

Sutter's face brightened as he saw the three men slowly come toward him. "Praise Jesus," smiled Sutter. He stood and, to Tasker's surprise, hugged him. Tasker used his remaining functioning arm to return the gesture.

On the ground, face down, with his hands cuffed, Wells said, "Hey, this is uncomfortable."

Jimmy Lail, in his Texas drawl, said, "You're about to be as uncomfortable as a June bug in a fishing tournament if you don't shut up."

All three men stared at him.

From across the street, Camy Parks cut through the crowd and ran toward them. Jimmy turned to face her and held out his arms. She ran past him to Sutter and kissed him hard on the lips.

Tasker settled back as he heard a host of sirens approaching from every direction. Then he laid back on the ground, shut his eyes and took the deepest breath of his life with his sore lungs.

Jimmy Lail's face flushed red every time he looked over at Sutter being treated by the paramedics, with Camy sitting next to him like a puppy. He'd just risked his life to save the city and she ran to that jerk. He tried not to glare but knew he wasn't concealing it well.

Sitting next to him, Wells, with his hands cuffed behind his back, said, "Women, they can be a pain in the butt." He nodded and smiled.

Jimmy looked at him and said, "If you open that redneck hole in your face again, you'll wish you were on that tanker." He nodded toward the still-burning hulk on the bridge; firemen were spraying it with a white foam.

Wells just shrugged.

Jimmy looked back at his former girlfriend and took a deep breath. He was a young, good-looking guy with a great job. What chick wouldn't want to hook up with him? He was just killing time with her anyway. He felt a little better until he saw Camy kiss Sutter on the lips again as the paramedics started to take him away.

Jimmy stared at them and said out loud, "I don't want to hear anything from you. You're in enough trouble." He turned to make sure his message had gotten through, but there was no one there.

Jimmy twisted his head in every direction, looking for the missing Wells, or Bolini for help. The crowd was milling all around, and Jimmy couldn't see any sign of the handcuffed man.

"Oh shit!" He started to run through the crowd.

thirty-six

a week later, Bill Tasker sat on his patio, Derrick Sutter in the lounger next to him. A week of rest had helped him recover only a little. He still wasn't supposed to drink beer because of the antibiotics and painkillers he was using, but he decided one Icehouse with his partner wouldn't kill him. Even though he had seen a lot of corpses that looked better than he did right now. He had thirty stitches in different cuts in his legs. Fifteen on his arms. Ten in one gash along his hairline. One wrist was broken, which he hadn't even realized at the time. Both legs had torn muscles, and his right ankle was sprained. He'd had to have a buzz cut to remove his burnt hair and allow the doctors to examine his head properly, and he had a couple of decent burns on his face and shoulder.

Sutter, on the other hand, had a bandage on his foot near his ankle and a pair of crutches. Dressed in a sharp pair of pants and button-down Oxford shirt, he was casually telling Tasker about his passionate affair with the lovely Camy Parks.

"I'm telling you, Billy, sometimes she's like a wild animal, and sometimes she really *is* a princess."

Tasker held up his hand. "I get the idea." He looked toward the sliding glass door. "My girls are inside."

Sutter shrugged. "Sorry."

Tasker asked, "How long you gonna be out of work?"

"They say I can be back at light duty next week. What about you?"

"Won't say. Need to be evaluated Friday. I figure two weeks."

Sutter smiled. "Why? Take some time. Two weeks ain't shit. You need a couple months, all you been through."

"How's Jimmy Lail doing?"

"Camy says he's obsessed with finding Wells. She says he's on surveillance everyday, looking for him." Sutter started to laugh. "You heard he had his car stolen, too?"

"Really. The Honda? Where?"

"Off Biscayne. The day we chased Wells. With everything else going on, no one made a big deal about it." He looked back at Tasker. "Camy says he doesn't care about the car, or anything but Wells."

Tasker nodded. "I know the feeling."

"But he's got help. Now the FBI knows what one of their snitches tried to do. They've got everyone out beating the bushes. Lot of local cops, too. But the FBI is definitely leading the charge."

"The name Eric Rudolph mean anything to you?"

Sutter smiled and nodded.

Tasker thought. about the similarity between the Atlanta Olympics bomber and Wells. Both had gotten away with it for a while. Rudolph had evaded a massive FBI hunt for five years, until some local cop found him digging in a dumpster. Tasker decided he wouldn't hold his breath until Wells was captured.

Sutter tapped a *Miami Herald* on the table between them. "You okay with this bullshit?"

Tasker smiled, looking at the headline: FBI AVERTS DISASTER. "Yeah, it's true. Bolini came through."

"But you risked your ass."

"We all did."

"I just think that's absolute bullshit."

Tasker shrugged. He really didn't care. He'd accomplished what he set out to do. Wells would turn up. Nuts like that always make mistakes. They'd have time to find him. No one had seen or heard from him or Alicia in the seven days since the tanker exploded. Tasker figured they were together.

Sutter looked at Tasker and said, "That reminds me."

"What?"

"You guaranteed me I wouldn't get shot by the FBI if I helped on this case."

Tasker smiled. "I think I said I could *almost* guarantee it." He sat up on the lounger. "Besides, what are you bitchin' about? The wounds are getting less severe every time. Next time it'll probably just be a graze in the arm."

Sutter and Tasker sat on his patio in Kendall and laughed together over all the things that had happened in the past few weeks. They laughed so long and so hard that Tasker's girls came out to make sure everything was all right.

Tasker put his arms around their small shoulders and kissed them each on the forehead.

"Yep, girls. Everything is just fine."

thirty-seven

daniel wells took the exit off Interstate 10, heading south toward New Orleans. They weren't going to stay here more than a night, but Wells needed to look around. He had an idea about his next show. It had been a long drive, but the kids had slept most of the way. Alicia had apologized from Tampa to Tallahassee about helping the cops, but he said he understood. He didn't know what he'd do, either, if someone threatened to take the kids.

It had been one wild week. Starting with his attempt to light up Miami . . . all the way to this road trip. He'd been lucky in Miami and knew it. When old Sal Bolini slapped the cuffs on him, he had tightened his fists and pulled his hand up so Sal had closed the cuff on his left fist instead of his wrist. Then, when the younger FBI guy was not paying attention, he had just stood up and walked away a hundred feet or so, letting the crowd swallow him up. The cops all rushing to the scene were too intent on the burning tanker to notice anyone filtering through the crowd. Slipping his left hand out of the cuff had been a lot more painful than he'd thought it would, but it only took a few seconds of determined struggle. A few blocks away, he'd found a tricked-out lowrider Honda, popped the window, jumped in and took the fast little sucker all the way to Tampa. He'd used a twenty he'd found in the car's console for some gas and a sandwich at the gas station on the west side of Alligator Alley.

Now he held the steering wheel to the Ford station wagon with his right hand because his left wrist was still sore from slipping the handcuffs in Miami. He had a white bandage over his knuckles on his left hand and still couldn't move his thumb. Considering the alternative, he wasn't upset by the injuries.

He had been a little disappointed that his stunt had not gotten more than a day's play in the national news, but the memory of that scene was burned into his head. He still felt the charge from it.

Alicia, snoring lightly, snuggled up under his arm closer. He hugged her.

Still, the tanker would be nothing next to his next plan. He smiled when he saw the sign for the Superdome, then glanced down at the book he'd stolen from the Miami Public Library: *The Principles of Nuclear Fission.*